Livy

A Love Story

Also by Gretchen Craig

NOVELS

Always & Forever
(The Plantation Series, Book I)
Ever My Love: A Saga of Slavery and Deliverance
(The Plantation Series, Book II)
Evermore: A Saga of Slavery and Deliverance
(The Plantation Series, Book III)
Elysium: A Saga of Slavery and Deliverance
(The Plantation Series, Book IV)

Livy: A Love Story
Tansy
Crimson Sky
Theena's Landing
The Lion's Teeth

SHORT STORY COLLECTIONS

The Color of the Rose
Bayou Stories: Tales of Troubled Souls
Lookin' for Luv: Five Short Stories

Livy

A Love Story

Gretchen Craig

Published by Pendleton Press.

www.GretchenCraig.com

Kindle e-book edition available from Amazon.com.

ISBN-13: 978-1522756262
ISBN-10: 1522756264

Livy
A Love Story

Foreword

Dialogue is always a challenge. If it's too daunting, we don't want to read it, but we don't want to "hear" characters who lived two hundred years ago talking like modern Americans either.

The task is especially difficult when trying to recreate how slaves spoke. People brought their African languages to the Americas, and there might be a number of groups represented on any one plantation. Adding to the complications, there was a Spanish period in Louisiana and there were German immigrants in significant numbers, but since the prevailing European culture was French, the language of Louisiana slaves would have been an amalgam with a dominance of French. However, blending African-nuanced French into a novel written in English is beyond my talents. Instead, I've tried to approximate the rhythms of Southern rural speech in my characters' voices.

As a Southerner, I quite clearly hear in my head the speech I've used in this book. Of course it is based on what I've heard all my life and partly on idioms and particularities I use myself. For instance, the common use of the word "gone" is a modifier: The milk is all gone. Some of us also use "gone" as a verb which rhymes with "bone": instead of saying "I'm going to get to that later," I might say "I'm gone get to that later."

Though I make no claim that my dialogue is accurate enough to impress a linguist, I've aimed to give a flavor of Southern rural slaves' speech. Perhaps you'll be able to "hear" it as you read as I do as I write it.

All things above were bright and fair,
All things were glad and free;
Lithe squirrels darted here and there,
And wild birds filled the echoing air
With songs of Liberty!

From "The Slave in the Dismal Swamp"
Henry Wadsworth Longfellow

Chapter One

The first time she saw him, he was grinning. The next time she saw him, he was whistling. A slave, working in the field, under a July sun. What was wrong with him?

Livy decided he was simple. It happened now and then, and no one knew why -- a child was born without the sense God gave hens. Instead this man was gifted with a strong body and a sunny disposition.

She kept her distance from him and everyone else on this new place. She had spent her entire twenty years on a plantation upriver, had known everyone in the quarters, had loved some of them. Livy didn't want to know these people. She wielded her hoe in the knee-high cane, weeding and keeping an eye out for snakes, and pretended she was the only one laboring in this field. She didn't mind hard work. She was used to it. What she minded was being forced to leave her mother and her sisters with no say-so. It was just easier to bear if she lived her life inside a dust-colored shroud where nothing could touch her.

"Hey, pretty girl." It was Zeb, the simpleton. He'd worked his hoe up the next row till he was even with her.

She ignored him.

"What's your name?"

She hacked at a bunch of crab grass with a savage blow.

"You been here, what, two weeks, and don't nobody know your name yet. You Suzy? No? I bet you a Rebecca."

So maybe he was not so simple, she thought. That teasing note was just a little too knowing to be simple.

"You act like you don't see me, so I can't see you neither? Well, I introduce myself anyway. I'm Zebediah. Zeb, to most folks." He leaned over to look up into her downturned face. "Sure wish I wadn't a will-o-the-wisp, cain't nobody hear me, cain't nobody see me."

Livy straightened, held her hoe up-right, and turned to him with a face she hoped would freeze him solid. "What you want?"

"I want to know your name."

She stared at him. Maybe he was simple. Then he smiled at her, and she saw the twinkle in his eye. Annoying, but not simple.

"Livy," she said, and turned back to her hoeing.

He chopped a weed with his own hoe. "Morning, Livy." And he set off down his row, like he was completely satisfied now he knew her name.

Next day, and the day after that, he said, "Morning, Livy." She ignored him.

Day after that, he said good morning, and then at sunset, he found her coming from the tool shed and said, "Evening, Livy." Two more days of good mornings and good evenings, he said, "My name's Zeb. You want to use it, it be fine with me."

He kept on with the good mornings, good evenings. Finally, she snapped at him. "What you want with me?"

He grinned and light shone off his face like a lantern. "I want you to call me Zeb. Good morning, Zeb. Good evening, Zeb."

She felt it first like a tickle behind her throat, then a tightening around her mouth, and then a tiny half-smile pulled at her lips. She tipped her head at him like she'd seen the master's women do and said, making it as formal as she knew how, "Good evening, Zeb."

Now the moon moved in behind his eyes and he glowed. "Good night, Livy."

~~~

After a long day's work, even if the night was steamy and still, people in the quarters slept hard. Livy shared a cabin with two other women. Etta, an old woman whose back was so bent all she was fit for was riding herd on the littlest children while their mamas were in the fields, and Grace, a dried up little woman with a limp who milked the cows.

Livy listened to their quiet, even breathing. She tried to match her breath to theirs. She tried to remember all the yellow things there were to look at. She did not allow herself to think of home, of her mama and her sisters back on the Griffin plantation. She didn't let herself think about being nothing more than a kind of
~~~

coin – the master gambles, he sells off a few slaves to pay his debt. No, better to tot up how many yellow things colored the world. Butterflies, daffodils, squash, baby chicks. Still, she could not sleep.

She rolled off the corn shuck mattress as quietly as she could and padded out to the porch. She could just believe it was a little cooler out here. Livy crushed a few leaves of the mint Etta had growing in a pot and rubbed them on her skin to discourage the mosquitoes, then settled on the top step to listen to the night music, bat wings whirring overhead, crickets sawing away in the bushes. A little sliver of moon gave enough light to see the outlines of the cabins.

A movement down the lane caught her eye. A man slipped into the cabin third down the row. That was Tish's cabin, Tish whose little boy Beesum toddled around with his fingers in his mouth. But why did a man have to sneak in to see Tish? Nobody would care. Tish was alone in her cabin, just her and the baby since her man run off. Run off and left her and their baby behind, that's what she'd heard.

Maybe he didn't run off though. Maybe her man was one of those maroons who hovered around the plantations to see their people or get food. Livy didn't see the point in that. Lying out in the woods, you still ain't free – hungry all the time, slave patrols after you all the time, scared all the time. You want to be free, then keep going till you be free.

After while, the man stepped out of Tish's cabin and closed the door real quiet. He looked up and down the lane, but Livy was sitting still and he didn't see her in the shadows. He crossed the lane and let himself into one of the bachelor cabins. She figured that was why this master bought her – he had too many bachelors on the place. Well, she didn't want none of them, so she wasn't gone be no help to him about that.

Pretty soon, here come another man. Jubal, it looked like. Jubal, the quarters' lover man who had two or three women pining after him all the time. She thought he stayed in the bachelor cabin at the other end of the lane. What did he want slinking into another cabin full of men?

Livy's mind wandered lazily over the possibilities. Maybe they were gambling in there, using carved wooden dice and pebbles instead of coins. But why be secret about that? Why be secret about anything in the quarters? They lived on top of each other, day in and day out. There were no secrets.

Except for this skulking in the night.

Sure as she'd ever been, she suddenly knew. They were planning to run.

Livy's pulse picked up. Running together, they'd help each other. Keep watch for each other when they had to rest, keep a lookout for the slave patrols, share the food they could forage.

~~~

The men sat in a circle around the candle placed on the floor, the windows all covered so nobody outside could see the light. Clem had the only chair, and Hector thought that was right since Clem must be near forty.

Hector looked around at the men, their chins and noses casting shadows in the yellow candle light. There was Pete, just hooked up with a woman, but he aimed to bring her with him. Clem, he wouldn't go, said his bones hurt too bad, but he help anybody thought they could get free. Clem's own boy run a few years back – nobody heard nothing about him, so they all believed he made it to freedom land. That was best -- believe he made it. And there was Samson, planned to come out in a year or two, when his oldest boy big enough to run with him.

That left Jubal. Hector had him figured for a wishful kind of man. He made time with three women, last Hector knew, no telling how many kids. He just liked dreaming about being a free man, but he was a help to them sometimes. He the reason they had a machete.

That meant only Pete was coming out with him, at least the only one this year.

"I found us a place," Hector said. "Eight or nine miles back in the swamp, maybe three miles from Flavian's camp."

"How much this place dry land and how much water?" Jubal asked.

"I reckon there's maybe twenty acres dry, two to four feet higher than the water."

"It got to be cleared, though."

"Yeah, it got to be cleared. We gone need saws and axes."

"And we gone need boats."

"Yeah. Either that or wade chest deep with the gators nipping at you. I've done it, but it wadn't no fun."
~~~

"I got a dugout started back in the bayou," Samson said. "Rate I'm going, it'll be ready in twenty, thirty years."

"Flavian don't mind you splitting off?" Pete asked.

"Nah. He all for it," Hector said. "A camp get too big, it make too much noise, leave too many trails, eat too much. He help us all he can, but we got it to do ourselves."

"Got something to tell you," Pete said. "I ain't going."

Anger flashed over Hector, but he kept his voice cool. "Why not?"

"Bess told me this morning. She pregnant. She won't go, and I ain't going without her."

Well, hell, Hector thought. All this talking and planning for nothing. He couldn't very well start a camp all by himself.

He guessed he couldn't blame Pete for not leaving a pregnant wife, but babies been born before in a maroon camp. It was up to Pete though.

"What about this Adam over at the Bissell plantation – he coming or not?" Clem asked.

"Yeah, he coming. Trying to get his hands on a axe."

The door handle jiggled -- Hector's hand was on his knife before he half knew the door was opening.

A woman stepped in and closed the door behind her. She was tall and slim, her eyes burning hot.

Sampson jumped to his feet, menacing her with his six foot bulk and his clenched fists. Judging by the looks on the men's faces, Hector figured she wasn't expected.

"I'm going with you," she said.

"What are you talking about, girl?" Clem said.

"You gone run."

"We ain't running. You think we fools? Go on back to bed. This here is a men's cabin."

Bold as brass, the woman brushed past Samson and sat down in the circle just like she been invited. "I'm going with you," she said.

"No, you ain't, cause we ain't going nowhere. Get on out of here," Clem said.

"I'm strong. I'm fast. I can run all night, steal food, cook, keep watch. I'm not afraid of nothing. I won't hinder you."

"No," Pete snapped. "Go on. Get out."

She had grit, Hector had to give her that. She stared at every one of them, not backing down one bit.

"She talk to the overseer, we in trouble," Jubal said.

"I won't never tell nothing to the overseer, never. But I'm going with you anyway, so I got nothing to tell."

"Your name Livy, ain't it," Clem said. "Livy, nothing we doing here got anything to do with you. We ain't running. Go on now, go to bed."

"I don't believe you."

Clem let out a great sigh and nodded to Jubal. "Take her back to her place. Livy, you make a fuss out there, wake folks up, they gone think you in here after a man. They all laugh at you from sunup to sundown."

"I'm going with you," she insisted as the men pulled at her.

Hector listened to the three pairs of feet on the porch and on the stoop. Then he didn't hear nothing else. At least she had sense enough not to cause a commotion out there.

"She gone be trouble," Samson said.

They breathed quiet for a few minutes, sweat trickling down their fronts and their backs.

"She want to go too bad to run her mouth off," Clem said. "We'll keep an eye on her. May be she can come out to the new camp with you, Hector."

"You taking your woman when the new camp set up?" Jubal asked.

Hector let out a breath. "When the boy old enough not to pick up a scorpion and put it in his mouth, Tish maybe come then."

"Me, I been thinking maybe me and my boy run," Samson said. "When he gets some age on him, maybe we run instead of coming out with you all. Head north till we hit the free states. Clem's son done it, some others must have done it, too."

Hector stared at the candle flame. It wasn't easy living out in the swamp and it wasn't any easier lighting out for the north. If it was easy, they'd have all done it by now.

"I ain't heard of nobody, but that don't mean nobody else never done it."

"Samson, don't you and the boy be running on your own," Clem said. "The odds ain't good, you know that. Go on out to the camp, make a new place. Hector gone need you and you be better off with him."

Samson ran a hand over his head and let out a breath. "It ain't time to do nothing anyway. The boy too young to leave his mama, too little to keep up. When the time come, I talk to you again."

"All right. Nothing more to do here." Hector got to his feet.

"Don't give up on us, boy," Clem said. "This ain't a small thing, running off. Maybe later on, some of us go out there with you."

He needed them now, Hector felt like shouting. But it wouldn't do any good.

Hector blew out the candle and slipped into the night. He was disgusted. He was disappointed. He'd seen it all in his mind, this new camp, clearing the land, building a place like the one Flavian had built. And now not even Pete was coming. He felt like punching something.

Once he found the trail heading back into the swamp, he made good time. The path took him through the back of the plantation deep into the woods to a pond that caught the moonlight so it was like a silver mirror with the moon caught in it. Hector skirted the marshy edge trying to keep his shoes dry, but it wasn't happening that way. Wet muck sucked at his heels and he was glad when the trail angled up a couple of feet onto dry land.

Owls hooted back and forth. Somewhere out in the marsh, a chorus of bull frogs sang to the skeeters. Come here, they croaked, hoping for a mouthful of bug. Plenty of bugs following him around. He entertained himself with the thought of having a frog tongue himself to turn the skeeters from a torment into a treat.

The dugout he'd left under a hanging willow waited for him like he'd told it to. He got in and shoved into the black waters. Flavian's camp was miles back in the swamp and Hector knew he'd never find it in the dark. He paddled and poled in the general direction, best he could tell from what stars he could see through the tree tops. When the sun sent a pearly gray light into the sky, he got his bearings.

People were up and stirring when he dragged the dugout up the bank. Still a little mist coming off the water, the heat holding off for another hour or so. Bacon scented the air and Birdie's two younguns were running around like wild Indians, but quiet like. Maroon children learned quick not to hoot and holler and carry on loud enough to bring the slave hunters down on them.

Flavian himself stood in the yard with his hands on his hips, waiting for him.

"How's it look?" Flavian asked.

Hector thought Flavian was the best man he knew, but he wasn't much to look at. Not puny, but kind of slight, not much meat on his bones. So Hector and the others didn't listen to him cause he was big and strong, and not really cause he was the smartest. Hector figured that was him, the smartest. What Flavian had was something else, a quiet something he carried with him.

"Look like the only one coming be this man Adam from the Bissell place."

"Well. It gone take time, that's all. And too many run off at once, that just stir everybody up. You got to remember too that everybody come out here got to be fed."

"I know it." Hector went on to see if he could get Birdie to feed him.

Chapter Two

Early morning, Zeb stepped onto the porch bare-chested to greet the dawn. Sunrise was his favorite time of day, the sun still out of sight but coloring the sky with yellow and pink. The birds trilled in celebration that they'd lived through another night, didn't get eaten up by an owl or a snake. "The sun, the sun!" they sang.

He reached his arms up to touch the porch eaves, stretching out the night's kinks. His mattress had gotten so thin, the ropes underneath bit into his back. Gone have to get him some more corn husks from the shed and re-stuff it.

Across the lane and three houses down, Livy stood on her porch openly staring at him. He grinned at her, she looked away. He knew he was a good-looking man – he'd had enough women prove to him that's what they thought. He hoped Livy would let him prove to her that she was a good-looking woman.

"Zeb, Mama Minnie say can you tie my hair."

"Sit down right here," he said. He sat on the top step and set his niece between his knees. His sister and her husband both died when the cholera swept through last year. Zeb, his mama, Minnie, and his grandma, Eva, lived in the same cabin, raising Faith and Hope.

Faith's hair was softer than wool, softer than cotton. He tied six knobs of hair with strips of calico, then pulled softly on one of them. "Ain't you the big girl? Pretty soon you have enough hair to braid."

"Mama Eva say she could braid it now would I sit still long enough." Faith heaved a sigh. "But I cain't."

He laughed and said, "Let's go eat."

With grits and bacon and fresh peaches in his belly, he worked steadily all morning, just one more hand out in the field, chopping weeds so they didn't drink up all the goodness in the soil before the cane got to it. Mr. Benning, the overseer, assigned each of them as many rows to hoe as he thought they could do in a day, then ambled off on his horse to oversee other crews felling trees or sawing wood or digging drainage ditches. Zeb had worked on all those crews. He didn't see much difference. Whatever the job, he bent his back and worked the live long day. Except sometimes felling trees you got to work in the shade.

He took off his straw hat and wiped his face with his sleeve. He looked for Livy and saw her the other side of the field, bent over her hoe. All she had on her head was an old red rag. She didn't wear a hat, she was gone get sun stroke. Before it got dark tonight, he'd cut some straw and make her one.

A swarm of colored dragonflies surrounded him all of a sudden. "Where you come from?" he murmured. There were blue ones, and green ones, and red ones. And oh lord there was one as purple as a morning glory.

Zeb smiled. They made the day worth living, a sight like that.

Behind him he heard Mr. Benning giving somebody a tongue-lashing. "You can't hoe any faster than that, I'll have you cleaning out the privies. Get at it."

It was Noah getting the scold this time. He was old enough the rheumatism had started creeping into his joints. Likely he was working fast as he ought to. They was all in this field for the long haul, anyway. Wasn't no point in hurrying through it.

Zeb finished his row and stepped over to the one Noah was working up. He started in and met Noah half-way.

"Thank you, Zebediah," Noah said. "Hot one, ain't it?"

Zeb fanned his face with his hat. "What you think, Noah? It better out here in this field in the summer, the sun cooking our brains, or out here in February, the north wind chilling us to the bone?"

"Well, Zeb. That's a question. I guess I rather be sweating out here in the sun than shivering in the cold."

Zeb grinned at him. "Me, too, old man. Let me do a couple more of my rows, then I come over and help you with yours."

"Your mama raised a good man," Noah said.

Zeb laughed. "I tell her you say so." He glanced up to check where Benning was. If the Boss seen him hoeing Noah's row, he'd holler at Noah again and likely give Zeb a whole acre to work. Zeb could hear the overseer's high nasal twang in his head: *If I'd known you could work that fast, Zebediah, I'd have given you a bigger chunk of this field for your own.*

Wasn't nothing out here his own. But he pushed the thought away. Didn't do no good fretting over something you couldn't change. Better to notice the dragonflies and be happy.

With determined cheer, he started on his next row and sang the first line of one of their favorites. "Deep river, my home is over Jordan. Deep river, Lawd, I wan' cross over into the camp ground." Noah took it up, then Rachel and Charlie, till high voices and low voices and the ones in between filled the air.

When the dinner wagon came, everyone left their hoe on the ground so they could find where to start up after they ate. They took their beans and greens and cornbread, all piled on top of each other in a tin bucket, to the shade of the wind break.

Zeb found Livy sitting by herself a little way off from the others. He took his bucket and sat down next to her. "Food ain't bad, is it?" he said.

She fished the spoon out of her bucket. "It ain't bad."

"You ever wish you worked in the cook house?" he said around a mouthful of beans.

"I did that, for a while. But they didn't like my face up there."

He looked at her, appraising the clear skin, the high forehead, the dark luminous eyes. "That hard to believe. What's wrong with your face?"

"It don't smile."

He drank from his water jug. "I seen that. What you saving 'em up for?"

When she didn't answer him, he glanced at her. She was staring into her bucket, her spoon idle in her hand.

"You got a bug in there?"

She looked at him then. "What you got to smile about?"

Zeb thought a minute. "I don't hurt nowhere. I got all my teeth. And this morning, I seen a swarm of dragonflies, all colors, even purple."

"Um" was all the answer he got.

"How about you, Livy? You got all your teeth?"

She gave him a nasty look. "What kind of question that for a man to ask a woman?"

He grinned and leaned over with a mock leer on his face. "You noticed I'm a man and you a woman?" The grin faded when she looked him in the eye.

He felt caught, her gaze full of resentful awareness and heat. She looked away first, and he felt the air whoosh out of his lungs.

"Why you do that man Noah's work for him?" she asked.

He looked at her, wondering why she needed to ask a thing like that. "Noah getting old, his bones don't move so easy anymore. Maybe someday, my bones get old and achy, and somebody come help me with my row."

"And you gone keep smiling till then, till your bones ache, smiling all the time?"

He stared at her, the bitterness in her tone sad and ugly. "Don't see no better way," he said softly.

~~~

That afternoon a patch of clouds floated between them and the sun, bringing a little relief. A light shower was even more welcome, but of course, afterwards, the ground steamed and the sun worked extra hard to suck up that little bit of rain.

Late in the day, Zeb had finished his rows and was working on Noah's when Mr. Benning came back. He sat on his horse and surveyed the field, seeing who was putting some elbow behind the hoe and who was just shoving at the weeds in the ground.

Zeb knew when Benning focused on him. It felt like his eyes were hot coals on the back of his neck. Maybe the overseer wouldn't notice who was hoeing what row, might not think about who he had assigned to which row. But, of course, he did.

He directed his horse between the rows until he came up to Zeb, Noah just a few yards away.

"Afternoon, Boss," Zeb said.

"You don't got enough work of your own, boy?"

Zeb turned an innocent face up and said, "What's that, Boss?"

How could Benning possibly be sure which rows belonged to him? They were in the middle of several acres of cane rows. Even he had trouble knowing which ones he was supposed to work, and what difference did it make anyway?

"You look like you helping work Noah's rows. That right, Zebediah?"

Zeb looked around him, trying to look puzzled, if not downright stupid.
~~~

"This not my row?" Zeb said and raised his brows in surprise to see Noah nearby. "Noah, you working my row?"

Benning spat in disgust. "Tomorrow you got yourself two more rows." He looked at Noah. "You, old man, better put some hustle behind that hoe in the morning."

As Benning clucked to his horse to move on, he deliberately stuck his foot out so that his boot in the stirrup caught Zeb right in the ribs.

Zeb stumbled back and grabbed at his side. Benning rode his horse on down the row, his fist resting on his hip, his gaze roving over the field hands.

Zeb couldn't breathe for a moment.

"I is sorry to see that, Zebediah," Noah said.

Zeb grinned at him, pain shooting through his side and around his heart and up his throat. "It ain't no bother. You just tell your littlest grandson, some day, he got to help out old Zeb."

That evening, after he'd had his supper and a wash, Zeb sauntered over to Livy's cabin, not feeling as easy as he hoped he looked. His ribs ached and he had to be careful not to take any deep breaths.

Livy was sitting on the porch stoop. He sat one step below her so their faces were about level.

"Evening, Livy."

She sighed audibly. "Good evening, Zeb."

"Thought I'd sit with you a while."

She nodded.

They watched the last of the sunset, then the purple moving in. "Be a dark night tonight."

She glanced up. "Yeah."

"I like a starry night. So many stars, you couldn't see all of them if you had a hundred eyes."

Livy looked at him. "A hundred eyes?"

"You ain't never seen nobody got a hundred eyes?"

"No, I ain't never seen nobody got a hundred eyes."

"Well, maybe tomorrow you come across somebody like that."

"Yeah. I maybe see a blue snake, too."

He touched her bare foot. "Now you know you ain't gone see no blue snake, Livy."

She moved her foot away. They sat for a while, watching the dark push away the last glow in the sky.

"If you was mad at that Benning this afternoon, I couldn't see it."

"Cause I wadn't mad."

"Why not? You wasn't doing no harm, and I seen him kick you in the ribs."

Zeb shrugged. "No point in getting mad."

She stared at him until he felt her gaze and turned to look at her.

"You know what I think?"

"What you think," he said, smiling.

"I think you too scared to get mad."

Zeb's shoulders tightened. "That's what you think, huh?" he said softly.

She nodded at him. He stared at her a moment, then unfolded himself from the steps.

"I'll go on and give you back your stoop," he said, and walked off into the dark.

Chapter Three

Zeb walked back to his cabin through the cooling dusk. He was angry. Or he was hurt. He didn't know which. He wasn't used to being either one. Just cause a man don't rile himself up over every little thing didn't mean he was scared. Livy had a hard heart, she surely did. Somebody must have treated her awful mean to make her so hard.

He went on inside. His mama and his grandma and the little ones were already abed, so there wasn't no candle lit. He jammed his toe against the table leg and bit his lip to keep from swearing. Nobody needed Hope to wake up and start in wanting to play when they was all done in for the day.

"You all right, Zeb?" his mama asked.

"Yeah, mama. Go on to sleep. That's what I'm gone do."

He didn't though. He lay awake with his arms behind his head for a long while, thinking about her.

Next morning at breakfast, Faith snuck an arm around Zeb so she could steal the bacon on his plate. He pretended not to notice until he suddenly grabbed her and her giggles rang through the cabin.

"Zeb, time me and you got out to the field," his mama said. Minnie was sun-wizened, a little bit plump, and a sweet woman. "Faith, you wipe Hope's face and get you on over to Etta's."

"Yessum."

The girls left with their great-grandmother Eva who would take them to Etta and then go on to the dairy barn. Zeb drank down the last of his cool cup of water and stood to go.

"What you got the blue devils about this morning, Zeb?" his mother asked.

He looked around the room like he'd find little demons hiding in the cabin. "What blue devils?"

"Whatever riding you. Something missing this morning – like you ain't hardly here."

"Mama, you watching too hard. I'm fine."

The overseer's bell clanged and they went out into the early-morning dew to start the day.

After they'd collected their hoes, Zeb and Minnie followed the others out to the fields.

"Mama," Zeb said after a while. "You think I'm a scaredy man?"

She walked on a ways without answering him. She knew Benning had kicked him in the ribs. She knew what he was talking about. Finally, she said, "Zeb, you the smartest man I know. You don't waste the life God give you feeling sorry and mean and sad. You learned before you was in long britches to look for joy in every day, for us here in the quarters just like for them living up in the big house."

Minnie stopped and made him look at her. "You find it, too, don't you, son? I see you finding it, like how you grin when Hope plants a sloppy kiss on your cheek. Like when you stop and listen to a mockingbird. You got the gift of finding joy, that's all. Don't matter other folks don't see that."

Zeb stared at the ground, wondering if it was true. He didn't feel scared, didn't feel mad, but maybe Livy was right. He was scared to be scared, scared to be mad. Or maybe it was right just to be happy.

"Go on with you, Zeb. You got them extra rows to get hoed."

The first ten minutes of hoeing, Zeb thought the pain in his ribs was going to put him on his knees. Then he warmed up and the pain eased some. Going to make it hard to do those extra rows, that was for damn sure.

The day's work done, sore and worn out, Zeb trailed along behind the others, his hoe over his shoulder. Livy wasn't far ahead. He wasn't up to stepping faster to catch her, but she turned around and waited for him.

"Good evening, Zeb."

He hesitated, but he wasn't gone be a child about getting his feelings hurt. "Evening, Livy."

She fell into step with him. "You got it done, didn't you? Them extra rows."

"Sure, I got it done."

She looked at him sideways. "Maybe I wadn't very nice to you last night. Maybe you don't get mad at nothing cause you ain't got no mad in you."

"Everybody got mad in them somewhere."

"Yeah? What make you mad?"

He thought for a few ambling steps. "I don't like to see nobody beat a dog."

They were approaching the tool shed where the others were lined up to turn in their hoes. It was almost twilight, the light softening and the air cooling.

"You ever been a whole day without smiling?" she asked.

"Like you, you mean? Don't think so. But I don't think I've smiled the last couple of hours either."

"Your ribs hurt, don't they? Still, I bet I could make you smile with three little words."

She handed over her hoe to the overseer's man and waited for Zeb to do the same.

"I bet you could, too," Zeb said as they moved off, "if they was the right words."

"You think you know what I'm gone say? Cause I think I see a little smile trying to make on your face already. So what you think the three words gone be?"

He grinned at her. "Kiss me, Zeb."

Livy laughed. First time he'd heard her laugh. "No, fool, they's not the words. They's 'Good night, Zeb.'"

"That don't hardly feel like enough for a smile."

She turned off the lane toward her cabin. "Seems to me like that's a smile on your face, just the same," she said over her shoulder.

Zeb almost laughed, but he caught his hand to his ribs instead.

~~~

All day long, Livy worked the cane, grown above her knee now. After a rain, it seemed to grow two inches between sunup and sundown.

In the quarters at dawn and again at sunset, in the field during the hot bright days, Livy watched the men she'd seen in the cabin that night. She knew all their names now except the one had
~~~

to be Tish's husband. She hadn't seen him again. Clem was the one had been in the chair. Pete and Jubal had dragged her back to her cabin. The other one was Samson. Not none of them wanted anything to do with her since then, but she caught a couple of them looking at her off and on. Probably wondering if she'd sidle up to Mr. Benning and get her a extra pound of bacon in exchange for telling him she'd seen them meet in the night.

She wouldn't tell, and she meant to be with them when they made a run for it. So she watched them. They didn't sit together at mealtimes, they didn't sit on the same porch of an evening to smoke a pipe before bed. They didn't seem to pay each other any mind. But sometimes they glanced at each other and seemed to mean something by it, as if their thoughts flew through the air.

So Livy dragged her corn husk mattress to the porch every night and slept out there, half-awake in case they tried to slip out of the quarters without her. She'd be ready to walk off this porch and run, no need to gather a bundle. She had the dress on her back and another one worn clean through on a peg in the cabin. She'd leave it for Etta to make rags out of. She had her shoes, the soles grown thin, but they were good for a while. She had her cook knife. And she had the pebble she kept in her pocket. She kept that because it was pretty. Not because Zeb had given it to her.

So she was ready. All she'd need to do was slip on her shoes, and they wouldn't be half a minute past her before she was on their trail. Once they were on their way, they wouldn't send her back.

Zeb would be the first one to miss her, she thought. He looked for her every day first thing so he could make her say "Good morning, Zeb." Then he'd smile and walk with her to the fields. She never knew another soul as happy as Zeb. She still wondered sometimes what was wrong with him.

Other slaves could have happy times now and then, sure they could. But this unrelenting good cheer made him look like a fool.

She didn't want anything to do with him anyway. She was running with Clem and them others. She didn't need to get messed up with some man who didn't seem to have good sense. No, she had no use for Zeb.

But she was aware of him, all the time. She knew where he was working, she knew when he stopped to drink from his water jug, when he straightened up and stretched his back for a minute. He wanted her, and she wanted him back. She was no virgin girl.

She had even had a babe three summers ago, but it hadn't lived. Loretta, she'd called her. But her baby hardly drew half a dozen breaths before she went back to God. It liked to have broke her, losing Loretta after she'd already lost Loretta's daddy.

She hadn't wanted to make friends here, but in spite of herself, she looked forward to those "mornings" and "evenings" he gave her. But she wouldn't give him any more than the same thing back. No touches, no lingering glances, not once she recognized there was a sizzle between them.

So she ignored the pull she felt when she was with him. She watched his big hands handle a dandelion before he blew it into the wind. She watched the way he walked, the hoe over his shoulder, loose in the body, at ease. But he wasn't no use to her.

~~~

Zeb was a frustrated man. He hadn't had to wait on a woman ever. He didn't go with the young girls or the women happy to be with their own men, but that left plenty other women glad to have him stroll with them into the barn of an evening where there was clean straw and only the horses to witness their doings.

But Livy. She wouldn't give him even a glimmer that she was interested. Once he'd got her to saying "morning" and "evening" back to him, she was willing to talk with him. She made him smile in spite of the fact she hardly ever smiled herself. But that was all, a little talking, a little teasing. No touching.

If he could kiss her, he could make her smile. He knew he could. And he spent uncomfortable nights imagining just how to make her happy on a pile of straw in the barn. But he didn't see he was getting any closer to her week by week. Maybe she really didn't like him. Maybe she really did think he was a scaredy man. His face felt hot at the thought.

He wondered if she'd thrown that pink pebble away. He had cleaned it off with water from his jug and polished it a little on his rough canvas pants before he gave it to her. She had held it in her hand, looking at it a long time before she put it in her pocket and went on about her business. He'd felt like he'd just given her a little piece of his heart and she'd tossed it in a black hole.

Livy was a hard woman, but behind that grim mouth and set jaw was a woman needed to be loved.
~~~

Meanwhile, even if he didn't have a woman, he had a family. Sunday afternoon after the preacher left, he hoed the little patch of garden behind the cabin, mended the chicken coop where a fox had been at it, banged down the nails rising up out of the porch floorboards, and helped his grandma Eva shuck corn. Water buckets needed filling at the well, and the girls needed somebody to be a daddy to them. He tossed Hope in the air, her squealing like a little piglet, and carried her on his shoulders down to the creek to get her feet wet. He helped Faith look for tadpoles and dig up worms for her fishing hook.

He was happy enough. The preacher told them that the life they led was the life God meant for them. Then he told them God was a just God, forgiving and loving and fair. Zeb could see a contradiction there, but he didn't dwell on it. He was a slave, his daddy and his granddaddy and he guessed his granddaddy's daddy had been slaves. Nothing to be done about it.

He knew some slaves who taken to lying out. Not just for a few days when they'd had all the work they could take. These were maroons, the ones who stayed out for months, even years. Some of them hovered around the quarters of this plantation and that one, stealing provisions, or picking up whatever their friends had left out for them on a tree stump or behind a log. He'd seen his grandmother, other folks too, take cornbread or a little meat, a handful of squash, some peas in a cloth bag and leave them out on the edge of the woods. Nothing left in that bag next day when she went to get it.

And some of the slaves run so deep in the woods or so far up the way north they thought they'd never be caught. Zeb knew some who'd run, but he never knew anybody hadn't been brought back in chains, whipped, even had his ear notched. As for Zeb, he wasn't worried about the whip or the knife. He was worried about what his mama would do if he ran. She'd be sick worrying, and she'd have to do all the chores herself, the girls too little and grandma too old. And he'd miss them. He didn't have much in this world, but he had his mama, his grandmamma, Faith and Hope, and they needed him.

And so he woke up in the mornings anticipating another day of blue skies, or rain, or heat, or cold, just glad to have another day on this earth.

He finished weaving Livy's straw hat, and the next morning as they collected their hoes he plopped it on her head.

She took it right off and looked at it like she never seen a hat before.

"What's this for then?"

"To put on your head, woman."

"Why you give me this?" Her voice was snappy, like she didn't much like him nor any hat either.

"To keep the sun off your head, what you think?" He smiled, but he worried she might shove it back at him. If she did that, he wasn't gone smile about it.

She turned it around in her hands, looking at it. You could almost hear her talking to herself, Zeb thought. What that fool done now, she'd be thinking. Don't want no fool's hat.

When she looked up at him, he had quit smiling. He waited, hoping she'd let him do this little thing for her. She looked into his eyes, seemed like a long time. Then she plopped the hat on her head. "All right," she said, and marched off with her hoe on her shoulder. Then he smiled.

Zeb worked. His ribs only a little sore now, he hummed the first notes of "O Canaan." Then Charlie picked it up and sang "I thought I heard them say there were lions on the way."

He was going to sit with Livy when the dinner wagon came out. Maybe he could get another laugh out of her today, but if he couldn't, it'd be fine if they just be together in the shade, enjoying their biscuit and bacon.

Chapter Four

Livy worked the other side of the field, her mind on what Zeb had done. Made her a hat. She hadn't asked for a hat. Hadn't asked for anything at all on this place. Why would she? She was leaving soon as she saw she had a chance. Clem and them others was up to something. Had to be they was planning a run, a bunch of them together. That would be her best chance, going with them. But what they waiting for, she asked herself. A new moon? A rainy night? What?

Day after day, she got herself close to Clem or Jubal, next to any of them, and hissed *I'm going with you.* They none of them ever answered her. They'd just move away from her, natural like, and nobody noticed.

Wednesday afternoon, the rain came down so hard, Benning sent them all back to the quarters. It felt like a holiday to Livy, sitting on the porch, listening to the rain and watching the lane turn to mud.

Later in the afternoon, when the rain let up, a small crowd gathered around Weasel, the funny man of the quarters. Leastways, he was funny some of the time.

Today, Weasel mimed a man hoeing weeds out in the cane, whistling, minding his own business. He straightened up his skinny old body and looked upward, nodding and giving little bows to somebody he was pretending was there. Livy figured it was supposed to be the overseer on his horse. Suddenly, Weasel doubled over and held his ribs. He pretended he could hardly breathe, clutching at his side. Didn't take long though before he straightened up, got hold of the imaginary hoe, started grinning and whistling like never was a finer day.

Livy saw Jubal elbow Zeb in his sore ribs and laugh at him. Zeb looked plenty embarrassed, but he smiled, of course. She might have known he'd be a good sport.

Zeb caught her eyes and stared back at her. She raised her hand, hoping he'd see it as friendly, not mean like some of them laughing at him.

Weasel made fun of a couple more folks, then the crowd broke up and here come Jubal stepping onto her porch. He acted like he was courting her, all pretty words and sly smiles, but she knew he was seeing two women on this row, and he hadn't come to her for loving.

With his arm around her shoulder like they were easy together, she walked with him down the lane toward the blueberry patch. There was still a light drizzle, but it was hot enough she couldn't tell what was sweat and what was rain. When they got to the back of the plantation, Jubal let go of her and they walked single file.

A hundred yards into the trees, Jubal stopped and turned to her.

"You know how to keep your mouth shut?"

"I been showing you I do."

"Ain't scared of nothing, you said."

She lifted her chin. "That's right."

Jubal stared at her, but she didn't drop her gaze.

"I'm gone show you the way to a place. You think you can remember the way and come back another time by yourself?"

"I don't see why not. What for?"

"I'm not gone tell you what for. You want in on this or not?"

She nodded. "Whatever I have to do."

He stared hard at her another minute, then turned and headed deeper into the woods where he picked up a path, a narrow one like the Indians made. She followed him half a mile. He stopped and said, "See that tree bent half way over?"

"I see it."

He didn't say another word, just kept going. They walked a long while, climbing over a fallen tree, crossing little streams running fast from the rain.

"See that? A oak tree with a hollow in it, three saplings nearby. Over there, a magnolia."

"I see."

"Come here." He took her to the hollow and had her reach up and put her hand inside. She withdrew a chunk of wood, cypress she guessed. Nestled at her feet between two big roots were more pieces of wood. A chunk of yellow pine, a piece of hard oak, and a smooth piece she didn't recognize. "What's that one?"

"Tupelo. These other two, they's oak, but see here how one of them is shaped like a little plate and the other one look like a finger?"

"Yeah, I see. And this black one, look like it got tar on it. These mean something," she said and looked at Jubal to tell her what.

"That piece of cypress you picked out of the hole, it mean on Wednesday night, there be a man here with a message for Clem. It mean you got to be here to get that message and bring it back."

"What the message gone be about?"

"I ain't gone tell you that. It won't mean nothing to you, but it will to Clem." He gave her a hard, searching look. "You know you could get killed doing this if Benning finds out. And if you tell him, thinking he'll give you a reward, then we kill you before we die. And that's a promise, girl."

Livy looked into Jubal's dark eyes. She didn't believe him. A master don't kill a slave could he help it; they was worth too much. And she wasn't gone tell, so his threat to kill her himself didn't mean nothing either. He just wanted to scare her. Instead of scared though, she felt a bubble of hope rising in her chest. "This mean you let me come with you then."

"It mean you gone earn the same chance to be free the rest of us got, that's what it mean."

Livy swallowed and blinked, trying not to let it show how her heart and her blood were racing. She was going to run, she was going to run so fast she'd feel the wind whistling by her ears. And she'd be with these men. Together, they would run all the way to Canada.

Jubal set the chunks of wood down next to the tree. "There be times you have to do this in the dark."

"In the dark? How am I gone find this place in the dark?"

"You been paying attention, ain't you? Same things here in the daylight be here in the night. You gone be able to have a lantern. Keep it half dark, nobody see a light back here."

Livy didn't mind the dark, but out here in the woods, alone? She could get lost, she could come up on a panther. She'd heard they was still bears in these woods.

Jubal must come out here in the dark some nights, she realized. To see if there were chunks left in the tree, to see if he'd need to come back any time soon.

"You don't do it, you better make Clem believe you keep this quiet. Or you life gone be short."

"I do it. Wednesday night, this other man, the messenger, he be waiting for me?"

"This time you go on Wednesday night. Sundays, you go in the daylight. You see what's in the tree, and if nothing in there, you wait a while, then you come on back."

"Why you let me do this, Jubal?"

His black eyes gave nothing back. He didn't like her, he didn't not like her.

"Cause nobody miss you on a Sunday afternoon."

~~~

Zeb was sitting on the porch with Hope in his lap, Faith leaning on him while Grandma told them a story about riding in a big ship all the way across the ocean like her grandmamma had done. About the wide blue sky, the deep blue sea, the white-capped waves stirred up by the wind. She didn't tell her girls about the sickness, the chains, the fear and the grief. But Zeb knew she would, when they were older.

He remembered her telling him about the rats that stole her grandma's food and nibbled her toes if she didn't kick and holler. But his mama had made her stop. "What the point of feeding him all that old bitter. They ain't no chains here, ain't no rats nibbling our toes. You let him be. He a happy boy. Let him be."

Hope was just about asleep, so he sat still. Best part of a little girl was when she went to sleep and a body could stop worrying she gone fall off the porch or find a worm and stuff it in her mouth.

"I take her into bed," Faith said. Scrawny little thing like she was, she gathered Hope up and pressed her against her chest, leaning backward to take her weight. She went on in the open door and Zeb heard her crooning when she put Hope down. She was a singer, Faith was, always making up some song and singing it to Hope soft and low.

Plenty of times like these when he felt peace wrap him up like a soft blanket. Faith inside humming and singing, Hope probably sleeping with her thumb in her mouth. Mama content to watch the dusk take the color out of the sky while Grandma dozed in her chair. Come Sunday, he'd go fishing. Faith wanted to bait her own
~~~

hook now, she so grown up. It was hard for her to be quiet, but he'd told her if she wanted to catch a fish, she had to be still. She was learning.

It was near dark when he saw Jubal come into the lane with his arm around a woman. Which gal he got to go out with him this time? He squinted his eyes and when he recognized Livy, he felt like his blood quit moving through his veins.

He had to coax every little half a smile out of her, had to press her to tell him good morning and good night, and she walked out with Jubal? She let Jubal have her?

There was no pleasure in him as the sun set, lighting up the few clouds left over in the west. No pleasure in the fireflies flitting around the cabins.

Why did she hold him off, every single day, and then walk out with Jubal?

He felt like he had ashes in his mouth when he finally lay down on his cot in the dark.

The next morning, Zeb saw Livy join the line behind him at the tool shed where they collected their hoes. He didn't turn around or step back to wait in line next to her. He didn't say good morning. Once he had his hoe, he passed by her still standing in the line. He felt her eyes on him, but he walked on.

Ahead of him Jubal was walking with Suzette, one of the women he visited pretty regular in the cabin she shared with her three little ones. Her man died same time Zeb's sister and her husband had, back when the cholera came through, and she seemed glad to have Jubal in her bed, even if her bed wasn't the only one he warmed up in the night. They talked and laughed and bumped elbows as they walked.

Well, if Livy wanted a man like that, nothing but smooth talk and here-one-night and there-the-next, then she got what she want in Jubal. It galled him bad. He was a better man than Jubal. Better for a woman. He would be constant with her, and kind. And he could love her good as any man.

The bile like to have drowned him for a minute till he shook himself. Temper didn't do any harm to nobody but himself, so he might as well just shed it.

He'd make himself think about something else. There was Noah ahead, walking like his knees were extra stiff this morning.

White speckled Noah's hair now, and his fingers were thickened and gnarled. He was old, Noah was. When Zeb was a boy and his papa had just died, Noah had taken him and Ned, his own grandson, fishing that afternoon, and every Sunday afternoon for the rest of the summer. Ned was long gone, sold off after he'd had his growth spurt and looked like he'd be a big, powerful man.

There was a time, after Noah's wife Em died, Zeb thought maybe he and his grandmother might take up together. But Noah's griefs never seemed to let him go, and Grandma Eva's either.

"Going to be a hot day," Zeb said as he caught up with Noah. "Ought to warm them old bones up good so you can out-hoe the rest of us."

Noah chuckled. "Like I did when I was your age. Hard to believe, ain't it, Zeb, that I was young and strong as you once."

"You still strong," Zeb said. "You just creaky. I think I hear that knee squeaking right now."

Noah laughed out loud. "Get on with you. I got hoeing to do."

Pretty soon, Benning rode through the field. He stopped near Noah and delivered the same threat loud enough for everybody to hear. "You put some muscle behind that hoe, boy, you don't want to be stuck ass-deep in the privy tomorrow." He snapped the short whipping stick he carried when he was on horseback, the crack reminding everybody of the big whip he kept handy on his cabin wall. He didn't use the bullwhip, but he liked putting the scare into the slaves with this smaller version, snapping it at them, sometimes drawing blood with a hard flick. The harm wasn't overmuch, but Zeb figured the threat made Benning feel good.

"Yassir, I workin," Noah said, calm as you please, and bent his back into it.

Mr. Benning gave Zeb a look when he passed him and went on to his other crews.

Zeb stepped over to Noah's row. "What he on you for, Noah? He catch you leaving food for the runaways?"

"Nah. I ain't done that in a while."

"Then what? He see you spitting in his coffee or putting burrs under his saddle?"

Noah snorted a laugh. "I ain't thought of the burrs under the saddle. Have to try that next."

Charlie in the next row said, "Nah, Noah. You don't want to go hurting the horse. Just find a couple of scorpions and leave 'em in his boots. When he put 'em on next morning, we hear some shouting and singing, I tell you."

Rachel, never far from Charlie, grinned. "I love to see that, I would."

When Charlie and Rachel moved on up their rows, Zeb lowered his voice. "What Benning got against you, Noah? Maybe I can fix it so he leave you be."

Noah shook his head. "You cain't fix it, Zeb, thank you for it just the same."

"Noah, tell me."

"I's just old, son, that's all. Some folks scared to be around us old 'uns. Scared they catch it." Noah laughed then, tickled at the thought. "And they will, they will."

Zeb didn't know what to say. Here he was, a big, strong man, but he had no power at all in this world. None. He knew it, and most of the time, he could forget it, lose himself in a song or a purple dragonfly, but sometimes, like now with Noah needing something he couldn't give him, Zeb felt the helplessness rising up in him.

He hoed his row, the sun burning through the thin white shirt on his back. He knew why Livy didn't smile. Wasn't no mystery in it. The helplessness got her and wouldn't let go. He straightened up and looked for her across the field of growing cane. She was wearing the hat he'd made her, her back to him, leaning into her work, the thin dress outlining her firm, curvy backside. She wasn't even smiling this morning after she been with Jubal yesterday. Seemed like she ought to be able to find something to smile about now and then. Why'd God put honeysuckle and blue birds on this earth if people wasn't supposed to enjoy them?

Zeb froze. A rattler was rattling his warning somewhere behind him.

Noah screeched. Then he shrieked. The hair on Zeb's arms stood straight up. He ran for Noah through the thigh-high cane, his hoe raised like an axe. Noah was on his back on top of crushed cane stalks, still hollering and gripping his leg.

Zeb saw the tail end of the rattles slipping away through the cane and chopped down with all his might. The snake twisted back and reared up to attack, but Zeb knocked it back and then sliced it into bits with the blade of his hoe.

People were crowding around Noah trying to help. He had his jaws locked so he wouldn't scream with the pain, but moan after moan pushed out of his lungs.

"Where he bit?" Zeb demanded.

"Look there on his calf." Blood oozed from two perfect holes, the muscle already swelling around them.

"Who got a knife?" Zeb said.

They looked at him with blank faces. Everybody in the field was stopped, staring. He stepped back and roared, "Who got a knife?"

Livy dropped her hoe and came running through the cane, crashing through and crushing the stalks. Another woman, Tunia, came running too. Zeb wasn't ever gone be out here without a knife again if he had to make one out of stone.

Zeb held his hand out for Livy's knife and knelt down. "This gone hurt, Noah."

"Just get it done."

Zeb made the cuts, let the blood flow.

"You gone have to suck it," Livy said. "Move over, I do it."

He shook his head. Zeb bent to the horrible wound and sucked. He spat and sucked, spat and sucked. His mouth was bloody and tasted like acid.

"That enough," Livy said. "That all you gone get out." He acted like he didn't hear her. She squeezed his shoulder. "Zeb, stop now."

He sat back on his heels and wiped his mouth with his forearm. Then he swiped at the tears on his face. "Let's get him out of this sun."

Charlie and Clem each took a leg and Zeb got Noah under the arms. Rachel followed behind with little short steps, trying not to outrun the men with their burden. Noah's eyes rolled up in his head and he fainted.

"Take him to my cabin," Rachel said. "Charlie and I got an extra cot in there."

They laid him in the cabin where it was cooler and the air smelled of bacon grease and onions.

"You got turpentine?" Zeb said.

Rachel already had the jug in her hand. She unplugged it and handed it to Zeb.

Noah's leg was turning dusky and was already twice as big as it ought to be. Zeb poured turpentine in the wound and all around it, rubbing away the dirt and blood.

"Good thing he still out," Charlie said. "He be howling he feel that sting."

Clem said, "I'll go tell Benning."

"Ask him bring the laudanum," Zeb said.

Rachel got a basin of water and a rag and gently wiped down Noah's face. He was groaning from deep in his belly before he opened his eyes.

"How bad is it, Zeb?" Noah asked.

"Bad enough to hurt plenty, I guess, but it ain't much. Might be if you play like it hurt real bad, you can lay up here enjoying yourself a whole week 'fore you have to take your hoe back out in that sun."

"It was a rattler, wadn't it?" Noah said on a gasp. "I didn't hear no rattle till it was too late." He hissed out a breath. "It a big one?"

"Nah," Zeb said. It had to have been six feet. A granddaddy rattler. "It a little ole thing. Probably had just enough venom to get himself a mouse for supper."

Zeb knelt on the floor next to the bed and grasped Noah's hand. The old man breathed in short little pants, trying to keep the pain from spewing out in a great shriek. "Zeb," he said between gasps. He didn't try to say any more and Zeb just held on tight.

Clem came back. "Where the boss?" Zeb said.

"Mr. Benning out where they cutting timber. He say he come when he get the chance."

Clem looked at the leg, then knelt down next to Zeb and gripped Noah's shoulder. "You hold on. The boss'll bring you some of that laudanum and send for the doctor. You feel better then."

"The doctor gone take off my leg, Clem."

"You have to let him do it, Noah. Ain't no way to keep that poison out of your heart you don't let him do it."

"I cain't work with one leg." Noah's voice trembled and he turned his head away.

"You don't got to worry. Zeb and me and some of the others get your rows done, and you can sit up on your porch and talk sweet into Eva's ear the live long day. You don't need but one leg to do that."

Clem got to his feet. "Rachel, you got plenty of water in the house? Firewood?"

"I got everything, Clem."

Clem turned back to Charlie and Zeb. "Boss said all us get back to work. Just Rachel, she can stay with Noah."

Charlie got to his feet, but Zeb stayed where he was and shook his head.

"Zeb."

"I ain't going."

Clem touched him on the shoulder. "Zeb, come on."

Zeb shook his head again.

Charlie and Clem went on to the field.

An hour passed, then two. Noah's leg was swelled so bad the skin had split and blood oozed out. When he was conscious, he was delirious.

Rachel dripped water into his mouth. Zeb never let go of his hand.

Another hour, and another. Zeb rested his forehead on the side of the cot. Hope had been dripping out of him as the minutes passed. The doctor better come soon and take the leg, or Noah wasn't going to make it through the day. As it was, he thrashed his head back and forth and muttered. He grimaced and squeezed Zeb's hand so tight it like to have broke his bones.

During their mid-day dinner, people congregated outside the cabin, waiting.

Zeb heard booted feet step onto the porch. Benning, at last. He'd have brought the doctor with him and something to ease the pain.

Benning stepped into the open door. Keeping Noah's hand in a firm grip, Zeb stood up.

The overseer took his hat off and wiped at the sweat on his forehead. He stood at the foot of the cot and looked at the leg. Then he looked at Noah, awake but hardly knowing himself. His eyes roved around the room, flitted over Benning, and then back to the patch of sunshine on the floor from the open door, then into the shadows, all the while a low groan rumbled from deep in his chest.

Benning took it all in, then nodded, his eyes on the grotesquely swollen leg. He took a deep breath, and turned away.

"This here for the laudanum, Mr. Benning." Rachel held out a spoon.

Benning looked at her. "He's out of his head, girl. He doesn't need laudanum."

Zeb fought to keep his voice steady and respectful. "When the doctor gone get here, Boss?"

Benning shook his head and put his hat back on. He strode out of the cabin.

Zeb stood like he'd been stunned by a blow to the head. No doctor? No laudanum? Suddenly he was striding after the overseer.

"Benning," he called. No mister in front of the name. "Noah need the doctor." When Benning ignored him, Zeb lengthened his stride. "He need the doctor today. I go get him myself."

Benning turned around. "You're going back to the field. All ya'll are going back to the field. Get on, now. That old man is going to die, and if he doesn't, he's not going to be of any use. You standing around gawking won't change anything."

Zeb's hands fisted. His chest heaved. He took a step toward Benning. Benning startled and stepped back.

"You gone get him a doctor or I'm gone beat you to a bloody mash."

"Ya'll better stop him," Benning said. "Get hold of him now."

Clem and Jackson grabbed Zeb's arms. "Zeb, stop this. Stop it."

He dragged them with him as he stepped on toward Benning. Pete and Charlie piled on, too, pulling him down, yelling at him. Samson kicked his legs out from under him, and Zeb bellowed like a gator caught in a trap.

Benning picked up a piece of firewood stacked on the edge of the porch and brought it down on Zeb's skull with a thwack.

Chapter Five

When Zeb woke up, he rolled over and retched. His ears felt like they were stuffed with cotton and his head felt big as a melon.

Late afternoon sun glinted off jars of vinegar, turpentine, and oil. The bars on the single window left a striped shadow on the dirt floor. The door was surely locked, but he stumbled to it and yanked on it.

So Benning had him locked up in the plantation's jail. Through the fog in his head, he wondered if there was worse to come. A whipping, maybe. Any boss would figure he'd earned it, threatening a white man.

Mama had told him and told him, growing up, how to get on. How to keep the boss from noticing him, how to keep himself free of the knotted scars the hot-heads wore on their backs. How to live, slave or not, and know the joy God put inside every man.

But joy didn't shut off the rage curling hot fingers around Zeb's heart. Benning had decided not to call the doctor for Noah, had decided to let him suffer, because he was old. Like he hadn't ought to be alive any more if he couldn't hoe a dozen rows in a day.

Zeb gripped the window bars and shook them till his shoulders burned. He wanted to shout and scream, he wanted to throw his fists into Benning's gut and pound his face. He paced the ten feet of floor and back to the window, over and over. There didn't seem to be any way to calm down. He couldn't let go of the fury burning him up.

Nausea rose up again, but all he had left in him was bile. His headache forced him to the floor, his head in his hands.

At dusk, someone called him quietly.

"Zeb," she said. He could just see her in the window.

"What you want?"

"Come here."

"I don't want you here. Go away."

"Zeb, come on."

He crawled to his feet and kept himself up with his hands gripping the bars.

Livy covered his fists with her hands. "Noah's passed, Zeb. An hour ago. I figured nobody want to tell you, but somebody need to."

Zeb stared at her. Wasn't nothing to say.

"Rachel said you held Noah's hand all those hours, Zeb. He knew you were there. And by the time you went after the boss, Noah was too out of his head to know nothing about you letting go. He died understanding you was there with him, Zeb. You was with him. You hear me?"

Zeb drew in a great shuddering breath and let it out again. He pulled his hands out from under Livy's and retreated to the deepest shadows. He sat again, elbows on knees, head in hands.

The moon was up when his mama came to the window. "You awake, Zeb? You head ain't broke too bad?"

"Mama." He got up and went to the window where he let her hold his hand through the bars.

"You head hurt, don't it? I brought you a comfrey. Wrap this cloth round your head, it ease the pain on the outside."

She reached through the bars to help him wrap and tie the poultice. Then she handed him a small jar. "This maypop tea. It help with the pain on the inside."

"Thank you, Mama."

"Now. This other jug just plain water. You drink all of it, hear? And this here's some supper."

"I cain't eat, Mama. But I'm glad for the water."

"We get you out of here tomorrow. Mr. Benning don't be doing nothing else to you. I gone talk to him in the morning first thing. I tell him remember you ain't never caused no trouble before, and you won't cause trouble no more. I tell him old Noah like a daddy to you, that's all."

"You don't have to do that, Mama."

"I will. First thing in the morning."

Zeb caught her hand through the bars. "Mama, I don't want you to say nothing."

"Zeb, you – "

"Mama, I ain't a boy no more for you to be taking care of. Leave it be."

She stared at him in what little light the moon gave them.

"All right, son. I won't say nothing."

Next morning, right after the bell clanged, Benning opened the shed door. "Get on out here."

Zeb saw he had the big whip coiled around his shoulder. So he was to be whipped. He didn't much care.

If there was to be a whipping, then there had to be a watching. Benning had everybody gathered round the whipping post where the weeds had grown high. Zeb glanced at the grim faces on the men and women he had known all his life. Whippings didn't happen often on this place, and when they did, every slave was reminded that's what he was. A little above a mule, and way less than a man.

Zeb didn't see his mama. He was glad if she'd stayed in the cabin. Break her heart to watch this. His grandmother Eva was there, though, right up front. She caught his eye and gave him a nod. She didn't look scared, she didn't look worried. A tall raw-boned woman, she was made of different stuff than her daughter-in-law.

"Clem, you and Jubal tie him to the post."

Jubal held a stick up to his mouth for him to bite down on, finished his knot, then looked him in the eye. "Show us what you made of, Zeb," he murmured.

First lash of the whip, all the fuzz left in his brain cleared right out. He grunted, the breath driven out of his body. Second and third lashes, his back felt like the whip was made of flames. He panted, keeping himself together. Fourth lash, a groan got away from him. He grabbed a deeper breath, determined that would be the last sound he made. By the sixth lash, he trembled from wrists to ankles and couldn't do nothing about it. But he was silent.

Benning was through. He coiled his whip. "You give me any more trouble, boy, I'll lay your back open till there isn't any skin left."

He turned to the crowd. "Ya'll got an hour to get Noah in the ground."

Clem untied the rope. Jubal took hold of Zeb's arm till Zeb could stand steady.

"Let go," Zeb said and pulled his arm free. He staggered the first few steps, the pain in his back so bad everything looked blurry and gray. He straightened up and blinked his eyes.

"Come on, Zeb," Eva said. "Let's put you some ointment on them cuts."

"Later, Grandma. I aim to bury Noah first."

She made him put his shirt back on so the flies wouldn't get in the cuts.

Zeb, Clem, Jubal, and Pete got shovels out of the shed. Most everybody followed them to the graveyard set on a raised patch of ground behind the quarters. A single spreading live oak shaded the graves laid out in rows, a slab of cypress marking the head of each one. Zeb remembered where his father was buried, three over from the tree. His sister and her husband were four back from his father, the two of them sharing their patch of the graveyard.

Zeb's shovel bit into the black earth. The sensation of fire licking at his back hadn't let up, but he couldn't tell the labor caused any more pain than he already felt.

Pete dug at the other end of what would be Noah's grave. Jubal said, "Leave off, now, Zeb. I'll finish up."

Zeb shook his head and kept digging.

When they were ready, some of them brought Noah out to his grave. The women had washed him and sewn him into an old quilt.

Etta, the oldest one on the place, talked to God about what a good man Noah was. She asked Jesus to bring him home where there wasn't no more pain, no more labor, no more sickness of heart.

Zeb stood with his feet spread apart, his heart a lump of lead in his chest as the people sang Noah on his way. Rachel's sweet voice called out, "Brother Noah gone to the kingdom, oh my Lord, oh my Lord."

Faith slipped up beside him and took his hand while Jubal and Pete lowered Noah into the fresh-smelling ground. All together, they sang, "By and by, Lord, by and by, there's a better home awaiting in the sky, Lord, in the sky."

Zeb threw the first handful of dirt onto the shrouded old man and stepped back while the others shoveled the grave closed. It was a good burial.

They headed back to collect their tools. Saws for the crew going to cut timber, scythes for those cutting grass, hoes for the ones going to weed the cane.

"Come to the house before you go to the field," Eva said. "We got to tend those cuts before they go bad."

Faith still had hold of his hand. Eva said, "Faith, honey, you go on and help Etta with the little ones."

She looked up at him with those big eyes, her face too serious for a nine year old. "You bleeding on the back, Zeb. You gone need me to come with you."

Lord, they hadn't let Faith watch the whipping? He looked at his grandma. "She didn't . . . ?"

Eva shook her head. "But everybody know about it."

Zeb squeezed her hand. "Grandma Eva and Mama Minnie gone take good care of me, Faith. You go on." She grabbed him around the waist and hugged him tight before she ran off.

His mama was waiting for him at the cabin. He could see she'd been crying, her face all puffy. She twisted her hands in her skirt and started to tune up again, but Eva said, "Stop that now, Minnie."

Zeb straddled a chair and endured the hot water wash, but when his mama rubbed witch hazel on the cuts, he shivered and like to have wept.

"You cut pretty deep, Zeb," his grandma said, handing him a cup of water sweetened with molasses. "Boss put his muscle into these lashes, yes he did. I reckon you scared him when you rushed at him, but he didn't give you but six. Could have been he'd give you a dozen or two."

Minnie slathered on a thick salve she made from suet and yarrow and comfrey, wrapped clean rags around him to keep his shirt from rubbing off the salve, and she had done all there was to be done. "You settle yourself down, now, son, and you won't have no more trouble. Noah be sad to see you whipped cause of him, you know that."

"Minnie," Eva said, her voice harsh, "he ain't done nothing a man don't do. He was taking care of his own, he was doing right. Staying out of trouble ain't always right."

~~~

The cane grazed his hips now as Zeb worked the soil around the stalks. Pretty soon the cane would be tall enough to shadow the ground and crowd out the weeds on its own. Then they'd be on to some other job on the plantation, Zeb didn't much care what.

Took days for him to not give a quick glance toward where he expected Noah to be wielding his hoe. Gave him a sick feeling when he caught himself at it. Folks seemed to think he was holding a grudge against Benning because of the whipping. But that wasn't
~~~

it. His blood rose remembering how Benning had looked at Noah, one of the best men Zeb ever knew, and nodded like it was all over and Noah lying there needing a doctor. Needing some of that laudanum for the pain. If the doctor had come, maybe Noah would be setting up on the porch, a one-legged man, but still breathing in the scent of the jasmine growing up the side of the cabin.

Noah just a *thing* to Benning, a thing to make the hoe move up the rows. No, it wasn't the stripes on Zeb's back that kept his jaw clinched. It was Noah in the bed, out of his head with the pain – and Benning not seeing nothing but a old slave, no use to him no more. That's what took the color out of the days for Zeb.

He worked, like he always did, even if cutting weeds pulled at the scabs on his back. Sometimes they opened up and bled. At night Minnie would dress his wounds all over again and wrap him in fresh bandaging.

He drew breath, but the life in him was beat down. A cardinal flitted by in front of him, a sight that once would have stopped him mid-stride to marvel at those red feathers. Now he saw it, and he didn't see it. The man whose heart had been made glad by a swarm of dragonflies paid no attention when a butterfly lit on a flower and slowly opened and closed its white wings.

What was inside him now was anger, coiled up like a snake ready to strike. Maybe Livy had been right. Always before, maybe he'd been scared to let himself see any cause to be angry. Boss kicks him in the ribs, he tells himself it don't matter, and lets himself believe it. What kind of man stays happy with a sharp-toed boot in his ribs?

He was hungry for somebody to mess with him. The boss steered clear of him. In a clear-headed moment, Zeb thought that might be why he was still a man standing in a field. If Benning looked at him funny, Zeb might have gone after him, and then Zeb would be dead. He wasn't so far gone he wanted to be dead.

Instead, he glared at Jubal. Jubal had been the one took Livy down the lane and out of sight of everybody else. Jubal had helped tie Zeb to the whipping post. Zeb jostled him in line at the tool shed, daring him to fight, but Jubal wasn't have any of it.

When he was with Faith and Hope, Zeb worked hard to look like a happy man. He didn't want little girls to see anything wrong in the world. Faith already knew too much, seeing his back all torn up in the evenings when Minnie dressed his wounds. But he tried to even if smiling at Hope toddling over to bring him her rag doll made him feel like his face was stiff as an old cow hide.

Livy started finding him on the way to the fields. "Morning, Zeb," she'd say. But he paid her no mind. She went on with it, "Morning, Zeb," "Evening, Zeb."

He stopped and looked at her one day at dusk when she'd come up to him in the lane. "You done made your choice. It wadn't me."

Next day, she shifted over to work a row next to him. "You wrong. I ain't with Jubal. I wadn't and I won't be." She moved off from him. She'd said what she wanted him to hear.

What did she think, he hadn't seen them come into the quarters that Sunday, Jubal's arm around her waist?

Just the same, he couldn't stop himself from noticing her every minute of the day. It hurt him just to look at her, wanting her so bad. He hadn't seen her talking to Jubal since then, though, had he? He didn't see Jubal pay her no mind, nor her pay any mind to Jubal. Maybe she told the truth and she wasn't with Jubal.

She was about as pretty a woman as he'd ever seen. Long slim legs, big wide cheekbones, a body to make a man want to grab her up and kiss her, her mouth, her face, her neck, kiss her all over. She said she hadn't let Jubal do that. And he knew she hadn't let anybody else get within kissing distance.

Sometimes he'd watch her and think maybe he'd go talk to her. He wanted to, even just to have her eyes on him. Other times, he'd think there wasn't no point in it. Not much point in anything, really.

~~~

Late in the afternoon, Zeb stepped over to the water cart to fill his jug. Clem walked up beside him like it just happened he came up to the cart at the same time. But Zeb had seen Clem eyeing him these last days, Jubal, too, and Pete.

"It was bad, Noah dying like that," Clem said.

"Yeah, it was."

"Seem like seeing Noah die so hard did something to you, Zeb."

Zeb took a big swig of water.
~~~

Clem took his turn at the spigot and let the water pour into his jug. "I always seen you as the perfect slave. Did what you was supposed to, did it with a smile. Didn't never complain."

"What good complaining do?"

"You right about that. Complaining don't do no good."

Zeb looked at Clem, measuring him. "You want something, Clem?"

"Don't want nothing, Zeb," he said, and stoppered his jug. "Just want to know if you still the happy slave, or if you ready to be something else?"

Zeb held himself very still. "What you talking about?"

"You wadn't never a complainer, and that's fine. We don't need no more complaining. We want anything different, we cain't wait for some chariot full of angels to come down and bring it to us. That's all I'm saying."

Rachel was coming up to fill her and Charlie's water jugs. Clem didn't say no more, just went on back to work. Zeb waited there a minute and let Rachel talk to him before he returned to his row.

Zeb wasn't stupid. Clem was talking about . . . Zeb wasn't sure. Running? Plotting some rising up against the master?

Crazy talk. Crazy. Zeb couldn't keep from thinking about it though. Then he'd tell himself again, crazy, crazy talk.

That night, Faith and Hope asleep, the cabin was quiet, just the sound of a little wind pushing through the trees. Zeb sat at the table carefully drawing Mama's cooking knife across the whet stone. Grandma dozed in her chair and Mama strained her eyes sewing a patch on Faith's dress by candlelight.

"Zeb," his mama said. "What Clem say to you today?"

Zeb didn't want to talk about that. He kept on pulling the blade over the whetstone.

"At the water cart, Zeb. That Clem, he always thinking something. I don't trust him."

"It ain't nothing, Mama."

"I know everybody on this place, Zeb. I knowed Clem since we was children on this lane. He want you scheming with him, don't he?"

"I ain't scheming, Mama. Don't fret over it."

He felt her looking at him. "I mean it, Mama. It ain't nothing."

She knotted the last stitch and bit through the thread. "I gone get ready for bed." She put her sewing away and went out to the privy.

His grandmother was awake, staring at him.

"Zeb, I never told, your mama never told you. About your daddy and your granddaddy."

He looked at her. "Sure she did. Daddy died in a fire. Granddaddy, well, I don't know nothing about him."

"She didn't tell you. My husband, your granddaddy, he ran, Zeb. He ran and he ran and we didn't never hear nothing about him again. He might have got picked up and sold to somewhere else, or he might have got killed, but I think he made it, Zeb. I think your granddaddy been living his life a free man somewhere up there in Canada."

Zeb set the knife aside. "I didn't know about that, Grandma. He run off and left you and the children?"

"I told him to go, Zeb. I told him, I send Abe after you when he old enough. He find you, you both be free, and maybe someday I come, too."

"But Daddy didn't run. He died right here. In a fire."

Eva shook her head. "No, that's what your mama told you. She don't want you taking after him. She want you safe more than she want you free."

"Daddy ran?"

"He ran. But they caught him and they brought him back dead."

Zeb stared into the candle. He didn't know any of this. He didn't know how to feel about it either. Didn't his daddy ought to have stayed and help raise him and his sister? And Granddaddy left Grandma and their children, too. He looked around the cabin. Didn't they need him, they with Faith and Hope to raise, the garden to keep up, the wood to chop, the water to carry?

"I know you got your daddy's blood in you, and I know what Clem got on his mind. What you gone do, Zeb?"

He rubbed his hand over his hair. "I ain't doing nothing, Grandma. There ain't nothing to do but get yourself killed. I ain't doing nothing."

Chapter Six

When the day's work was finished, they had maybe an hour before dark to collect the children, wash faces and hands and get ready for supper. Used to be, Zeb's grandma slipped out of the cabin sometimes, toting a sack of biscuits or corn, whatever they had left on the table. She'd been doing that long as he could remember.

Zeb had followed her when he was a boy, wondering where she went with their leftovers. Along about twilight, she'd mosey along like she had no place in particular to be and end up at the edge of the plantation, almost to the woods. She'd take a casual look around and then set her sack inside an old hollow log lying on the ground. He'd been so young, he'd wondered if she was feeding a raccoon or maybe squirrels and rabbits. He followed her again next time she fixed a sack, hoping he'd see the critters she fed. That time, she lingered a while as the sky turned dark and the north star shone out. In a little bit, here come a man and a woman. Zeb knew them. They used to live down the lane, but he hadn't seen them in a long time.

Eva opened her arms and the woman stepped in and got a hard hug. Then the man hugged grandma. They talked real low for a few minutes. The man got grandma's sack and they eased back into the darkening woods.

Zeb understood then they were laying out, hiding from the overseer and the master, trying not to be slaves. He worried how they were going to find their way in the dark woods without a lantern.

"Zeb?" Grandma didn't sound glad to see him standing in the darker shadows under the oak tree. "What you doing out here?"

He came on out and took her hand to walk back to the cabins. "I wanted to see where you going with that sack, Grandma. I didn't know you was helping the runaways."

"You old enough to follow me out here, you old enough to not tell nobody. You understand that, Zeb?"

"I won't tell nobody."

She squeezed his hand. "Then let's go on back and get to bed."

Zeb figured she had spent a lifetime sneaking food out to the maroons who had run from the master but lingered on the edges of the plantations, the ones didn't want to leave their families or didn't see any likelihood of traveling north through a whole world of slave hunters. He liked that his grandma did it when there were runaways in the neighborhood. But she'd been caught more than once. She had scars on her back to prove it.

Before Benning's time, when that other overseer had loved the whip, Zeb had had to half-carry her back to the cabin, blood pouring out of the lashes. When he told her she got to quit helping the runaways, she said, "Not till I dead."

What she had done was be more careful. These days, she waited till Benning had done his rounds, till his dogs were asleep under his porch, till he himself had gone to bed. Then she eased through the shadows to the spot where the runaways knew to wait for her, and she eased back into the cabin while it was still dark. She could have been a ghost, she was so quiet.

Zeb watched Eva pack a sack with boiled eggs, two baked potatoes, and a wedge of cornbread. When she walked around the table, there was a hitch in her step. Her hip was bothering her tonight.

"I take that, Grandma."

She shook her head. "I do it."

"Grandma, I'll do it for you. Just tell me where you leaving your sack this time."

Zeb's mama strode across the little room and stood between them. "Zeb, you ain't getting into that. You get yourself another whipping, a worse one maybe. You stay out of it."

"Mama – "

Grandma talked over him. "Hush, Minnie."

How many times had he heard his grandma tell her that, like there wasn't no need to make a fuss over every little thing. Now he thought about it though, mama mostly fussed if she was afraid he would get into trouble with the overseer. She couldn't bear the thought of it.

"Zeb," Grandma said. "You stay put. God give me this to do and I gone do it."

"Grandma –"

She held her hand up to stop him. "Zeb, you a good man, but this be my task before heaven and I aim to do it long as I can walk."

"All right. But I do it when you want me to."

Not but one night later, Zeb leapt out of bed, his feet on the floor before he was good awake. Lantern light flooded the cabin, showing his grandma heaved up on her elbow, squinting, and his mama with the covers pulled up to her nose.

"Stay where you are," the overseer said, his voice quiet. He didn't want no crying babies in the night. "Zeb, get back in the bed." Benning held the lantern high, chasing shadows all the way to the corners.

Zeb heaved a sigh and sat on the edge of his cot. Wasn't the first time Benning had come in, no knock, no by-your-leave. He was looking for runaways, or even for some slave run off for a lying-out, just taking a few days for himself, willing to pay the price when he come back. Nobody from here had gone off in a long while, but could be somebody from the next planation up or down the river had. Wasn't nothing for it but to sit still and let him have his look.

Benning stepped up the ladder leading into the loft. Nothing up there but a dried-up mattress. Benning climbed back down, took a quick look under the beds. Looked for signs the floorboards had been disturbed.

"A boy has run away from the Benoit plantation south of here. I ever catch you hiding a runaway, Eva – " He didn't say what he'd do, and he was right if he thought that was more frightening than a specific threat. "So he's not in here with you, but I think you've been leaving food out for him." Eva was still in her cot, leaning on her elbow watching him. "No sir, Mr. Benning. You told me not to do that no more, so I ain't."

Benning stared at her, a little smile on his face. Wasn't much going on down here the overseer didn't know about, but Zeb figured he didn't know nothing about what Clem was up to.

"If I see you sneaking out the back way to let the others know I'm coming, there will be trouble in this cabin. Stay put, all of you."

Benning closed the door softly behind him, hardly making a sound on the floor of the porch.

The corn shuck mattresses rustled in the dark as the three of them shifted, getting settled.

"You gone get our rations cut again, you don't quit it."

"Hush, Minnie," Eva said. "We got neighbors, don't we? We got cousins right here on the lane. Nobody in this house gone go hungry."

"Grandma, you too slow with your bad hip. Somebody seen you out there with your sack and told. You best let me leave the bundle from now on."

"Zebediah," Eva said, "I been leaving bundles out there longer than you been alive. You leave me to my own."

Zeb didn't know when he'd heard so much frost in her voice. Not when she was talking to him, anyway.

"Besides," Grandma said, "Benning don't need nobody telling him. He knows I be the one leaving food out there. Just ain't worth his trouble to catch me at it hisself."

Mama went back to sleep first, he could tell from her breathing. Faith and little Hope had slept through the whole thing, and he was glad of that.

Grandma said into the quiet. "Zeb, that runaway a boy not more than fifteen year old. He got to eat."

Took Zeb a long time to sink back into sleep.

~~~

Sunday afternoon, Weasel commenced to gather people around to watch his nonsense. Livy had decided she didn't like Weasel. Nothing seemed to happen Weasel didn't know about, and sometimes he was more mean than funny. She was sitting on her porch and she could see his tomfoolery just fine, but she had other things on her mind. Jubal had given her a job to do, and it wasn't going to be easy.

Weasel strutted around his little square of the lane swiveling his hips, looking over his shoulders and batting his eyelashes. Next he put on a big face-splitting grin and swaggered, rolling his big shoulders. Then he grabbed one of the women and made her stand still where everybody could see her, made shaping gestures all up and down her body to show how desirable she was. She just stood there, so he took hold of her hips and made her stick one hip out with her hand just so. She played along then and smoothed her dress over her breasts, making everybody titter and snicker.

Weasel turned back into the swaggering man with the grin and sashayed around the woman, looking her over, nodding his
~~~

head. "Morning, Livy," he said loud enough for everybody to hear. The woman simpered and said, "Morning, Zeb."

Oh my Lord, Weasel was poking at her and Zeb. A couple of women looked at her and smirked, everybody else laughing. She liked to have choked, everybody making fun like that.

Then Weasel reached out a finger and touched the woman meant to be Livy. He jerked his hand back like he'd been burned and stuck his finger in his mouth. Tried it again and got another burn.

Everybody laughed and whistled, but Livy's face felt so hot she thought maybe she really would burn anybody who touched her. She didn't look to see if Zeb was standing there watching. She didn't see how she could meet his eyes and everybody looking at them and laughing. Her stomach was threatening to heave up all her dinner.

She didn't quit gulping air until Weasel went on to pick on somebody else. Somebody eating too much, looked like. Livy didn't watch.

She had no idea people seen her and Zeb like that. Like they was lovers.

Lovers on the outs. Leastways, he was on the outs with her. She didn't like to think how sad that made her. Pitiful kind of courtship, saying "Morning" and "Evening," first him at her and now her at him.

Courtship? Her mind had slipped that word right in there and she didn't mean to have no courtship. But Zeb was such a tender man, the way he loved those little girls, and that old man Noah.

When her man was sold off the other place, Livy thought she'd die. Her heart had been so full of love, and he had been so fine, and such fun. And they had a baby coming. Sometimes she wondered if her baby would have come out stronger if Livy hadn't been so grieved and heartsore the last weeks before she was born. But Mama had said no, that baby knew she was loved, even before she saw the light of day.

A baby Zeb gave her would be loved, too. She didn't tell herself she didn't want him. She did. But making a baby with a man meant a kind of belonging she didn't want anymore.

She could be friends with him though. Zeb wanted her company as much as he wanted her body. At least she thought he did. Maybe that was foolishness. Maybe men didn't think like that.

But she sure did like the man.

Weasel was poking fun at old Isabel who'd gotten so she couldn't remember where she left her hoe or her drinking jug. Pure meanness, that was. But while folks was watching him cut up, she could do what she had to do.

Inside the empty cabin, Livy slipped a coil of wire out of her rolled-up mattress and put it in a sack.

She carried the sack behind the crowd still watching Weasel, hoping anybody saw her they'd think it was full of blueberries. Likely they wouldn't think about her and her sack at all, but she felt like that stolen wire was glowing hot and red and would burn right through the bag for all to see.

"Want you to do something," Jubal had said. She was drawing water from the well when he came up to her one evening. He and Bettina was to the well before she was, but he teased and flirted with Bettina and got her to fill her bucket ahead of him. When Bettina was gone, that's when he told her he gone give her a job.

Whatever it was, Livy was willing to do it. "What?"

"Smithy got in a barrel of wire this week. We got use for a piece of wire. You get it, you take it to the tree and leave it."

She looked at him with her head tilted. He think she was made out of air, could just walk into the blacksmith shop and walk out again with a piece of wire and nobody see her?

"How'm I supposed to get this wire?"

"Smithy gone leave a coil on top of the anvil when he quit tomorrow night. You walk into the shop after dark, pick up the wire, and walk out again."

"Just that easy, huh? And what if somebody see me?"

"That's why you going in the dark. Watch what you doing, don't let nobody see you."

She had worked all the next day with fear creeping around the edges of her spine. If somebody saw her, somebody like Weasel who seemed to know everything that went on, she'd be whipped for a thief. Where she came from, sometimes they even branded a thief, right on the forehead. So she wouldn't get caught, that's what she told herself. She'd wait till everybody gone to bed, she'd just slide through the dark, get that wire, and slide right back to her bed. She should pick the stitches in her mattress a little beforehand so she could hide the wire in there till Sunday afternoon.

She'd lain on her mattress on the porch while the quarters settled down. Grace swore rubbing fresh thyme on her skin worked better than mint to discourage the mosquitoes, so she smelled like a garden lying there in the open air. Across the way, Mayella's baby had the colic and was crying like he never be quiet again. Down the lane, somebody was quarrelling, but they hushed pretty quick.

Long time after it seemed everybody'd gone to sleep, Livy slid off her mattress and padded down the steps barefoot. She kept to the moon shadows all the way to the blacksmith shop. When she stepped into the work room, she felt the heat still radiating from the furnace. She didn't have any trouble spotting the anvil. It was bolted onto a tree stump two feet across and four feet high. And on top of it, a coil of wire.

And now here she was, in the light of day, ambling through the quarters with the wire like she had never stolen anything in her life. When she was well into the trees, she hurried on to the old Indian trail and hiked the path to the oak with the hole in it.

She was to leave the wire in the tree and check to see if there was a piece of wood in the tree hole. She was reaching into the hole when that man Hector came out of the woods quiet as smoke.

"I'll take the wire. You name Livy, ain't it?"

"Yeah."

"You give Tish something for me?"

"Why she don't come for it herself?"

"Tish ain't venturesome like you."

He handed her a burlap bag. "This here's palmetto heart. You take some of it for yourself."

Livy asked him, "Why don't you go on and run you want to be free? What you waiting for?"

"Running is for fools. Slave patrols get you long before you make it all the way free."

"You'd rather live out here like a wild animal."

"You don't know much for a gal wants to get herself out from under the white man's boot."

She stared at him. He wasn't raggedy. He wasn't skinny or sick or scared.

"You got a camp back there, don't you?"

He hefted the wire. "Thanks for this," and went on up the trail without looking back.

Livy sat down with her back to the tree. So Clem was telling the truth when he said they weren't running. Not all the way running anyway. They was going to a camp back in the woods. Or the swamp. Livy didn't like the swamp.

She wondered how many there'd be in that camp. Sooner or later the slave hunters would find them out there and then they'd be done for. Unless they had guns. She'd heard sometimes maroons would show up in town, bold as brass, with furs or cypress tubs or game to trade. They could have guns.

She wondered if a body could stay in a maroon camp for a while, scout out the next camp to the north, move to it, and then to the next and the next until someday she would be all the way to freedom land.

She leaned her head back and looked at the sunlight filtering through the leaves. Nothing said she had to go with them. Nothing said she couldn't run off on her own. She'd go back upriver and collect her sisters and mama and they'd run on together.

But Isabel would be having her baby soon. Mama's knees were bad. And Cassandra would never leave Mama.

Then she was on her own. She could stay here and live out her days on this place. Maybe with Zeb. She let herself think about Zeb for a minute, but then she shook her head. No Zeb, no settling down. She could not get this terrible yearning out of her heart. She was going to have to run or join Hector and the other maroons. What was it like, living in the swamps, wondering every minute if the slavers were coming for you? Or a gator, or a cottonmouth.

Probably no worse than running, listening for dogs on your trail, hungry, scared, maybe lost.

She wanted to be free, but she didn't want to be run down by a pack of dogs. She didn't want her back cut up by the lash. And that might be what happened if she took off, alone, or into the swamp with the others. How much did she want it?

Chapter Seven

Late Sunday afternoon, Zeb, Samson, and Pete came back from the bayou with a string of catfish. Seemed like every child on the place was screaming and laughing. They were playing Red Rover, two lines linked arm in arm across the lane, challenging the opposite line to send a challenger to break through.

"Red Rover, Red Rover, send Faith on over."

Zeb stopped to watch Faith dart across the lane and try to slip under the linked arms to score a point, but they were ready for her. She bounced off the barrier they made and landed on her bottom, which seemed to be the funniest thing to happen in a hundred years. Faith grinned and brushed off her behind, wiggling it at the enemy side before she dashed back to her own.

Zeb saw Benning before the children did. The master's wife was with him. He couldn't think when he had ever seen a white woman down here. When the children saw the two of them, they dropped their linked arms and stared. Seemed like every sound got swallowed up and buried.

The woman had hair the color of straw. She had on a pink dress made of some stuff that looked like it floated around her. Her shoes were white with a raised heel. Hard to take your eyes off her. But it wasn't because she was a woman and he was a man. Everybody on the lane, men, women, boys and girls, were staring at her.

Benning said something to her and she nodded.

"All ya'll little girls, come on over here and line up in front of Mrs. Dietrich." He gestured to show them where he wanted them.

The children looked at each other, their eyes big. The girls stepped forward and lined themselves up.

"Mrs. Dietrich needs a little nigger in the house to fetch and carry for her," Benning said. "She needs a smart girl, a good girl. You girls stand there and let her look at you. If she asks you a question, you answer her."

He nodded to the master's wife, and she walked slowly along the line, examining each girl. There were eleven of them spread out, their bare feet dusty from the dirt lane. Some of them wore dresses too big for them, others' were too small. All of them had their hair neatly braided and tamed. Zeb noticed the older girls stood straight and stiff, afraid to move. The younger ones couldn't be that still and fidgeted. Faith, he wasn't surprised to see, rocked back and forth on her heels. She looked like she was curious and maybe a little excited to see the white lady down here.

Lord, don't let her choose Faith. He couldn't bear the thought of her spending all her time at the big house, coming down to see them a little while on a Sunday afternoon. Maybe not even that.

Mrs. Dietrich paused in front of Samson's girl. Sarah had a little bit of a stutter, and when the woman asked her a question, she was too tongue-tied to get an answer out. The mistress shook her head in disgust and moved on. Samson's whole body seemed to sag in relief.

But Faith, bless her, didn't have a bit of shy in her. The mistress asked her a question, Zeb couldn't hear what, and Faith grinned that big grin of hers and whatever she said made the mistress laugh.

Mrs. Dietrich turned to the overseer and said a word or two. Benning took Faith by the shoulder and moved her along in front of him. The three of them, the white mistress, the boss, and Zeb's niece walked on out of the quarters.

Zeb felt like somebody tied a rope around his chest and twisted it tight. Samson and Pete were both looking at him, studying him. They wonder what it was like to have a child taken off, just like that? They wondering what it felt like?

He handed the catfish to Samson and walked on to the cabin on legs that felt like tree trunks. Mama stood on the porch, Hope in her arms. She'd seen the whole thing. He glanced at her face, and then he couldn't look at her anymore. She followed him in the cabin and handed Hope to him. She climbed onto her cot and turned her back to the room.

Grandma Eva stood up from bending over a pot of beans at the fire. "What wrong with you, Minnie?"

Mama didn't answer her, and Grandma turned to Zeb. "What happened?"

Zeb told her. Grandma sat down heavy on the rawhide chair.

Nobody said anything. Hope fell asleep on Zeb's shoulder and he put her down on her pallet. He sat down in a straight back chair. Last winter when he'd stretched the hide and cut it and tied it tight across this same chair bottom, Faith had sat with him, chattering the whole time. When he brought it in, ready to sit on, she'd announced to her grandmother and great grandmother, "We finished," like she'd done half the work herself. Zeb had grinned at the time, tickled at her.

"Well," he said. "I expect she be better off up there. Easier than out in the fields or in the laundry."

"She gone have to go to work soon, anyway," Eva said. "This way, she be out of the weather."

"Not like she sold off the place. We see her now and then."

Crickets, the sound of voices out in the lane. Hope's soft breathing. Dark seeped into the cabin but they didn't light a candle. Finally, the quarters grew quiet and they went to bed.

Zeb didn't sleep much that night, nor for the nights after that. It was hard to work all day when he hadn't slept, but he could do it. He told himself the same things over and over. This be better for Faith they make her a house slave. She wasn't all the way gone, just a few hundred yards away was all. She'd come down and see them every chance she got. And she was almost ten. The boss would've been putting her to work in a few months anyway.

But she'd have been home with him and the two mamas and her baby sister every night. She'd have got to grow up with her family around her.

Sometimes he felt resigned. This was life. It wasn't so bad. Faith would have plenty to eat up there at the house, wouldn't have to hoe out in the sun, or work her woman's body down till she was a old woman by the time she was thirty.

Other times he felt a hot red wave of fury well up inside him. His jaw ached from clenching it all day and into the night. He could hardly eat he was so full of bile.

And what good it gone to do be angry? This what it meant to be a slave. No use being angry. No use at all.

The weeding in the cane fields done for now, Benning set them to other tasks. Zeb and Jubal and Charlie went up into the vegetable patch behind the house where the master's cook got her peas and celery and peppers. He dug sweet potatoes and picked corn, trying to remember why he used to smile all the time, before Noah, before Faith.

He sat in the shade to shuck corn. No more than a hundred feet away, the master's little girls were having a tea party on the lawn. They had a small table and little chairs to sit on. They had a teapot and little cups. They wore white dresses with ribbons and laces and more ribbons in their hair. The oldest one was a big girl, maybe eleven or twelve. The other two were about the size of Faith. They didn't have no work they had to do, didn't have no thought of living anywhere but with their mama and daddy.

And here come Faith carrying a tray with little cakes on it. She carefully set a plate down next to each girl, then placed white napkins next to the plates. They acted like they didn't see her, like their napkins and cake just appeared out of the air.

Faith stepped away and stood in the shade, her tray held before her, her gaze far away.

The oldest girl spoke and gestured with her hand. Faith moved out from the shade and stood in the sun so her body blocked its heat from the white girl. Faith, who could hardly slow her mouth down from sunup till sundown, didn't say a word.

He wanted to go over there, take Faith by the hand, and walk her home to the cabin. He wanted to hear her chattering and singing to her baby sister.

Jubal sat down next to him and started rubbing the dirt off the potatoes with his hard hands.

"That your girl over there, ain't it?" Jubal said.

Zeb didn't feel like talking. He shucked another ear of corn.

"Those little white girls gone be children a long time yet. Look like Faith's childhood be over." Jubal reached for another potato. "How you feel about that, Zeb?"

Zeb fixed him with a stare. "What difference it make how I feel?"

Jubal just nodded his head.

~~~

Zeb had changed, Livy could see that. She'd wanted him to be a man, to know he was a slave and to resent it as much as she did. But it hurt to see what he'd lost. He didn't pause to look up at the clouds in the sky or to say a friendly word to whoever was nearby. He didn't talk to nobody, didn't smile at nobody.
~~~

When the boss took Zeb's niece up to the big house, she'd seen how Zeb had closed himself off from the rest of them. Mean as she knew it was, she was a little glad Zeb knew now how it was to feel like some dumb animal, no more control over himself than the cow out in the pasture.

It wasn't a awful thing, the girl going up to be trained as a house slave. Some of the mamas and daddies in the quarters probably be glad if it were their gal that had been chosen. But sometimes it wasn't the worse things that pushed a soul into a deep pool of bitter.

She had been numb with despair when she learned the master had sold her and she'd be leaving the place, the only place she'd ever known, and leaving her mama and sisters, too. What pushed her from despair to this relentless, simmering anger, though, had been when it was time to go. She wanted to step over and hug Isabel and Cassandra, to hug her mama good bye one more time. And the overseer wouldn't let her.

Didn't have to be the worst thing that ever happened to put you in that place where mad was with you every minute.

Looked like for Zeb, the boss's wife taking his niece up to the big house was what had put him in the same place she was.

Course he was still mad at her about Jubal, too. A couple of days after Noah died, she'd come up beside Zeb when he was outside with the littlest girl. "Zeb," she said. "I'm sorry for Noah having to die like that."

He'd picked the little girl up and put her on his shoulders like she wasn't even there.

"I shouldn't have told you you smile too much," she said softly. But she didn't know if he heard her cause he walked off without looking at her.

So he hadn't believed her when she told him she wasn't with Jubal, and it didn't sit well with her whenever he give her the shoulder, like she was an awful person. Well, he was hurting, and a tender man like Zeb, he didn't deserve to hurt.

So she had started in on him like he'd done to her. Good morning, good evening, every day. He wasn't answering her, but she hadn't answered him for a long time, either.

Those mornings and evenings were what Weasel had heard and made foolery out of, but that hadn't stopped her from working at Zeb to let up being mad.

And what were Jubal and Clem and Pete thinking? They were keeping an eye on Zeb. They didn't trust him now he was as mopey as she'd been? Or maybe they liked him better this way, now he wasn't like some floppy-eared puppy. She watched them look at him, like they was measuring him, then murmur together. They was thinking something, she knew that.

Livy watched him too. Now that she had let hope creep in, thinking maybe she'd get free going with Clem and the others, she could let herself feel a little good sometimes instead of all the time bad. She noticed the way Zeb's thin white shirt clung to him when he was sweating out in the sun. She noticed how easy it was for him to work just about twice as fast as she could. He was a strong man, a good man. When she was alone in her bed, she imagined him lying there with her, her hands roaming over those smooth muscles in his back, his hands on her. She was still young. She could have other babies. It'd be nice to have babies with a man who knew how to smile. But Zeb wasn't smiling no more. And she wasn't gone be on this place long enough to think about babies.

~~~

When the mid-day dinner wagon came out to the fields, Livy collected her bucket and spoon. She usually sat with the women now, talking a little, making an effort to be part of the people here. She didn't want the boss to notice her one way or the other, like he might if she didn't talk to nobody. Better she fit in. And they was nice women. She'd be leaving them soon, but she could be nice, too.

There he was again, Zeb going off to eat his lunch under a different shade tree. That wasn't right, the friendliest soul on the place eating all alone. Somebody ought to be nice to Zeb for a change, try to get him smiling like he used to. Livy looked around – nobody paying any mind to where Zeb ate. So that somebody gone have to be her. Didn't mean she was gone be his woman, didn't mean she was gone stay here on this place.

He was mad at her though – he likely wouldn't smile for her either. But she'd try. She trailed along behind him and sat down next to him.

Zeb glanced at her and went back to spooning beans in his mouth. She spooned half a boiled onion out of her bucket,
~~~

hesitated, then ladled it into Zeb's bucket. "I don't want no onion," she said.

He gave her a look, then stared at the onion. He ate it, but he didn't look at her again, didn't say nothing.

She never had felt shy with him before, but she did now. She took a breath and told him again, "I'm sorry I said you smile too much. I miss your smiles."

He sat still with his spoon poised over his bucket. He turned his head and looked at her.

"What it take to make you smile again?" she said with a scared little smile of her own. "Three little words?"

A glint shone in his eye. "Depends on what they is."

She'd meant to be friendly, that's all, but now she felt like her eyes were stuck, gazing into his, her pulse pounding in her throat.

"What if they was, 'Kiss me, Zeb'?"

He smiled and it was like the sun peeking out from behind the clouds. "I don't want no peck on the cheek, Livy."

She shook her head. "No pecks."

"I might want more than one," he said.

"Don't be greedy. One just fine to start with."

They looked around them. Most everybody was ahead of them, their faces turned the other way.

They both leaned in and kissed, only their mouths touching.

Livy had never been kissed like this before, the merest brushing of his lips across hers, soft and warm. Then a little pressure, his mouth opening. He ran his tongue along her bottom lip and dipped in behind it. She opened her mouth to him and gave him everything. Though their bodies were inches apart, their whole selves were behind that kiss.

When she thought she might bust from the pounding in her chest, he pulled back.

"I been waiting for that," he said.

She let out a sigh so big it could have stirred the leaves in the trees. "I been waiting for that, too."

She leaned in again. Just as his mouth came to hers, she murmured against his lips, "You taste like onions."

"Your fault, woman." He closed the smidgen of distance between them and kissed her again.

Chapter Eight

Zeb and Jubal and Pete were still assigned to the cook's garden, weeding, digging potatoes, getting the ground ready for the second planting of corn seed.

Dinner time, Zeb sat down under a big oak with his dinner pail. He wished Livy was sitting next to him. This evening, he'd take a minute, go pick her a ripe peach out of the orchard on the way back to the quarters. Maybe take her for a walk before it got too dark. He kiss her enough, she'd come round, might even move into the cabin with him and the family.

Mama had the same idea. That very morning at breakfast, she'd said, "I was thinking, Zeb, we could clear out the loft, put a mattress up there. If you want to bring that girl to stay with us."

Zeb looked at her like she was crazy. "What girl?"

"Don't you go teasing me, Zebediah. I seen you with that Livy plenty of times, and then she come sit with you with her lunch bucket."

"So you seen me eating dinner with Livy and you think she ought to come stay here?"

She laughed. "I seen more than eating dinner."

He'd grinned at her. "Saw her give me her onion, did you?"

"She give you more than an onion."

They could clean the cobwebs out of the loft, air it out, could have their own space. She wouldn't have to be lonely no more. He thought a moment. He wouldn't be lonely no more either.

Jubal come with his dinner and sat down with Zeb in the shade. They ate a while, comfortable together.

"I got me two girls, three boys," Jubal said.

Zeb knew that. Everybody on the place knew who had what children. Even if every one of Jubal's babies was born to different mamas, he still looked after them, took them fishing, showed them how to tie knots.

"Look to me like, lessen somebody do something, my children gone be living the same life as me and their mamas when they grow up."

Zeb tensed. He didn't encourage him. Jubal would get to it or he wouldn't.

"I rather do something, Zeb. What about you? Someday you have a houseful of younguns. You want to see your own girl taken out of the cabin and set in somebody else's house when she still just a little gal? You want your sons working the live long day so a white man can live in a big house and put ribbons in his little girls' hair?"

A mockingbird was chasing a squirrel across the yard. Zeb watched that instead of looking at Jubal.

"Some folks say we ain't got it bad here," Jubal went on. "The master and the boss don't be quick with the whip. When somebody sick, Benning don't fuss while they lay up a while. They pretty good to us."

Jubal took his time, eating, wiping his mouth with the back of his hand. When he did speak, he acted like he was just talking about how bacon made the collards taste good. "But say my boy want to have a little farm, raise a few cattle. Say he want those cattle and all his hard work to belong to him and his sons and his girls. He gone be able to do that?" Jubal shook his head. "Not lessen somebody do something."

Zeb finished his dinner and set his bucket aside. He lay down on the grass, his arms crossed under his head. The sun filtering through the canopy made patterns on the back of his eyelids, dark and light.

"Some of us gone do something so our children don't be slaves. You be one of us, Zeb, we do it together."

"No," Zeb said, and settled his hat over his face.

After that, Jubal didn't want no more to do with him. That was fine with Zeb. But Zeb didn't forget what he'd said. He thought about it during the day as he went about his work, he thought about it sitting in the cabin with his mama and grandma before they went to bed. When he woke up in the morning, that was what came to mind first. Doing something, Jubal had said.

He'd always believed in living the life God put out for you, taking pleasure in the taste of cane juice on your tongue, in the sun on your face on a cold day, in cool water sluiced over your head on a hot one. Wasn't it better to *live*? He'd always thought so.

Why get yourself killed trying to change what can't be changed? A dead man don't get no pleasure out of nothing.

But Jubal talked about doing something. If he meant a rising up, his head was full of clouds. Zeb hadn't heard of many revolts, but he never heard that a one of them had succeeded. The white man had all the power. He had weapons and horses and . . . Zeb thought about that. Why were weapons and horses enough to keep all of them down? There were many more black slaves than there were white men.

He figured people just didn't never see living any other way. Who on this plantation had ever known a free black man? But they knew there were some. The tinker man who came through twice a year said there was a black farmer a few miles up the river who owned his own land. He said there were black people in the city who owned stores and houses and even carriages. Lots of them were poor, too, who took in washing or cleaned out the gutters, whatever work they could get. But their sons and daughters decided what they were going to be. Maybe she would be a washerwoman, or he would muck out stables, but they would decide for themselves.

Yes, everybody in the quarters knew there were free black people. They just didn't let themselves think about it. Black people were strong, stronger than white men who never worked a hoe or an anvil, but they didn't let themselves think about why weapons and horses were enough to keep them down.

They were afraid. Soon as he thought it, Zeb realized how much fear he carried around himself. He had never heard about his grandfather, and he hadn't remembered his own father coming back dead. But since his grandmother told him, he'd been having little flashes of memory. He must have been little, and he must have buried that day deep, but he thought he could see a man's body, limp and discolored with bruises, coming into the quarters in a blue cart. He thought he heard somebody scream. He thought he could remember the terror and the awful grief that engulfed him like black flood water.

He had been afraid ever since. You don't be a happy slave, you be a dead slave being brought home in a cart.

Jubal wanted him to do something. Well, when Benning wouldn't bring the doctor for Noah or even give him a dose of laudanum, Zeb had done something. He wasn't sorry he'd done it. Wasn't even sorry he got six scars on his back, but it hadn't saved Noah.

He could see now, though, how he'd been hiding from himself. Faith had been walked right out of their lives. They hadn't let her come back down here even once. And Zeb had said nothing to the boss. Hadn't asked him if maybe Faith could sleep down here every night. If maybe Faith could go up there a half a day instead of all day and all night. Wouldn't likely have done any good, but maybe it would have. He should have tried.

But if Jubal meant turning rebel, people white and black getting killed? Then waiting for the militia to come cut them down like scythes swinging through dry grass? Didn't have anything to do with being afraid. There just wasn't any sense in it.

Still, there was plenty to get angry about if you let yourself. He could have a moment here or there, with Hope, with Livy, when he felt glad, but most of the time, he suffered from a low-grade burn. Instead of stepping onto the porch of a morning and breathing in the dawn and the gladness of being alive, he stepped out there and thought about how many children lived on this lane, how many of them gone spend their lives hoeing and chopping and pulling and pushing.

Felt like Mama tip-toed around him now. Like he was an egg and she was afraid she'd knock up against him and crack him open. She was afraid, always had been, he'd end up like his daddy, so she had taught him how to be a slave and still smile. That wasn't wrong. But it wasn't right either.

Grandma got up from her chair soon as Mama went out for a last visit to the privy before bed. She had a little box she kept on the high shelf. Zeb didn't know what was in it, had never asked, but he figured it held the treasures she'd collected through life. He didn't have a box, but he had a place on the shelf for a piece of gnarled wood looked like Jesus, and a rock with a spiral shell buried in it. Things he'd picked up here and there.

Grandma opened up her box and handed Zeb a clay pipe. "This here belonged to your granddaddy, Zeb."

He handled it gently. The bowl was nicked and discolored. The stem had a long crack. Felt like he wasn't careful, it would crumble in his hands. "Why you give me this now, Grandma?"

"I think maybe it be time, Zeb. I think I see your granddaddy coming out in you."

They heard Minnie's steps on the back stoop.

"I best keep it for you," Grandma whispered, and slipped the pipe back into her treasure box. "But it yours, Zeb. It belong to you now."

When Zeb's mama came back in he was still wrapping a tight cord around a bunch of straw to make a new broom. Grandma was putting her night gown on. When he got the broom finished, he blew out the candle and went to bed.

Chapter Nine

Zeb, Jubal and Samson were clearing the weeds out of a drainage ditch down by the blueberry patch when here come the white girls, all of them carrying little baskets. Faith was with them, wearing a new dress. It was blue and had ruffles around the hem. Too big for her, but she'd grow into it. He bet she thought it was the prettiest thing she'd ever seen. He bet she was full of smiles when she put it on in the mornings.

He straightened over his hoe, hoping he'd get to talk to her, but when he caught her eye, she gave him a little hidden wave down at her side and turned away.

Zeb's throat tightened up. They told her she couldn't even talk to them? Faith wasn't an orphan. She had family. He could feel the blood pounding in his temple. She had a family who missed her.

Zeb put his hoe down and stepped up out of the ditch. He would give Faith a hug, ask her how she did, tell her Hope got a new tooth.

"Zeb," Samson said, his hand on Zeb's arm.

Zeb shook him off. He strode through the blueberry bushes and called her name. "Faith."

Faith turned. A nine year old girl shouldn't have a look like that on her face, ever. He saw her mouth say Zeb, but she didn't say it out loud.

The oldest white girl, the one about two years older than Faith, saw him coming. She marched over, grabbed Faith's hair and slapped her hard across the face.

"I told you, you are not allowed to talk to niggers anymore."

Zeb stopped where he stood. He wanted to give that white girl a slap on the backside. And he wanted to gather Faith into his arms and take her away from there.

The white girl tilted her chin up and stared at him. Then she smiled, and he liked to have done something stupid. Something that wouldn't help Faith, and would likely get him killed.

Faith's eyes were squeezed close. She wouldn't look at him.

Samson came up behind and put a hand on his shoulder. "Come away, Zeb. Come away."

He turned on his heel and strode off. Didn't know where he was going and didn't care. He kept on, his long strides eating up the ground. When he stopped, he was deep in the woods on a narrow path. He followed it, walking hard like he could leave the hurt behind him. He couldn't think with the blood pushing through his brain so hard. All he knew was rage so hot he didn't know how to live through it. His breath came in harsh, shallow pants, all he could do to pull in a little air.

This was why Jubal talked about doing something. This was why his daddy and his granddaddy had run. This rage that tore around inside a man till he couldn't just *be* anymore. Jubal must feel it, too. And now Zeb had to find a way to breathe enough to get through this day and the next and the next.

And Faith had to find a way to live up there with people who were mean to her, day in and day out. How she gone grow up to be when she never saw anybody who loved her?

He couldn't guess how many miles he'd gone on that trail before he turned back. By the time he cut off into the woods behind the quarters, he felt heavy as an ox. Like he went into the woods a young man and was coming out old as Noah.

Jubal was waiting for him, standing with his arms crossed over his chest.

~~~

Jubal knew a man didn't have a clear head when he was in a passion. And Zeb was in a passion. This kind of pain was why people were willing to risk everything to get away. Not pain from the whip. The pain from feeling helpless, seeing somebody you love suffer and not being able to do anything about it. What kind of man didn't fall into a passion over that? Zeb had just been sleeping all these years. He was smart. He was strong. He smiled all the time, but that didn't mean he didn't have backbone, it just meant Zeb had kept childhood's blinders on. Safer that way, Jubal understood that.

But Zeb was awake now. And they could use him. Flavian had a carpenter, a smith, a tanner, a hunter. They needed people to raise the food, people who knew how to do whatever come up.
~~~

They were trying to build something out there, not just hiding out so they could live like creatures of the swamp for the rest of their lives.

Looked like Zeb was settled enough after marching up the trail for a few miles. Maybe his blood was calm enough he could hear.

He turned them toward the pond on the far side of the fields. They ought to be working that ditch next to the blueberry patch, but Benning had checked on them just before Jubal had come looking for Zeb.

"Where's Zebediah?" Benning had said.

The little girls were all gone back to the house by then, their pails full of blueberries. It had hurt his heart to see Faith with her eyes cast on the ground, her face closed. She'd always been a laughing little thing. Happy, like Zeb.

"Zeb gone to the privy, boss," Jubal told him.

"You three finish up here and get on over to the saw pit, see if Owen can use you. They got a pile of logs to cut through."

Jubal and Samson had worked fast as they could to get the ditch cleared out so it would look like they'd all done a three man task. Samson had gone on to the sawpit where there were probably a dozen men taking turns at the six foot saw, one man in the pit under the log, the other on a platform over it, pushing and pulling the saw through tough old hickory. Wore the men out in ten minutes and another team would take their place.

Benning likely wouldn't notice whether Zeb and Jubal were there or not as long as there were plenty of men working the pit.

They sat on a grassy bank. Jubal waited for Zeb to ask him what he wanted. But Zeb wasn't talking.

"You remember when I talked to you about doing something? Something to keep our children from working sunup to sundown and getting nothing for it?"

"I hope to God you ain't talking about a rising up. You get us all killed."

"We ain't that stupid. When did anybody ever win a rising up? I know all about that last big rising. My daddy was a young man then, marched along the river road toward New Orleans with all them others like they was gone take over the world. He was one of the lucky ones, kept his head attached to his body, and he talked about it all the rest of his days. You probably heard them stories, too."

"Yeah. That's why I been thinking you was stupid."

Zeb wasn't trying to be funny, but Jubal laughed anyway. "You remember Hector?"

"Sure. Been gone a while now. Except I seen him sliding through the dark into Tish's cabin a couple of times."

"He been out at Flavian's camp. You may not know Flavian. He's from the Brown place down river from here. He got enough people now and Hector gone split off and start a new camp back in the swamp."

Zeb's gaze was on the pond, thinking. Jubal was glad to give him the time.

Finally Zeb looked at Jubal. "So you going out there with the maroons. They got any children out there? Is it safe for a couple of little girls?"

"You want to see for yourself, Hector can take you there."

Zeb nodded, his thumb rubbing across his chin. "Yeah. I want to see it."

"Your grandma been feeding runaways all these years, Zeb. Later on, when we got a place made, she be welcome. Your mama, too."

"Who else going?"

"I ain't ready to tell you that. But the thing is, Zeb, you build yourself a camp, you don't need to be sneaking to the edge of the plantation for your grandma's little sacks of food. Some of them out there make tubs and troughs and such out of cypress, hunt for pelts and game, and they go right on into the market at Donaldsonville, even New Orleans. They careful, know who they can trade with. Come back with powder, shot, tools, wheat flour, whatever they can't make."

Zeb sat with his arms around his knees. Jubal knew it was a lot to think about. It was a risk. A big one. They wouldn't never be safe, not really, out there in the swamp. Between slavers and storms, animals, hardship – "You won't have no easy life, but Zeb, you won't answer to nobody but yourself out there."

"You keep saying 'you,' Jubal. You ain't going out ?"

Jubal contemplated his dusty bare foot. "Some folks don't have the stomach for living rough like the maroons do. They want a roof over they heads and a bed and knowing that there be food on the table morning and night. You gone have to do without that for the first year or so. Then you have a camp like Flavian's where you can raise your kids and live out your lives without nobody's boot on your neck." Jubal shrugged. "My three boys, two little girls, they all too little to take out there anyway, and I ain't leaving them."

"I don't know that Faith big enough either," Zeb said. "Don't know if that the right thing to do."

"Maybe not, but they need a man like you, Zeb. Somebody strong, good with his hands. I been working with you my whole life. Nobody here a better worker than you. And I seen you fix that broken pump with wire and a bent hoe blade, worked fine until smithy could make a new part. You be welcome out there, Zeb. You and yours."

Zeb ran his finger over his top lip, thinking. He'd be taking Faith away from her grandma and her great-grandma and her baby sister. And running off – he'd always thought that was craziness. She had all she needed to eat, she had a roof over her head. What kind of life would she have with him out in the wild?

Jubal clapped a hand on his shoulder.

"Come on. We better sneak over to the saw pit and act like we been there all afternoon."

Chapter Ten

Slapping at mosquitoes and wincing at the sting of sweat rolling over fresh bites, Hector dredged up all the patience he had in him. He was crouched behind a patch of wild hawthorn on the edge of the last field of the plantation. Another twenty minutes, it'd be dark and he could ease on into the quarters.

All those months ago when he'd run off, he hadn't planned it. Benning had told him he'd have to take down the fence he'd spent the whole day putting up and do it over tomorrow. Wasn't nothing wrong with that fence a little tweak wouldn't have fixed, but no, he was supposed to tear it all down and do it again. And Hector had spat.

Benning had kept his body real still, but the look on his face was black. He could do murder right on the spot, and there wasn't nobody this side of God to say a white man done wrong.

Good sense had Hector saying, "Sorry sorry Boss. I didn't mean to spit so close to your boot. No sir, I never do something like that." He'd bowed his head and looked sorry indeed. And he was sorry. It was about as dumb a thing as a slave could do, and for what? He was going to have to work all day tomorrow doing something, anyway, might as well be taking the fence apart and putting it back up.

He was too proud. His mama had told him that since he was twelve years old. You act so proud, you get yourself a world of pain, she'd say. Pride don't get you anything good in this life. And, fool that he was, he'd been proud of that fence that wasn't even his.

Benning hailed some men working fifty yards away and they come running. "Get hold of Hector here. Take him over to the blacksmith and tell smithy to put the ball and chain on his leg. I'll be over directly."

Hector went cold from his head down to his toes. It wasn't hard to imagine what dragging around a ten pound ball would do. It'd tear up the flesh around his ankle, for one thing, and nag at him every step of the day. For how many days? For as long as Benning said, that's how many.

The men's grips on his arms were loose, Hector not giving them any trouble. They all knew there wasn't nothing to do but go on over to the blacksmith shop and get him fitted with the ball Smithy kept back of the shed; didn't get much use, but it was there and ready.

They wasn't talking, any of them. It was a dread thing what the overseer was doing to Hector, and they had their own thoughts whizzing around in their heads.

His mind was whirling with anger and fear and indignation. He'd done wrong, and he'd been dumb as a donkey, but he wasn't gone wear no chain and ball.

It was easy for Hector to jerk away and run like a rabbit for the woods. Far as he could tell, they didn't even try to stop him.

He ran and he ran till he was at the far end of the plantation where the cypress trees lined the edge of the swamp. The water wasn't deep here, but it was deep enough to keep the dogs off his trail. And back here was nothing but wilderness. No roads, no squared off tracts of ownership. He could lose himself back here long as he wanted.

And that's what he'd done. Been more than a year now. First days he'd been hungry and bug bit and scared. And felt like the biggest fool God ever made, cause here he was lost out in the swamp, and Tish and his boy were back in the cabin without him.

Tish would spend the nights crying cause he'd run off and left her. He thought about going back. Benning wouldn't kill him. He was worth too much to the master to kill him. But he'd do more than punish his body. He'd humiliate him and try to take every smidge of pride he had left and stomp on it. What'd he have left to offer Tish if he wasn't a man anymore? No, he wasn't sorry enough to go back and face that.

When Flavian found him, he was curled up in a ball on a piece of dry, bushy, buggy land, panting from the stomach cramps. He'd eaten a lizard and discovered for himself why nobody caught and raised lizards to eat.

Flavian helped him into the dugout and took him back to his camp. He'd never been so glad to have a roof over his head or a piece of cornbread to fill his belly.

Took him six days to get his strength back. He missed Tish and the baby so bad it hurt, but he liked it in the swamp. They'd built three cabins, were putting up a fourth as they got the timber. Everything happened slow out there. They didn't have many tools, and they spent most of the day hunting and trapping and gathering roots and wild fruit.

But there was an ease living in the swamp. He never knew how heavy slavery was till it was off his shoulders. He felt lightened. He felt a creeping joy stealing in.

They didn't have much extra, but they had enough. They didn't have to sneak up to the slave quarters and beg for food like some runaways. But several of the men did sneak back so they could see their mamas or their wives. Once Hector learned his way through the swamp, he did the same.

First time he slipped into the cabin in the middle of the night, he liked to have scared Tish half to death. Then she'd cried while he held her tight. They woke up the baby so he could talk to him and hold him and kiss him. When Beesum went back to sleep, Hector had loved Tish till nearly daylight, the sweetest loving he ever did.

Tish told him Benning had sent the slavers and a pack of dogs after him, knowing there wasn't much chance of catching him once he got in the swamp. But she was scared they would find him, here or in the swamp. She told him not to come back. But he couldn't stay away.

It was dark now, just enough light to keep from walking into a ditch. He had business before he could see Tish, though.

The lane through the quarters was empty and still, but Zeb's house still had candle light leaking out the window cracks. Hector scratched on the door and stood to the side so the light wouldn't hit him full on when the door opened.

Zeb came out and closed the door behind him.

"Ain't seen you in a while, Hector," Zeb said not much louder than a whisper.

"Jubal say you want to see the camp."

"I'd like to see it, but I ain't likely to come out there to stay. And if I ever did, I'd be coming with a nine year old. Be good to know what I'd be getting her into."

"The camp ain't much yet. You'd be helping build it. We'll see Flavian's camp first. It settled, probably put your mind at rest about what we gone do."

"How safe is it out there, Hector? You ain't taken your own family with you."

"That's cause Tish won't go, Zeb. She want a roof and a bed, she don't want Beesum walking into the water and getting caught by a gator. She got a good imagination, Tish do."

"Any children out there?"

"Some in Flavian's camp, sure. They growing up fine."

"And the slave hunters?"

"We doing all we can to be safe, Zeb. I show you Sunday. We leave early and you get back late, all on a Sunday, Boss won't know you been gone. But it gone cost something."

"What?"

"It ain't no small thing to show you where the camp be."

"All right, then. What?"

"We need a axe."

Zeb gave a soft snort. "You need a axe. Then you gone need a mule. No way I can walk off with a mule or a axe."

"I'll come Sunday before daylight. You got the axe, I take you."

Hector left Zeb to figure it out and stepped like a cat through the shadows toward Tish's cabin.

Zeb would be a good man to have with them. Everybody got along with Zeb, and that was a help when a bunch of men lived on top of each other. Zeb was a good man all round. He'd figure out a way to get that axe.

Tish had already blown her candle out and the cabin was dark when he eased the door open.

"Tish?" he whispered.

"Hector." There was a little sigh in her voice that pulled at him – it hurt she was lonely without him.

She scooted over and made room for him on the bed. This hot a night, she didn't have no covers and no clothes either. He shucked his off and climbed in with her. She smelled good, like she'd bathed in mint water. He ran his hands all over her body, wanting to touch her everywhere at once. She grabbed his face in her hands and kissed him, claiming him with her mouth.

When they lay still and drowsy together, Tish's head on his chest, he wondered how he could leave her again. He always thought that, but he always left.

"Let's don't wake Beesum tonight. He's cutting a new tooth, and he miserable when he awake."

"All right. Maybe he be up before I leave anyway. I can stay till near daylight this time."

"Why you staying all night?"

"I'm gone take Zeb to see Flavian's camp. He maybe bring his biggest girl out."

"That gone be hard. The little girl, Faith, she been taken up to the big house. She don't come down here at all."

Hector's fingers played in Tish's hair as he thought. It wasn't a good thing when a bunch left a plantation together. Made the master that much madder, and that much more determined to catch them. Slaves were worth money, even little girls. But it looked like the only way to get Zeb was to take the girl with him, and he'd sure like to have a man like Zeb out there.

That woman Livy wanted to come, too. They'd be getting more men, and a camp with no women didn't have no family feeling. But the master might call the state militia after them if all three came out and once, plus Adam from the Bissell place.

They needed a flood, that's what. Then they could make out like a bunch of people drowned instead of running off. Weren't no runaways, Boss, just drowned and lost slaves, people would say. But Hector didn't figure he could conjure up a flood.

What needed to happen was to just take the woman. She wanted to come now. This minute, most likely. Maybe he could talk Zeb into waiting a few months.

~~~

How was Zeb supposed to get a axe? That's what the tool shed had a lock on the door for, so a man couldn't just walk off with a axe or a hoe or a machete. More than one way to use a axe, after all. Every rising up Zeb ever heard of had started at the tool shed.

How could he ever get away with it? Couldn't carry a axe hid in his hat. He thought about sticking the handle down his pants leg, the blade at his waist. Might work. But, lord, if it didn't, there wasn't any explaining what he was doing with a axe down his pants.

He needed to do it though. Needed to see what it was like out there. The scared look on Faith's face when she saw him coming to talk to her in the blueberry patch, of her lowering her eyes with a big red handprint across her cheek – he didn't forget that, ever. But taking her off to live in the swamp was a fearsome thing. Probably a crazy thing to do. Faith wasn't the first child to be taken up to live with the white folks, after all. Likely it would come to
~~~

nothing, this scheme of Hector's, but he'd go see what was what out there in one of those maroon camps.

Next day was Saturday. Zeb was supposed to be clearing a ditch today, so he lined up at the tool shed and got his hoe. He'd decided the best way to get the axe was to just ask for it. If he acted sneaky, he'd be caught for sure.

"Got some saplings to clear out of that ditch, Boss. Need me a axe, too," he said.

There really were saplings to be chopped down. He really did need the axe. Still, sweat popped out on Zeb's forehead. But asking was the hard part. At the end of the day – well, Zeb and everyone else knew Benning was a careless man at the shed. If he took a tool from every man and woman come up in the line, he was satisfied. So with any luck at all, it should be easy enough to hide the axe and simply turn in the hoe at quitting time.

Benning reached behind him for an axe and handed it over, just like that. The cold sweat on Zeb's back began to dry as he walked away with a hoe over his shoulder and the axe in his hand.

He followed his crew to the overgrown drainage ditch. They'd cleared half of this ditch already, he and Samson, Jubal, Alfa, and Wally, so there wasn't any reason for them to wonder why he had an axe. They'd all seen the ten foot tall saplings growing up from the bottom of the ditch.

He chopped down the saplings first thing, laid his axe down out of the way, and tossed the saplings on top of it.

He spent the rest of the day trying not to think about that axe. Didn't let himself even look over that way. Jubal probably seen what he did, but Zeb had waited for the others to be busy hacking weeds before he'd set it down. Come quitting time, they'd all be thinking about supper and getting off their feet. They weren't gone think about that axe.

Once they finished clearing out the ditch, they started piling up the brush to burn. "I'll get the saplings," Zeb volunteered. No reason then for anybody else to come over here and see the axe laid flat in the weeds, no reason at all.

Come quitting time, they walked back to the shed. Zeb could almost feel that axe lying behind him in the high grass, he was that scared, but he didn't turn around to check it couldn't be seen.

The man he had to watch was Wally. He was a worrier, Wally was, got to be the first one at the bell every morning, got to be sure he turned in his tools clean, got to be sure Benning happy with him all the time.

Zeb's stomach clenched imagining Wally turning around and calling out, "Hey, boy, don't forget your axe."

To distract Wally and the others, too, Zeb kept everybody talking about going possum hunting next full moon. Jubal helped out, being the best talker on the place. So their crew was last lining up at the shed without nobody standing around behind them.

Sweat poured off his forehead and down his neck. This was a crazy plan. Anyone could happen up on that axe out by the ditch. And Wally would be sure to mention it was Zeb who left it out there. All that trouble, for nothing.

He was next in line to hand his hoe to Benning. His hands on the handle were slick with sweat, but he handed it over like it was any other day. Benning didn't even look up at him.

He felt sick to his stomach as he walked away, wiping the sweat from his face. Now all he had to do was wait till near dark and take that axe somewhere nobody would happen up on it.

He sat through the longest supper he ever ate, trying to be cheerful so his mama wouldn't notice how antsy he felt. Soon as dusk was underway, he perched Hope on his shoulders and announced the two of them were going to take a walk in the cool, maybe see some fireflies. Nobody seeing a man with a child think anything going on, and it wouldn't do Hope no harm. She was happy up there where she could see everything different, her little hands wrapped around the top of his head.

He moseyed this way and that until he was finally at the ditch. Like he was setting Hope down to walk a little bit, he bent and took up the axe.

Hope back on his shoulders, he ambled along, cutting through the tail end of the lane to get to the woods trail, hardly anyone around. Just Weasel and a couple of Fancy's kids sitting on the stoop. Looked like Weasel found him a bee hive somewhere cause he was breaking off pieces of honeycomb for the little ones to chew on.

Weasel too busy licking his fingers to pay any mind to Zeb, but his gut knotted up anyway and he felt the blood pounding in his temples. It was dark enough, he kept telling himself. Nobody notice no axe. All they see was him giving Hope a ride before he put her to bed.

Just off the trail was an ancient oak tree, the kind whose huge limbs hung down low and made a kind of room under the branches. He set Hope down and whacked the axe into the trunk high up over his head, then headed back to the quarters with a sleepy girl in his arms.

He was a damned fool, trying a stunt like this. And he hadn't made up his mind he was taking Faith and running for that island anyway. Damned fool! Could have been enough light in the sky that somebody seen that axe at his side.

His heart pounded so hard he felt light-headed. The master could sell him off for this if he wanted to.

Chapter Eleven

Took ten days to get word Hector coming for him. Zeb waited on the porch in the dark, trying to tell himself this wasn't nothing. Just slip off the place for a day. There wasn't no real risk to it. Not like he was running away – he'd be back before dark.

His daddy and his granddaddy had run away. He couldn't get that out of his head. What were they like, his only male kin? Were they dreamers, like Jubal? Or hard-headed, or desperate? What did it take to make a man leave everybody who loved him behind, to take such a terrible chance? He didn't know if he was the same kind of man as them at all. Sure, he was going out there to look at the camp, but his mind wasn't made up to more than that. Could be he and his mama and grandma were too soft on Faith, worrying all the time that her life wasn't perfect when nobody's life was perfect.

Wasn't just Faith, either, who would give up Minnie and Eva and Hope. He would, too. He wasn't afraid of the hard work it must take to build a maroon camp, but maybe he was a little afraid of leaving everything and everybody he'd ever known, of taking the kind of leap his daddy and granddaddy had. Got his daddy killed, maybe his grandpa, too. He thought it again -- sometimes being scared was just good sense.

And what about Livy? He didn't know how he could stand to leave her. That day they'd kissed, he thought she was gone be his from now on. But she didn't allow no kissing every day. Just now and again, maybe, she said. And she meant it. They hadn't kissed but once since then, a hand's breadth of space between them. Still, she sat with him at dinner time, talking, making him smile. Sometimes he got a laugh out of her, too.

Love was growing between them, he felt it. But she was all the time telling him, with words and without, that she didn't want no man. Zeb didn't believe her. They just needed time together.

Auntie Jean's old dog Possum snuffled in his sleep under her porch next door. Probably chasing rabbits in his dreams. Not another soul to be seen or heard. For now, there was only the setting moon, a few clouds, and the smell of honeysuckle to keep him company. Another half hour, some of the mamas would be up, starting a cook fire, seeing to the children. Hector needed to come on if they were going to be gone before folks started to stir.

~~~

Livy had pulled her mattress on the porch to sleep so Etta's snoring wasn't so loud and because she had still not given up the notion that Jubal and them was going to sneak by her cabin some night on their way to freedom. The moon being behind her side of the row, she was in deepest shadow, but she could see Zeb setting on his porch across the way. He couldn't sleep?

Or maybe he was waiting for something just like she was. She'd seen him storm off the other day, so mad it looked like his whole head was swelled up. It was cause of that little girl they'd taken up to the house. Faith, her name was. Those white girls been mean to her again, that's what Etta said, and Zeb taken it hard.

A while after he strode off so mad he didn't even see her watching him, he come back onto the place with Jubal walking alongside him. She hadn't noticed Zeb and Jubal spending any time together before this.

And since then, he hadn't been the same old Zeb at all. He still smiled, but it didn't half the time reach his eyes.

And it wasn't because she wouldn't let him kiss her. It scared her, how much she wanted his kisses, so she was careful with herself.

"I want another one of them kisses," he'd said, tempting her when they was walking back to the quarters late in the day.

"Zeb, I ain't gone give you no more kisses. That time, it was just for fun, cause you a man and I a woman and you was looking sad. It ain't gone be more."

He wheedled at her, grinning. "I could look sad again." And he tried to pull the grin off his face and hung his head. But he couldn't keep the fun out of his eyes. She wanted to grab him up and kiss him from his eyes and ears to his toes. He knew it, too.

"Don't I look sad, Livy?"

She laughed and took his hands so he couldn't press her body against his and kissed him. My Lord, how that man kissed. He
~~~

wasn't thinking about Jubal nor nothing but her when he pressed his lips to her. A woman knows something like that.

She loved breathing in the scent of him, sweat and sunshine and something else that was just Zeb. But she hadn't let him kiss her again even though all the time, she felt Zeb's pull on her. She could have a life here with Zeb. Have babies. Her heart ached for a life with Zeb. But she'd still be full of that fire that said you got to get free.

She didn't think she could get over that, not even for Zeb. Who'd she be if she wasn't waiting for her chance to run?

Maybe Jubal got Zeb thinking about running, too. Wouldn't that be something.

~~~

The moon was near down when Zeb saw Hector slip out of Tish's cabin. Zeb stepped quietly off the porch and met him in the lane.

"You got the axe?" Hector whispered.

"I got it."

Hector motioned with his head and they walked out of the quarters and into the woods.

"Where is it?"

"We ain't to it yet."

When they found the old trail, Zeb stepped over to an oak with drooping branches, reached up high, and worked the axe out of the trunk.

"Not much of a hiding place, Zeb."

"You didn't see it, did you?"

"No, I didn't. It still dark though."

"People generally look at the ground when they walking in the woods, day or night."

"All right. We got the axe. Let's go."

Hector led the way to the dugout under the willow tree and poled them into the swamp. Mosquitoes plagued them, but Zeb expected that. They arrived at Flavian's camp when breakfast was over and the maroons were busy with the day's tasks.

Two men were sawing a log into rough planks. A woman had a cypress trough she was stirring dirty clothes in. The camp looked
~~~

tidy and orderly. And dry. Zeb had worried about that, wondered if they lived with their feet in the muck.

Flavian helped pull the dugout onto the landing.

"Who you got here, Hector?"

"This is Zeb. Show him what you brought, Zeb."

Zeb offered the axe to Flavian, who hefted it and then tested the edge with his thumb. "What you gone do when the boss finds out he got a axe missing?"

Zeb shrugged and slapped at a mosquito like he wasn't scared down to his bones about that axe. "I ain't gone know nothing about it."

"Come on. I'll show you the camp."

Zeb stepped into the cabin Flavian shared with his wife and two kids. Had a dirt floor, a loft, two windows. Wasn't big, but it was big enough. Another family cabin, and a bachelor cabin with half a dozen cots in it, a crudely made plank table, and logs upended to sit on.

Outside, a chicken coop stood on stilts. Two hunting dogs snoozed under a gum tree. They'd built a work shed for cutting cypress logs into tubs and paddles and bowls, whatever they could take to the market in town or to the mill where they always needed scoops and rakes and bins and didn't care who they got them from.

Somebody was digging sweet potatoes out of the garden situated in a cleared space where the sun could get in. A boy maybe twelve was picking beans.

It looked like a home, Flavian's camp did. Nobody had any fat stored around their bellies, but nobody looked hungry either.

Flavian kept up a steady chatter about how if you burned mostly bark for cooking it didn't make much smoke. Didn't light any fires that could be seen in the dark. Pretty basic steps to hiding out.

"The slavers never find you out here? You got lookouts?"

Flavian gave him a look. "They's been close a few times."

"You gone fight if they find you?"

"Yeah, we gone fight."

"What you got to fight with besides your fists?"

Flavian eyed him. Zeb understood. If he were to go back and tell the boss what kind of fight the maroons could put up, it wouldn't be good for the maroons.

"He brought the axe," Hector reminded Flavian.

"How I know your Mr. Benning didn't give you that axe so you could come out here and see what we got?" Flavian's voice had an edge to it.

Zeb held Flavian's gaze. "I cain't prove it. I cain't even tell you I'm coming out here for sure. I don't take it lightly, running away like you done. Maybe I won't."

"Then you seen enough," Flavian said. "Hector, take him off from here." They were sent off without any breakfast. Zeb guessed he had riled the man beyond where his hospitality went.

When they were away from the camp, Hector poling and then paddling them deeper into the waterways, Zeb said, "Flavian gone lay into you for bringing me out here?"

"He get over it when he see you come with your girl. A man means to do mischief ain't likely to bring a little girl with him."

"I told you. I ain't made up my mind to do such a thing."

"Come on. We got time, I'll take you to where the new camp gone be."

Hector's place was an island amid the swampy waters. Underbrush was sparse with a canopy of cypress, gum, red maple, and locust trees blocking the sun. A black willow hung down over the water where they beached the canoe.

The air was heavy with scent and so humid that a man's sweat hardly dried on his body. The trees overhead made the air seem green, and the water smelled fresh, probably cause there was a little current pushing past the island.

Birds liked it here. A big white stork with black edging on its wings waded nearby. A heron with a yellow crown eyed them for a moment, then went back to his prowling through the shallows.

"Pretty, ain't it?" Hector said.

Zeb nodded. It was. He walked on, eager to see how far the land reached before he hit the other side. Some of the trees boasted of air plants with cream and purple flowers growing way over his head. Ferns crowded each other along the island's fringe. It took him near ten minutes, walking slow, before he came to the far banks. A lot of room for a few people.

"We get enough tools, we can cut trees, make some cabins, some furniture. We got your axe, Adam's axe, and we'll get more. It's a start."

"This water here safe to drink?"

"I been drinking it. It's safe enough – it moves here, the water does. You see that?"

"Yeah, I seen it."

"We cut some trees, get some more sunshine in here, the mosquitoes move back into the shade."

Zeb nodded. He wandered along the shore, taking it in. He looked out over the water surrounding them, at the thousands upon thousands of cypress draped with gray moss. Hard to see more than a hundred feet through it all. Ought to be safe from the slavers, way back in here. If they ever found the place, it'd be by luck. Or by somebody turning traitor, like Flavian feared. Even if the slavers came, Faith wouldn't come to no harm. She just a child, and they'd want her whole.

"What do you think, Zeb?"

Zeb nodded. "Faith could grow up here without nobody telling her she a nothing. Could grow up knowing who she is." But there wasn't nothing to eat on this island. Likely they could fish, but . . . Well, the longer he was out here in the swamp, the crazier it seemed to bring a child out here to this wild place.

Back at the dugout, Hector handed Zeb a cup. He dipped into the water and tasted it. "Not bad water," he said. He drank that cup and another. If he didn't get sick to death from it, then the water at least was good.

Paddling away from the island, they passed the biggest gator Zeb ever seen sunning itself on a bank. Must have been long as two men put together.

He broke into a sweat just thinking about what an animal like that would do to a human being. To a little girl. And there wasn't no way to keep one off the island Hector decided was his. No way at all.

It took them the rest of the day to paddle and pole back to the plantation. Zeb had no way of knowing whether Hector took him a roundabout way to disguise the route to the hideout, but even if he didn't, Zeb didn't see how he could find his way around out here anyway. That cypress tree had knees growing up around its base, and so did that one and that one and that one. He supposed he would learn it eventually, just as Hector had. Unless Hector was just wandering toward the plantation cause he couldn't help it.

They beached the dugout under the willow and Zeb shoved the drooping branches aside to emerge on the edge of the woods behind the quarters. "You coming in?"

"Yeah. After dark. Too late to go back now. I'll have another night with Tish and the boy."

Zeb had nearly an hour before dark, so he treaded careful when he reached the other side of the woods. He could see the orchard and the first cabins of the quarters from where he stood. Looked quiet.

He stepped from the trees to head for the cabins. What if the Boss had come through the quarters? He did that once in a while, just strolling through of a Sunday, seeing how everything was. What if he had done a count in the tool shed and knew he was short an axe? He'd be tearing the place apart, counting people, asking people who saw what. If he found an axe missing, and Zeb missing – he didn't like to think what would happen.

His urge was to stride, to get in the cabin quick as he could, but he forced himself to stroll.

~~~

Livy had been waiting out here near the trail head an hour or more thinking Zeb would be coming back this way. She had paced for a while, wrought up with hope and possibility. If he'd gone hunting or fishing, some of them would have gone with him, but she didn't see nobody else missing for the whole day. And the way Zeb had been acting lately, and him walking along with Jubal? He'd made up his mind to be a maroon out on Hector's island. That was all it could be.

They could be together, the two of them, and be free. Never in her life had she been so full of longing and worry.

When she heard him coming, she took a deep breath and stepped into the path. "Hello, Zeb."

Zeb startled. "What you doing out here, Livy?"

"Waiting for you."

No smile for her, not even a little one. That not like Zeb either.

"I got some business, Livy. I gone have to get on." He tried to step around her like he had somewhere he had to get to.

Some of that worry eased off. She was right, she knew it. Falling into step with him, she said, "I reckon you need a little help with your business."

He gave her a sharp look.
~~~

"There a bunch of folks between you and your cabin," she said. "I think we better do this together."

He came to a dead stop. "What you talking about?"

"Folks need a reason for you being gone all afternoon. I gone be your reason." She mussed her hair and rebuttoned her dress so the buttons were all off one hole.

"What are you doing, Livy?"

"We got a secret, we gone keep it a secret. You been to see Hector's place, ain't you?"

He stared at her like she was a woman could read minds. Then the worry lines crossed his forehead. "You in this, Livy?"

"I aim to be."

"Livy, stay out of it. Things go wrong, you got to be able to tell Benning you don't know nothing about it."

"I do know about it, Zeb. When you go, I'm going with you."

He shook his head. "I ain't going, Livy. It's just a little island out in the swamp, nothing but brush, trees, water, and alligators. I'm not taking a little girl out there. She safe where she is. She'll make do."

She dropped her hands from her buttons, her lungs feeling tight and small. She couldn't understand him, a strong man, a smart man. How could he stand being a slave? "What about you, Zeb?" she said softly. "You don't want to be free?"

He closed his eyes and shook his head. "Freedom cost too much, Livy. It cost leaving my family, and maybe they get cut by that whip cause I run off. It cost my mama grieving cause I been tore up by the dogs or the whip. My daddy gave her that grief when he run off and come back dead. I don't want to do that to her, and if they kill me or maim me, what good I be to Hope or Faith either one?"

Dear, sweet Zeb. He didn't have it in him to want what she wanted, to want to be free so bad it overshadowed the dream of a life together. It hurt, loving him like this, and not seeing in him the man she wanted him to be. She reached for him, meaning to place her hand on his cheek.

He shrugged her off. "You think I'm scared. Yeah, I'm scared. And not just of dogs and whips. I got one life, Livy, and I don't think spending it to raise two little girls be a bad way to use it."

He turned to stride off and leave her, but she caught his arm.

"You think I don't know what it mean to run away? I'm going, Zeb. Even if you don't. But I rather go with you."

He stared at her as she stepped close. "I wouldn't talk nobody into running. I know the chances ain't good. But if you was to run, I'd go with you. To this camp, or to wherever north takes us. But even if you don't come, I'm going out there to Hector's island."

He touched her cheek, his fingers cupping the curve of her jaw. "I want you, Livy. I want to love you and wake up beside you of a morning. I think about it all the time. But it ain't just you and me I got to think about."

She stepped away from him. "I could love you, Zebediah. I guess I already do. But I got to go."

They held each other's eyes, silent and sad.

"Well, then," he said.

So that was it. He wasn't coming with her. Abruptly, she turned her back on him. Why'd God put this wild rage to be free inside her and then send her to this peaceable man?

"You crying, Livy?" he said quietly.

She sniffled and wiped her hand across her face. "Crying is for fools. Fools like you and me both, I guess." She turned back to him, her chin tilted up. "You still need me to give folks a reason for you being gone all day. Case anybody ask."

His thumb traced a tear track on her face. "You'd do that for me? You thinking I'm nothing but scared, and you'd let folks think I had you out here in the woods?"

"I don't think you nothing but scared, not anymore I don't. And you ain't going to have me out here in the woods, anyway."

"I'm not?" He brought her into his arms and there was that sweet smile she loved.

They kissed till they were both about ready to lie down in the grass, but Livy found her head. They ought not to be making themselves crazy for each other when nothing gone come of it.

"I just doing that so folks will see our lips all swelled up," she said.

He laughed out loud. "Let's go in then and let them see what I done to you."

Her poor heart, Livy thought. She was singing inside from those kisses and furious with herself for it.

Chapter Twelve

The next day, Monday, they were all finishing up their noon dinner when the bell started pealing.

"What's that all about?" Samson said.

"Don't know," Pete said. "Maybe Boss gone give us all peach pie and candy cause we work so hard."

"Yeah, I reckon that's right," Samson said.

"Nah," Jubal said. "He got a dozen dancing girls come to give us a show."

"I wouldn't mind watching dancing women. You reckon they wearing clothes?"

"Charlie, you devil," Rachel said, coming up behind him. She grabbed at his arm and gave him a pinch.

"Ow, woman," he said and grabbed her up under his arm.

"Zeb," Samson said. "You got you an idea? Or you expecting dancing girls, too?"

"Me? I think he calling us all up there to tell us we got the rest of the week off. No field work, no garden work, no timber work, nothing."

They walked on toward the bell yard imagining what they'd do with a week of free time.

Livy came up beside Zeb and held him back a little. As they followed the others to the gathering place, she whispered, "What's wrong?"

"Like I said, Boss gone give us a week off." He tried to smile like it was all a joke, a funny joke, but she didn't look like she thought it was funny.

"I mean what's wrong with you."

He hesitated, then he told her, "Boss might be missing a axe."

She drew in a big breath. "Shh," he said and squeezed her hand. He was scared, but he didn't mean for Livy to be. He had enough scared for the both of them.

When they reached the yard, Livy pulled on him to stand up front, right under Benning's nose. "Smile at me, Zeb," she whispered. She leaned in to his arm and made calf eyes at him.

She was smart, Livy was. Right up front where Boss would see them making love eyes at each other. Zeb not a man thinking about no missing axe. He thinking about the woman clinging to his arm.

Two white men, strangers, stood at Benning's elbows. They were greasy-looking fellows, and they were armed.

Benning climbed on the stump so he could see everybody and they could all see him. He tapped the small whip against his boot top, watching them gather.

"All right," he said. "Listen up. We got a serious offense here, and I mean to get to the bottom of it. Some one of you has stolen an axe."

Not a one of Zeb's people made a sound, but he felt the sudden tension rise up behind him like a wall of nails.

Benning looked over the faces turned up to him, lingering on one here or there. Jubal, if Zeb had to guess. Maybe Samson, another. But Benning didn't glance at Zeb standing six feet away.

"I spent a few minutes thinking that it was just a mistake. One of you got back from the woods or the fields too late on Saturday to turn your axe in. The shed was closed up. So you meant nothing by keeping the axe over Sunday.

"But nobody left it leaning against the shed door for me to find when I opened up this morning. Nobody brought me that axe and said, 'Sorry, Boss. Here's the axe I had from you on Saturday.' "

He scowled. "No. What we have here is not an innocent occurrence. What we have here is theft." He nodded at the two white men. "These men and I, we will tear this camp apart till we find this axe. Now, you don't have to think very hard to know what I will do to the man who stole it."

Zeb heard the rustle of people shifting their weight from one foot to another. Livy nuzzled up against his shirt sleeve and squeezed his arm to make him look at her, then gazed at him like he was the moon and stars. Neither one of them thinking about no axe, no sir.

"But this can end without anyone getting hurt. You got maybe five minutes to get back to your cabins, where you will stay until our search is complete, no matter how many days it takes. But if in those five minutes, the thief puts that axe out in the middle of the lane so I see it first thing when I come down, then nobody has to get lashed, nobody has to get chained, nobody has to get cut."

Zeb closed his eyes. This could be bad. Boss could decide to punish somebody, anybody, to try to flush out the thief. Zeb couldn't let another man take a whipping for him. He'd have to confess. What would he say when Boss demanded to know where the axe was now?

He better think of a story. Either that, or he better be ready to run.

"Zeb," Boss said. Zeb opened his eyes, his spine quivering like jelly. "We need somebody probing the privies. You and Pete, get a couple of shovels and meet us in the quarters."

Some other time, he'd have heard jeers and teasing at being singled out for such loathsome duty, but no one said a word. Silently the people moved together to return to their cabins, Livy giving his hand a quick squeeze before she let him go.

Zeb and Pete were on the third privy, sick with the smell, when Mama hissed at him. "Come on out here – something going on with Weasel."

Zeb dropped his shovel and walked between the cabins, Pete behind him. Weasel was making a scene out in the lane like he always did, only this time Benning and the other white men were standing there staring at him. Weasel was on his knees, blubbering. Blubbering? Weasel? Didn't seem likely.

"What's going on?"

"Weasel fessing up – he took the axe you digging for," Grandma said.

How could this be? He caught Jubal's eye, who shook his head the least bit and looked away.

"I never meant to steal no axe, boss, just to borry it. I won't never borry no axe again, I promise."

"Well, go get it," Benning said.

Weasel clasped his hands together and bowed his head.

"Weasel. Where's the axe?" Benning snapped.

"Well, that's just it, Boss. I don't got the axe no more."

Benning took a deep breath, leaned all his weight on one leg and smirked at the other men. "All right. Let's hear it."

Weasel looked sideways to where Fancy was standing with her two little ones, watching him make a fool of himself.

"Fancy needed honey, she said. She'd be sweet to me, she said, was I to bring her honey."

Fancy rolled her eyes and put her hands on her hips while half the people tittered and smirked.

Weasel wiped his nose and left off crying. "But, see, Boss, I too old to be climbing trees."

Zeb doubted that. Weasel was wrinkled and leathery, but he still worked a hard day just like the rest of them.

"So I ambled by the saw yard where they got the axes leaning around and I picked one up. Just to borry it. And I sneaked off an hour or two and walked into the woods. And there was a bunch of bees right out there, built themselves a hive in a tupelo wadn't no bigger around than this." Weasel held his hands out, fingers curved to indicate the size of the tree trunk. "So I chopped it down and got me the honeycomb out of there."

Weasel held his arms up. "See? I still got the bee stings."

"So you got the honey and you came back to Fancy, and you got you some sugar." Benning was enjoying this, Zeb thought. He grinned at the other white men and had that gleam in his eye men get when they talk about women.

Weasel's face suddenly glowed, his mouth wide in a happy grin. "Yes, sir. I got me some sugar."

Fancy threw up her hands and strode off.

"So." Benning wasn't smiling anymore. "Where's the axe now?"

Weasel lowered his head, miserable.

He's overdoing it, Zeb thought. Nobody gone believe him he act too much like he stupid. He glanced at Livy across the way. Her fingers covered her mouth, all her attention stuck on Weasel.

"That's just it, Boss. The axe got itself lost out in the woods."

"Got itself lost, huh? Well, you'll just have to find it."

Weasel shook his head vigorously. "I done looked, Boss. I went back to the woods when I remembered I didn't bring the axe back, but I couldn't find that tree nowhere. I looked and looked."

"You'll look some more, then." Benning scanned the people watching. "Zeb, Pete, you go out there with him. Find that axe. The rest of you, you got work to do. Get to it."

Looking sorrowful, his shoulders bent, Weasel said, "Come on, boys. It just trees and trees out there, but we go look."

In the woods, the air was still and heavy. Sweat rolled off their backs, inviting the mosquitoes to plague them. Pete lagged behind since he was actually looking for a felled tree.

"Why you doing this, Weasel?" Zeb asked.

He shrugged, no sign of the sorrowful fool in him. "Don't cost me nothing but pride. I got plenty of that left."

"Boss not gone be happy with you we don't come back with no axe."

Weasel gave him a shrewd look. "What makes you so sure we not gone find an axe out here?"

Zeb clamped his jaw shut and looked away.

Weasel snorted a laugh and headed toward a sunny spot among the trees.

"I done looked over that way," Pete called. "Nothing there."

So the three of them spent the rest of the afternoon wandering through the woods, Zeb and Weasel just waiting for Pete to give up.

"Where the hell are we?" Pete finally said. "I done lost my bearings."

"We head that way, we likely pick up the old Indian trail," Weasel said.

Pete gave him a look. Pete probably been thinking all this while, Zeb figured. But he wouldn't say anything.

"All right. Lead on, Weasel the Woodsman, you suddenly know you way around out here."

"Maybe we spot us another bee hive on the way back," Weasel said with great cheer. "You boys young enough to climb right up to it, then we all get some sugar tonight." He looked at Zeb and winked.

When they got back, they found Benning at the tool shed, the two hired men gone.

Benning glanced at Pete's cheek, swollen up from a yellow jacket bite. "Well?" he said.

"They's a lot of woods, out there, Boss," Pete said. "We didn't find no axe, no felled tree neither."

Hands on his hips, Benning turned a narrowed gaze on Weasel.

Weasel held his palms up. "Like I told you, Boss. It got itself good and lost out there. I sorry as I can be, Boss, sorry as I can be."

Zeb could hardly breathe, waiting to see if Benning swallowed Weasel's silly story. Not a man on the place would forget an axe, leaving it out in the woods, when he wasn't supposed to have it in the first place. Weasel wasn't near old enough to have a brain that full of holes.

Benning glanced at Pete, who looked disgusted. Then he looked at Zeb, who kept his face blank.

He shook his head and let out a sigh. "Weasel, you are a sorry piece of shit. You'll spend the night in the stocks, and stay locked in till I let you out sometime tomorrow."

"Boss," Weasel whined. "Every bone in my body gone hurt you put me in the stocks all night."

"I imagine you're right. Zeb, you tell Fancy she can bring him water," and then Benning laughed, "and some of that honey if there's any left."

~~~

The sun about down, Zeb rocked Hope to sleep on the porch. A strange world, Zeb thought. Here he was rocking his baby girl like it was any other night, and he'd had about the worst day of his life. Worse even than when Noah died.

He was going to lose Livy. He didn't know how he was gone keep on when she left him. And if Weasel hadn't stepped in? If Zeb had had to fess up to save somebody else from taking his punishment? He broke out in a cold sweat all over again.

Was this some sign God giving him? Getting away with the axe show he was meant to go on out to the island? Or maybe God didn't know nothing about it cause He busy with somebody else's problems. But oh my Lord, he prayed, I thank you for saving me.

He should thank Weasel, too, he thought with a grim smile. But any thankyou would best be left unsaid.

Livy stepped onto the porch and sat on the floor next to Zeb's chair.

"That's a sweet child you got there," she said softly.

"Especially when she asleep."

Livy smiled. After a while, she said, "I had a baby."

He looked at her, surprised. Why hadn't he known that about her?
~~~

Across the way Anna stepped into the lane and hollered for one of her boys to come home.

"I named her Loretta. Perfect little girl, sweetest rose bud mouth."

"You lose her, Livy?" Zeb asked.

"Yeah. I didn't have her but half a minute. I don't know why. She just wouldn't breathe, no matter what we did."

Zeb touched her hair.

Anna had to call her boy again, and this time you could hear trouble in her voice if he didn't come tearing home.

"Weasel know it was you?" she said.

"Look like it."

"Why you think he did it?" Livy asked.

"I don't know. I never thought Weasel had much thought for anybody but Weasel."

"Sometimes there be more to a person than show on the outside." She leaned the back of her head on his knee.

"Like with you," he thought she said.

Chapter Thirteen

After another day's work in the punishing heat, every tired muscle and bone complaining, Zeb lifted the long pump handle and gave it a hard push. Sweet water gushed out and splashed in the puddle below. He stuck his head under the stream and drank noisy gulps of water, gave the handle another pump and sluiced cool water over his bare chest and back.

"You a sight, you are," Livy said.

He grinned. "You sneaking up on me so you can get a peek?"

"Don't need to peek you standing out here in the middle of the yard."

"Come on, I'll pump for you."

"I get my dress front wet, I'll have to fight all the men off me."

"I'll help with that. Come on, it'll cool you off."

"I come for something else, Zeb." She took his hand and tugged. "Walk with me."

"You looking mighty serious. Where we going?"

"You'll see."

She took him deep into the peach orchard. The peaches were all gone by now, but there was plenty of leaf .

"I hope we gone do out here what I think we gone do."

"Depends on what you think we gone do," she said, giving him a look from under her lashes and laughing at him.

She pulled him down to sit with their backs against the short trunk, the leaves hanging down over their heads. He reached for her, but she held her hand up. "I want you listening, Zeb."

He breathed in and sighed. "What, then?"

"You ain't acting like you used to."

Livy knew him, he realized. She wasn't fooled by a laugh or a smile. "I don't feel much like I used to."

"Whether you do or not, you got to act like you do. Boss ain't a stupid man."

"He believed Weasel lost a axe in the woods."

"Well, he a little stupid then. But Zeb, you don't want him paying any mind to you. And some time, he gone notice. Where be the Zeb used to smile all the time, that's what he gone think."

"He knows why. Cause of the way he let Noah die. Cause the white lady took Faith away."

"He gone think you ought to be over that by now. He might wonder what you thinking about that you so serious all the time."

He knew what she meant. "And he got a missing axe."

"Yeah."

He rubbed his thumb across the back of her hand, thinking. He nodded. "I guess I better smile more then."

"And I can help with that," Livy said.

Moving to straddle his legs, she cupped his face in her hands. Her kiss was sweet and tender.

His hands moved down her back, shaping her waist, her bottom. They kissed until Zeb's blood pounded and his body ached to be in hers. His hand behind her head, he leaned her back to lay her on the earth.

Livy put her hands over his mouth and whispered, "No, Zeb."

He pressed his forehead against hers and groaned. "God, Livy."

He struggled to get his breath slowed down. She was breathing in little pants herself.

She kissed his cheek, his jaw, his neck. "I want you, Zeb. But we can't be making a baby now. You see that."

He leaned back to look at her. "You said 'now.' That mean if things was different, you'd be my woman."

She looked into his eyes like she could see straight through. "I ain't nobody's woman, Zeb, and things ain't different. This is just for now."

He heard enough sad in those words to match his own. That's why he kissed her some more, keeping his head best he could.

Finally Livy pulled away with a little laugh. "The mosquitoes eating me alive," she said.

"All right. We'll go in."

Hand in hand, they walked through the dusk back to the quarters.

"My mama say you welcome to move in with us, Livy."

"She say that?"

"She did. Said she'd sweep the cobwebs out of the attic, make us a new mattress."

"I didn't think she liked me."

"You don't give nobody a chance to like you."

"Well, I been friendlier lately."

"Just don't get too friendly with none of the men around here."

She held his arm close. "You a jealous man?" she said, teasing him.

"I didn't know it till I seen you with Jubal. But yeah, I'm a jealous man."

She nuzzled the top of his arm. "Zeb." She wasn't teasing now. "Don't go forgetting. I'm leaving when Hector give the word."

He turned her around and wrapped his arms around her like he could keep her with him if he just held on tight enough. He kissed her, hard.

"Zeb," she gasped against his mouth. "Somebody gone see us."

"Let 'em."

~~~

It was easy for Zeb to smile the next day. He felt like smiling. And he'd begun to see the fun in the scavenging he did for Hector. Nobody asked him to, and he didn't take no risks doing it, but if he found a nail on the ground, he pocketed it. Found a scrap of leather near where Emil cut out rough shoes for them to wear and pocketed that, too.

Hector and whoever went out there with him would need a hammer and a saw, but folks were more careful about putting their tools away since the axe went missing. Not likely Benning would be as forgiving as he was to Weasel if it happened again. There would be other chances, though, for things that wouldn't be missed. He liked to think whatever he salvaged would make life a little easier for Livy if she really did leave him to be a maroon out in the swamp.

He was thinking maybe she was softening toward him. Maybe she'd decide she couldn't leave him. He prayed for it, but he knew he was only hoping. There wasn't no sureness about it.
~~~

Though he ached for Livy, his worry over Faith had eased a bit. He'd been seeing her out and about with the white girls, not grinning or singing like she used to, but she had a little spring back in her step. She looked all right. Maybe she was learning how to handle that mean sister. Maybe she was growing a thicker hide so the meanness didn't bother her anymore.

The next time he saw her, he thought he was wrong about that. That oldest girl must have come from an evil seed. Marvina, he heard her sisters call her.

Miss Marvina had Faith following her around outside to hold a parasol over her so the sun didn't touch her. The older girl seemed to be making a game of it, turning suddenly, marching quickly and then slowing, so that Faith could not possibly keep the parasol over her head.

Zeb watched them from across the rose garden where he was helping out the gardener for the day. The white girl, dressed in a pretty yellow dress with ruffles and lace, stopped abruptly so that Faith bumped into her.

Miss Marvina whirled around. "Don't touch me, you filthy thing!"

If this had been a quarrel with another child in the quarters, Faith would not have been able to resist. With a sly grin and a wicked gleam in her eye, she would have slowly reached out to touch the angry child. But this was not the quarters.

Faith stepped back, her head bent. Zeb couldn't hear what she murmured, but whatever she said, Miss Marvina was satisfied. She flounced away, on to her next devilment.

Faith saw him thirty yards away, him standing there stunned at the meanness in the girl, sick at Faith's hurt. Then Faith opened up the clouds for him. She looked right at him and slowly shook her head in disgust. Isn't that girl the most pitiful, cussed child you ever seen? She might as well have said it out loud it was so clear. As if that spite had just rolled off her back.

He laughed, relief welling up in him. He'd made the right choice for Faith. She didn't have to hide out in those swamps where he couldn't keep her safe. She was finding a way to still be Faith and live in that house. He'd tell Mama and Grandma tonight, and they'd feel like singing.

The rest of the day, Zeb hummed and sang the old songs, feeling easy about Faith for the first time in weeks.

After supper, he strolled across the lane to Livy's cabin.

"It gone rain," she said. "You want to come in, say hello to Etta and Grace?"

"Nah. I just want to see you a minute."

He pushed her back into the shadows of the porch where dusk had already begun. He nuzzled her neck, expecting her to shove him away and give him a scolding, but she put her arms around his waist. He was gone win this woman yet.

"We ain't gone stand out here loving on each other where anybody turn his head this way can see us."

"There ain't nobody gone look this way." He cradled her head in his hands and kissed her. No delicate feathering, no sweet tasting – he pressed against her mouth, demanding entrance. When she opened to him and he felt that last little tension leave her body, he softened his kiss.

She finally pulled away. "We gone have to stop this or I'm gone pull your clothes off right here on the porch."

He laughed softly. "I wouldn't stop you."

She pushed at his chest. "Let me go. All the dogs gone wake up and howl they hear me doing what I want to do to you."

"All the dogs, huh?"

"The cats, too." She pecked him on the cheek hard and fast. "You go on now."

He ran his thumb across her mouth. "Come to the hayloft with me."

Livy reared her head back as if she could see his eyes in the growing dark. "Zebediah, I ain't going to lie with you in no barn."

"Ahh, Livy," he said and hugged her tight. With a brief kiss, he let her go. "I'll see you in the morning."

He eased his way into his own cabin so as not to wake Hope. By the candle's light he saw his mama was leaned into her hands, sobbing. Grandma looked like she be happy to kill somebody.

"What happened?"

"Sissy, up in the laundry," Grandma said, her voice low and harsh. "She say the master's wife gone take a trip. All the way to some place called Charleston. She taking her girls with her. Faith, too."

"For how long?"

"Sissy don't know. Maybe from now on. Master got him a woman down in New Orleans, one of them octoroon gals, and the missus found out. She say she ain't living with him no more. She going home to her mama in Charleston."

Minnie curled over the table top and hid her head in her arms. But Eva, stalwart, ferocious Grandma, looked at him with those glittering dark eyes and asked him without words -- What you gone do about this, Zebediah?

"When they supposed to leave?"

"Sissy say it take them a week to get all them trunks packed. Maybe next week Wednesday, maybe Tuesday."

Zeb let himself down into a chair. He couldn't conjure up the least memory of the island, of the swamp. His mind was a blank.

You got to think, he told himself. He looked at his mama and grandma. They was as different as two women could be, and they wanted different things.

What mattered, though, was what was best for Faith.

"All right," he said softly to his grandma, and she nodded like she heard what she wanted to hear.

Zeb slipped back outside and found Jubal on Ruby's porch. "Let's take a walk," he told him.

Jubal had a youngster in his lap and the baby's mama at his side looking at him like he was a piece of red candy God gave her. He scowled at Zeb, but he handed the baby to Ruby and came off the porch.

It was nearly dark and the wind smelled like rain, so Zeb stopped not far beyond the last cabin.

"What?" Jubal said.

"I need you to get word to Hector."

"Why should I?"

"It's Faith. I got to get her away from there and there ain't no time for waiting."

"She getting fed. She out of the rain. Hector ain't moving out there hisself till harvest is over. "

Zeb's blood began to rise. "They gone take her away far from here. I got to get her to the island before that happens." He bit the next words out: "Tell me how to send word to Hector."

Jubal looked at him hard. "I'll think about it."

"Tell him I can get a sack of beans, a sack of corn. Maybe some sweet potatoes ready to dig up. Tell him we got to come out now."

Jubal only said, "Best wait till after harvest."

"You the one pulled me into this, and now you not gone let it happen? What the hell's the matter with you?" Zeb fought with himself to keep from plowing his fist into Jubal's face. Pivoting on his heel, he marched back into the lane. By the time he got to Livy's house, he'd banked his anger low enough to deal with it.

When she cracked the door open and saw it was him, she said, "I ain't going to no barn."

"Something happened."

"Just a minute." She closed the door and reappeared a moment later buttoning up her dress.

They walked silently past the other cabins, some candle lit, others dark. Samson's dog followed them for a bit but decided he'd rather sleep.

Far enough away from the cabins not to be heard, Zeb stopped. "I got to take Faith. In the next few days. I can't wait."

"What's happened?"

He told her what he knew. They had to get word to Hector to meet them with the boat, and they didn't have any days to waste.

"Jubal gone send him a message?"

"He ain't in any hurry, but you walked out with Jubal that time. You know something about how he sends word to Hector?"

He could see the glimmer of her smile. "Yeah," she said. "We don't need Jubal."

Zeb grabbed her to him and hugged her hard. She chuckled and hugged him back.

"What we got to do?" he asked.

"Today Tuesday?"

He thought a minute. "Yeah. Tuesday."

"Then we got to go tonight. We gone need a lantern."

So it was decided. No more dickering with himself. No more fretting about Faith living up there in the white house, no more telling himself she was fine, no more wondering how he'd keep breathing and eating if Livy was gone. Gladness and hope suffused his spirit, and he felt he could do anything.

Livy stepped close and wrapped her arms around his waist, her face pressed against his chest. "We gone be together, Zeb. It what I prayed for."

He squeezed her tight. "Me too, Livy." He gave her a lingering kiss on her neck and then broke it off. "We got to go."

He tiptoed back into his cabin to get the lantern while Livy put her shoes on. His mama had gone to Auntie Jean to tell her about Faith. Grandma Eva still sat at the table staring at the candle flame. "I need the lantern, Grandma."

He took the old box lantern off the mantle. "We got any more candles?"

Eva lumbered across the room on quiet feet and rummaged in the box the other side of the mantle. "How many you need?"

"I better take all three."

She handed him the flint and steel. "Put that in your pocket."

He lit one of the candles, lodged it firmly in the lantern, and lowered the black-out panels on all four sides, leaving only a sliver open for air.

"Go on to bed, Grandma. I gone be gone a while."

"This dangerous, what you doing?"

"No, Grandma," he whispered. "This tonight ain't dangerous. Go on to bed."

Livy waited for him in the dark. Together they walked out of the quarters and found the path into the woods. Once they'd stumbled in far enough to risk the light, Zeb opened one panel of the lantern and they hurried on until they met the old Indian path.

"This way," Livy said. "You can give us some more light now."

The owls were swooping through the trees, possums rustling in the bushes as they waddled down their nocturnal paths. Somewhere out here no doubt there was a puma on the prowl.

Livy reached for Zeb's hand and he squeezed it. "We be all right," he told her. "None of these creatures interested in us."

" 'Cept for the mosquitoes."

"Yeah. They always interested."

It took an hour for them to reach the old tree.

"It's a long way for Hector to come check this tree every week. You, too, and Jubal. What they got to message about that's so important?"

"I think it mostly cause Hector be lonely out there, and he worries about Tish and the boy. This way, he know they all right without having to come all the way into the quarters. And I think he waiting for Jubal or some of them to come out with him."

"I didn't think Jubal would leave all them kids of his."

"Maybe not. Maybe he just likes having secrets, pretending he a big bad runaway."

She held the lantern to the bottom of the tree and picked up a handful of wood chunks. "See this one? The one with the black tar on it. That the one mean it's urgent. This here cypress one mean he got to come Saturday night."

Livy put the two pieces of wood in the knot hole. "There. This is all I know to do. All Jubal know to do either."

Zeb knelt down and put a fresh candle in the lantern.

"What happens he don't come? What we gone do then?" she said.

She'd said "we" again. He could hug her for that. She'd be with him. Maybe that ought to worry him, having to protect both Livy and Faith; it made him feel stronger instead. But -- if there was no boat to take them into the swamp, it would change everything.

"I'm taking Faith on Sunday before daylight. If Hector's here, good. If he ain't, then Faith and me, we run for it, far as we can get before they miss us, then we hide out."

He straightened up once he had the new candle lit. She was staring at him. He'd said Faith and him – she thinking he'd leave her? He reached for her hand.

"Livy, if Hector ain't here, I want you to go on back while you still can. Won't nobody know you come out here with me if you back in your cabin before daylight."

When she didn't answer him, he held the lantern high so he could see her face. She was looking at him with her big eyes. "If Hector ain't here to meet us and take us in the boat," he said, "it be too dangerous. Understand?"

"I understand just fine. But I going with you and Faith, Hector here or not. *You* understand?"

Zeb's chest ached, the possibilities clear to him. They could have a new life out at Hector's camp, Livy his woman, Faith growing up loved. Or they could be dragged back to the bell yard in chains.

"I probably can keep us hid till after the master's wife gone off without Faith. That might be all I can do. They catch us, they take us back, and the master gone make an example of us. They'd whip you, Livy. I might do something crazy I see them whip you. You got to stay back if Hector don't come."

"He will come."

"Promise me, Livy. If Hector ain't here, you go on back."

"I won't promise."

Zeb crushed her to him. "Livy. I can't take you with me there no boat here."

She cupped his cheek with her hand. "The boat gone be here. My bones know it."

She kissed him and his body turned hard so fast he felt dizzy. He touched his forehead to hers. "Your bones, huh?"

"Yeah, my bones know it. Let's get home. My feet ache."

Chapter Fourteen

By Saturday, Zeb had bagged all the foodstuffs and odds and ends he'd gathered and raised them into the tree where Hector had docked his boat last time. All he had left to do was figure out how to get Faith out of the big house.

He imagined himself sneaking into the house in the dead of night, bumping into furniture, blundering into the master's room, never finding Faith at all. He imagined seeing her out in the yard and hissing *psst* at her to come behind the bush where he was hiding, the mean girl catching them, shouting and screaming till the master came out and locked Zeb in the storage shed.

In the end, he decided his best chance was simply to ask. Late in the afternoon on Saturday, he approached the back porch of the big house. He thought he would knock on the door and ask Jessup, the house man, if Faith could come visit in the quarters overnight, but then he saw Missus was on the back gallery arranging a vase of flowers.

His throat nearly closed he was so tense. "Missus?" he called softly.

She put her flowers down and leaned over the balcony rail with a scowl on her face. "Did you say something to me?" she accused.

Zeb nearly groaned. He could see where Miss Marvina got her hateful streak.

He took his straw hat off. "Yes, Missus."

"Well, what is it?" she snapped.

He twisted the hat around in his hands. "They say you going to Charleston and Faith going with you."

She stared at him. He might have been a dog just peed on the rug.

"We gone miss Faith, Missus, when she go off. I was hoping you could let her come down to the quarters, let us have her tonight and tomorrow so we can say good-bye to her."

She waved a hand at him impatiently. "Have her back in time to dress the girls for supper tomorrow night."

Zeb bobbed his head again and again. It wasn't hard to act subservient when he was scared and grateful at the same time.

"Faith!" the missus hollered. "Come out here."

Faith stepped onto the gallery wearing the too-big blue dress. "Yes, ma'am?"

"Be back here by five o'clock tomorrow afternoon. Any later than that, and I'll take a switch to you."

Zeb saw confusion cross Faith's face, then she saw him standing in the courtyard and looked at him like he was Jesus come down from heaven.

She raced down the back stairs and plowed right into him. He grabbed her up, her gangly legs dangling down to his knees. She wouldn't let go of his neck, so he carried her all the way back to the cabin.

He hadn't told his mother or his grandmother what he was doing, so when he walked in the door with Faith, they both froze like they were part of a picture, Mama with a cooking spoon in her hand, Grandma with four plates to set the table for supper.

"We need another plate tonight, Grandma," Zeb said.

The spoon dropped to the floor, the plates clattered to the table. Then Mama and Grandma were all over them, hugging and kissing both of them.

Hope toddled over and pulled at Faith's skirt tail. That's when Faith let loose. She grabbed Hope up and sobbed into her little sister's neck.

Mama and Eva carried the girls to the bed so they could all be touching, all crowded together. Zeb pulled out a chair from under the table and grinned at the sight of them, all talking at once.

Then he had to force the grin as he blinked back tears. He was going to miss this, all of them together. He didn't know when he would see them again, but he hoped to come back for Hope when she was older. If they really did make it out in the swamp, really did build a home where the girls were safe.

While Minnie and Eva got supper on the table, Faith sat on the floor between Zeb's spread legs and played acorns with Hope.

Zeb tugged on a pig tail. "You got a pretty ribbon in your hair."

"I got a white one, too. Miss Ellie, she the youngest, she like to play with hair. Miss Joanna let her do her hair, too, but not Miss Marvina. She don't like nobody touching her."

Was now the time? He could say, *How would you like to never go back to the big house again? How would you like to run away with me to live in the swamp with the gators and snakes and water all around?* A lot of people were afraid of the swamp, and with good reason.

He should be enjoying this last time with the five of them together, but he was suffering with doubt. Was living like that, worrying about floods, animals, hunger, was that really better than Faith putting up with a mean mistress? There were the two younger white girls who seemed to be good to her. She would never be hungry, never be in danger if she stayed on, even in this Charleston place.

But maybe she'd grow up to be scared all the time, like she had to watch every step and every turn of her head. Maybe she'd grow up forgetting how to feel her heart happy when she see a thousand lights shining on a stream in the sunshine, or catch the flash of silvery fish in the water.

Dark fell and they lit the candles. Zeb watched Faith grab an acorn out of Hope's pile to make her cackle.

Either way, go or stay, Faith had a hard life ahead of her. And she was too young to decide. He decided for her, for the hundredth time. Faith would not grow up without love and laughter and hope.

Mama called them to the table for supper and heaped beans and rice on Faith's plate. "You eat all that, I give you another biscuit and molasses."

Faith kicked her legs back and forth under the table as she ate. She hadn't done that in a long time. And she talked with her mouth full, another habit Mama had trained out of her. But she was excited to be home, so very happy to be where she belonged.

"In the morning," she announced, "I gone play with my friends. We gone run and run. Those little white girls don't never run. But Carly and Beau, we gone run and run. And then, Zeb and me going down to the creek and fish, ain't we, Zeb?"

"We got lots of fishing ahead of us," he said. He had his hooks and string wrapped up in a piece of cloth in his pocket. They were going to be eating a lot of fish from now on.

Zeb waited until Hope had finally calmed down enough to go to sleep, curled up with Faith on the bed. When he saw Faith's eyes droop, he cupped her jaw.

"Don't go to sleep, honey. We got to talk."

He helped her climb over Hope without waking her and took her to the chair to sit in his lap.

His grandma already sat at the table. She knew what was coming, he could see it in her eyes, but Mama was gone be hard hit.

"Sit down, Mama." She wrung out her dish rag and smiled as she took a chair.

"Faith, listen close," Zeb said. "We gone make some big changes. You listening?"

All her sleepiness disappeared. "What kind of changes? I don't have to go to Charleston with those white folks?"

"No, you ain't going to Charleston. You and me and Livy – you remember Livy?"

"She the pretty one you sweet on."

"Yeah. You and me and Livy are going to go away early, early in the – "

Mama knocked her chair over she stood up so fast. "No. No, no. No. You ain't doing this."

Zeb let out a breath and looked at his grandmother. She gave him a nod.

"Mama, I thought it out. It's best."

"Nothing's best if it means living like a wild animal in the swamp. Nothing's best if you end up caught and dead."

"I know you scared, Mama. I know your heart broke when they brought Daddy back. But we're not going to die. We're going to live out there in a camp, like the other maroons. We'll make a life for ourselves out there. We'll be free, Mama."

"They'll come after you, they got dogs – "

"You always worrying, Mama, but not everything bad you think of gone happen in life."

"Faith be safe up there in that house. They feed her all she want, don't they, Faith. She got shoes on her feet, you see that? And a ribbon in her hair. She better off with the white folks."

He shook his head. "No, Mama. They gone take her away."

Mama pressed her clasped hands to her breast. "Don't do this, Zeb. She just a little girl."

"Minnie." Grandma reached up and took one of Mama's hands, a rare moment of tenderness for her. "There more to life than being safe."

"Safe mean you *got* a life."

"No, Minnie. Zeb and Faith, they ain't cows in the field don't hardly know they alive, don't know sad or happy. Cows, they just breathing. That's not what we want for Faith."

Faith slid off Zeb's lap and walked around the table to wrap her arms around Mama's hips. In a voice so small Zeb hardly heard her, she said, "I don't want to go nowhere with them white people, Mama."

Mama clutched at her, tears flowing over her cheeks, her chest heaving in the effort it took not to sob.

Grandma picked up the fallen chair and led Minnie to sit down. "You hold on to Faith, and you listen."

"Zeb, don't do this," his mama sobbed.

Lord, it tore him up. But he had to do it.

"Please, Zeb."

"Hush, Minnie," Grandma said, as she had so often before, but this time she said it softly, with kindness. "Zeb got his father's blood in him, and his grandfather's too. He a smart man, and he gone do this. Understand?"

Mama shook her head no and clung to Faith.

"Go on, son," Grandma said. "How you gone do this?"

"In the morning, before daylight, Faith and me and Livy going to the bayou. Hector gone meet us there with a boat."

Zeb didn't mention the possibility, maybe the likelihood, that Hector wouldn't be there. Let Mama have at least that much assurance, that they would be safely at the camp long before Faith was expected back at the house.

"Livy and I both been collecting food and gear we gone need. We load it into the boat, get in ourselves, and Hector gone take us to the island he been clearing, miles and miles back, where nobody gone find us."

He didn't know if his mama even heard him, but he kept trying. "I been to this island already, Mama. It's a good place, with lots of birds flying around and singing, fresh water flowing by, flowers in the trees."

Faith wasn't missing a word. "There be others girls for me to play with?"

"Not right away, honey. Later on, when other children come, you gone be the big sister."

Faith twisted in Mama's lap and touched her cheek. "It gone be all right, Mama. I be with Zeb."

Good-hearted little Faith. She sat still and let Mama weep over her, holding her tight.

Zeb felt like weeping too. He met his grandma's gaze. She nodded at him. "You doing the right thing, son."

He closed his eyes, so very grateful for that benediction.

Chapter Fifteen

Zeb slept a few hours, but he sat the rest of the night on the porch, waiting for the first hint of dawn. Even before the sky lightened, the birds took to singing. He went back inside to find his grandmother up and stirring a fire.

"We don't need to eat, Grandma."

"I know you ain't got time for me to make biscuits. I just wanted a little fire to see by."

Zeb leaned over and touched his mama's hand. She was wrapped close around Faith, the two of them nested like spoons in spite of the heat.

Mama was awake. "It time, then."

Grandma handed Zeb the candles and her flint and steel. "I get me another flint. You take these." She took her box of treasures from the shelf.

"Grandma, I can't take Granddaddy's pipe. It be broke before the day over."

"No, that ain't it." She handed him a scrap of red cloth with a needle stuck in it. "This here for Livy. Tell her it a wedding present."

Zeb put it in his pocket and wrapped his arms around her. "Thank you, Grandma." He stepped over to Hope's cot and gently ran his fingertips along her soft cheek.

Mama pulled the dress over Faith's head, her still half-asleep. "I got to pee," Faith told Mama.

"Use the pot, then. We don't want to open the door but once." She put her hand on Faith's chin and made her look at her. "You understand you got to be quiet?"

Faith yawned hugely, nodding but unimpressed.

They were ready. Mama stood in the middle of the floor, looking old and lonely. Zeb took her gently in his arms. "We gone be all right. I promise. And later on, we come back one night so you can see how Faith growing tall and strong. "

She heaved a sob against his chest, but she gulped in a big breath and held herself in.

"Take care of Hope, Mama. We love you. Faith, tell Mama good-bye. We got to go."

Mama trembled, and her breathing was ragged, but she managed not to cry. Zeb was proud of her, giving Faith a good send-off.

"All right," he said.

Grandma opened the door and he and Faith slipped out into the dark.

Livy was waiting for them in the lane. The three of them quietly left the quarters.

When they were into the woods, Livy said, "Hector's here. I watched for him last night and seen him come in to Tish's house."

A huge breath escaped from Zeb's chest. "Thank the Lord."

It was too dark to keep going. They stopped at the tree Zeb had hidden the axe in and waited for the sun to come up. In ten minutes, they could see enough to find the path. By the time they reached the pond, they could make out individual trees. They kept going.

At the bayou, they found Hector's boat pulled ashore. Zeb retrieved the bundles he'd hung from the branches overhead. Livy got Faith settled in the center seat.

"We gone have to squeeze together," Livy said.

"That 's all right. I cold anyway."

"Remember how good it feel cause later we gone think we stepped into the devil's oven."

Zeb had done everything he could do. He stood at the boat's prow with his arms crossed and waited.

The sky was still dark gray with just a slender band of light low down in the sky when Hector sauntered into the clearing.

"Morning."

Zeb flinched at Hector's too-loud good cheer, but nobody but the birds would hear.

"Everybody ready?" Hector said.

"Let's get on."

With sunrise, the bayou began to waken. A fish jumped in the water. Birds flitted from one tree to another. Livy nudged Faith and pointed to a pink spoonbill catching the light under its wings as it flew overhead.

Hector steered from the back, Zeb paddled in front. Zeb was keenly aware he was lost. He supposed he could backtrack and eventually find himself back to the plantation, but it would require blundering among the hummocks, islands, and pools of the backwaters. He would learn it, he supposed, just as Hector had.

They were all hot and tired by the time they reached the island. Faith drowsed against Livy's arm and was befogged when Zeb lifted her out.

"We're here, honey." He set her down and held his hand out for Livy. Bless her, she gave him a smile full of sunshine when she stepped ashore.

"This it, huh?" she said, looking around. Her smile didn't dim in spite of the fact that most of the island was covered with trees and vines and palmettos.

Hector had made progress with the axe Zeb stole. The clearing was a good thirty feet wide along the shore and maybe thirty feet deep, and along the back edge he had constructed a lean-to constructed of sapling poles and palmetto leaves. They'd be out of the rain then and that was something.

Zeb and Hector unloaded the bundles of food and odds and ends he and Livy had collected the last weeks.

"I'm off. See you in a week or so."

Zeb turned to him, shocked. "You're not staying?"

"Not yet. Told Flavian I'd help build the last cabin before I left him."

Zeb just looked at him.

"I owe him, Zeb. You'll be all right. I left you the axe, a fishing pole in the lean to, and a bucket for water. You got a knife, right?"

"Yeah. I got a knife. And fish hooks."

"You'll be fine, then."

And just like that, Zeb and Livy and Faith were alone in their new home.

Hector was right. They'd be fine. He just hadn't prepared himself to face . . . all this . . . without Hector's experience to guide them.

Livy stood in the sunshine, turning slowly, her arms stretched out and her head tilted back. "Feel that, Faith? Feel it?"

Faith stretched her arms out, too. "What we feeling, Livy?"

"This what freedom feel like. Come here, Zeb. Feel it."

He watched her instead, and felt like he used to do before Noah died. That feeling he'd had when all the colored dragonflies had swarmed around him.

Livy twirled over to him and grabbed his hands, pulling his arms wide. He'd never seen such a smile on her face. She felt it, too. He grabbed her up and kissed her hard.

"Come here, Faith." He grabbed her close, too, and hugged the both of them.

Livy broke free and danced away, her arms flung up. "Free!" She twirled once more and slowed to a stop. "Zeb," she said, near to tears all of a sudden. "We did it."

She clapped her hands over her face, then swiped at her tears. "We gone be happy, here, Zeb. You and me and Faith, we a family now."

Later Zeb would think about the knot of worry building in his chest. But not now. This was a moment to be happy if there ever was one.

"Come on, let's look around."

There were patches among the cypress and tupelo and gum trees where the sun shone. They could plant their first seeds in those natural clearings and slowly enlarge them to have garden plots.

"Look up," Livy told Faith. "See up there?" She pointed to pink flowers growing high on the tree trunks.

"How they grow up there without no dirt?"

"I don't know that, but I know they called orchids. They had them back where I come from."

They waded through the shallows along the shoreline and came to a sort of pool and in it otters were playing in the water. They watched for a while, such a happy sight. Zeb agreed they were cute as they could be, but he thought he'd be willing to eat one just the same.

Farther on, they found a stand of wild iris, dozens of deep blue flowers with a core of golden yellow.

"Can I pick them?" Faith asked.

"We ain't got no jar to put them in. They live longer you leave them where they are," Livy said.

"Someday I get me a jar."

"Then we'll pick all we want."

When they got back to the clearing, Faith wandered into the lean-to.

Zeb froze when Faith screamed. He sprinted toward her, but he held back when he saw Faith scratch up a clod of dirt and hurl it at the black snake nestled in a corner of the shelter. It stirred. She hurled another clod at it, and it slithered away.

Livy stepped up beside him.

"You see what she did?" he said, so proud he couldn't stop smiling. That knot in his chest eased loose. "Faith, you just made yourself the owner of this whole island. What you gone call it?"

She twisted her mouth, thinking. "We could call it Iris Island. Or Orchid Island." She murmured the two names to herself a few times. "I gone call it Orchid Island."

"Orchid Island," Livy said, trying it out. She leaned in to Zeb and smiled up at him. "We're home, Zeb. Really home."

He glanced around the barren clearing, at the tangle of trees beyond, and was humbled that a woman and a little girl stood in the same jungle and swamp and saw a home surrounded by blue irises and pink orchids.

~~~

Zeb reminded them to be mindful of smoky fires. They built it under the overhang of the lean-to so what little smoke they made would be broken up by the palmetto roof. For supper they roasted sweet potatoes they'd brought with them and the fish Zeb caught with Hector's pole.

No plates. No spoons. One cup Livy thought to bring. But they feasted.

"What's the first thing you gone do in the morning, Faith?"

"You mean after I pee?"

"Yeah. After that," Zeb said, smiling at Livy.

"Well," she said, "there not gone be nobody to play with. Not gone be no kitty cats either. Maybe I just fish."

"Fish for breakfast be good. What you gone do, Livy?"

"Hard to know where to start, ain't it? We need something to sleep on besides the dirt. We need to get some beans planted. We need to know what else they is to eat around here. But nobody gone ring a bell out here for us to get up. Maybe I sleep until the
~~~

sun been up an hour. Maybe that's what I'll do my first day of freedom."

"You remember where the otters played in that pool? Let's go back and dip ourselves in there before it gets dark."

Faith helped him put the fire out and held his hand on the way to the bathing pool. "What you gone do in the morning, Zeb?" she asked.

"Well, we got an axe. We got trees. And I got a strong back. I'm gonna chop me a cypress down and start hewing out a dugout."

He turned his head to look at Livy walking behind him. She met his eyes and nodded. Likely she didn't like being marooned out here either. One thing to choose to stay put on one little island, another one to be stuck on it.

~~~

Livy followed Zeb and Faith to the other side of the island. When had God decided to be so good to her? There was Zeb, moving brush aside for Faith, ducking his head for overhanging branches. A kind man. A brave man. And he was hers.

At the water's edge, they shucked off their clothes and hung them on branches. Zeb helped Faith step through and around the cypress knees and into the water. Then he turned back to Livy and held his hand out.

Her whole body thrummed, looking into his eyes, taking his hand. A free man and a free woman. Like Adam and Eve starting over on an island in the swamp. With Faith, they'd make themselves an Eden.

Her hand trembled when she touched his. Zeb's smile was slow and knowing. She was his, too, that smile said. She felt like the first woman, the most beautiful woman, the only woman.

She gave him a teasing look back, lingering at his manhood, making him stir.

Zeb laughed. "Come on in here before I embarrass myself."

She stepped into clear cypress-stained water with a soft little current to keep it fresh. Likely there were leeches in these waters somewhere, and hidden dangers, but Livy's paradise provided this sweet little pond.
~~~

The lash marks on Zeb's back were still pink with scar tissue, but he only shook his head when Livy wanted to touch them. "Don't think about it no more. That was another life."

"All right," she said.

"They don't hurt him no more, those cuts," Faith said. "I asked him and he said no."

Zeb heaved a big splash at Faith and got her giggling. The three of them played, pain and fear and anger forgotten. Livy washed Faith's face, then Faith said, "Let me do yours." And Livy's heart was won.

They stepped back onto the bank, their wet feet picking up the damp black earth. Faith picked her foot up and scowled.

Livy gave her a hug. "We not gone have clean feet on this place. It be all right."

When dark fell, Faith fell asleep as soon as she lay down in the lean-to, her head cradled on her arm. Livy sat with Zeb at the edge of the water, their arms hooked around their knees, and looked at the night. Too many trees, too many clouds to see the sky, but there was enough moon to see the cypress all around, straight as sentinels, and a glimmer of light on the water.

Zeb nudged her with his elbow. "I think we ought to get married," he said.

Livy snorted. "You got a preacher hiding in the bushes?"

"Come here." He shifted onto his knees and pulled her onto hers. He took both her hands and gazed at her face. He meant it. This beautiful man meant to marry her.

She tilted her face to him, only able to see the outline of his jaw and the gleam of his eyes.

"Livy. I say this before God. I will love you and take care of you all my days. I am your husband until I leave this world."

Livy's heart pushed against her lungs so she could barely breathe. "Zeb. Zebediah. I say this before God. I will love you and take care of you all my days. I am your wife until I leave this world."

Their clasped hands between their chests, Zeb leaned in and kissed her, his mouth warm and gentle and sweet. Livy closed her eyes, her whole body softening, aching for his.

He lowered her to the ground. "I'm gone get dirt on your back," he murmured.

"It'll wash off."

He lay beside her, his big calloused hand lightly playing over her neck, her breasts, her belly.

"This dress too hot, Zeb," Livy whispered.

"I can take care of that."

He unbuttoned her slowly, his knuckles brushing her breasts. He trailed his fingers up her leg, pulling the skirt up. "Lift up," he said.

She lifted her hips and he slid the dress up to her waist, shifted her, and pulled it over her head.

She reached for his pants, untied the drawstring, and tugged. The fabric snagged on his erection and he chuckled. "Let me do it."

And then they were skin to skin from toes to mouths. She ran her fingers through the soft springy wool of his hair. His hand traced her spine, caressed the curve of her waist, and palmed the roundness of her bottom.

He feathered kisses on her neck, traced her ear with his tongue, and stroked her breast. She explored the hard planes of his back, the taut muscles of his buttocks. When he took her nipple into his mouth, her private place melted, opened, and wanted.

His fingers drifted down her body, lingering at her navel, circling, probing, and then drifting into the soft nest of her womanhood. He stroked her gently, pressing his palm against her mons. With a groan, Livy held his head and kissed him, her mouth wide-open like she could swallow him whole.

He dipped his finger into her passage, causing her hips to jerk. "You ready for me, Livy?"

She hooked her leg around his hips in answer.

His slow slide into her was the sweetest moment she'd ever known. Her whole body hummed, and when he withdrew and slid in again, she drew in a gasping breath.

He gripped her buttocks and shifted the angle of his gentle thrusts, growing deeper and more insistent with every penetration.

His tongue pushed against her lips, invaded her mouth, licked her inner cheek. Livy wrapped both legs around him.

"Livy," he groaned. "I can't make this last."

"We make it last next time."

She arched, drawing him in and squeezing him with her inner muscles.

The rhythm of his thrusts quickened, the power in his body thrilling her, taking her higher and higher.

Light and heat flooding her senses, his hips pounding against her, she held on and soared with him, above the treetops, into the sky, until one deep, powerful surge thrust her into the stars.

She cried out, ecstasy climbing from deep in her body into the sky. His breath hard and fast, his hips pummeled her until one final lunge released all his heat into her.

He panted a moment, relaxed on top of her, then he rolled off, taking her with him, their bodies still joined.

When he could speak, he placed his hands around her face and kissed her. Her hips bucked against him again and he held her until her final spasm left her limp in his arms.

"It's true," she whispered to him. "We married, Zeb."

Chapter Sixteen

The first days on Orchid Island went well. They had fresh-caught fish to eat and potatoes from home. Livy planted squash seeds and hoped there was time enough for a crop before summer's end. Zeb found a good sized cypress and began the laborious process of chopping it down, one man with one axe.

Faith made him proud. She didn't scream any more when she saw a snake, which turned out to be pretty near every day. She pelted it with whatever was at hand and hollered "Shoo" till it slithered off. Zeb taught her how to recognize the poisonous ones and told her to call him if she saw a cotton-mouth or a copperhead.

He taught her how to light a fire using the flint and steel.

"I never learned to do that either," Livy said.

He looked at her in amazement. "You can't start a fire?"

"Never had to," she said.

Zeb winked at Faith. "She's spoiled as that Miss Marvina, ain't she?"

"I am not," Livy declared. "Look at these hands. I can shuck hard corn with these hands. And hoe all day without no blisters."

"Come on, Livy," Faith said kindly. "I'll show you what to do."

Hiding her smile, Livy did as she was told. "First, you get you some little bits of this and that for kindling, like chips from where Zeb hacking at that tree."

Before long, Livy and Faith were the proud makers of fire on Orchid Island. The two of them spent most of the day together and Zeb would hear them mimicking the birds they heard. At night, they laughed themselves silly trying to sound like bull frogs. Zeb was the champion at gator grunts.

Livy set Faith to gathering moss to make mattresses. They would have to cure the moss to get rid of the chiggers, but all things in good time. Building a camp out here was going to take time, lots of time.

And some luck, he began to realize. Their fourth day, a rainstorm came through. It wasn't a hurricane – he'd lived through one of those and knew this was nothing like what the wind was capable of. Still, the trees whipped around, and the rain fell in a solid curtain.

The water rose. No higher ground to retreat to. No canoe to float in. The closer the water crept to the lean-to, the tighter Zeb's shoulders got. At least it's daylight, he kept telling himself, and with the wind blowing the rain under the lean-to, they couldn't get any wetter than they already were.

Faith huddled in Zeb's lap, his back sheltering her from the worst of the rain. Livy cuddled next to him, shivering. The wind caused the lean-to to lean some more, but it held.

An hour, no more than that, and the storm moved on. The water creeping over the banks toward the lean-to retreated in little rivulets.

Zeb exchanged a look with Livy over Faith's head. They needed to get a cabin built.

They needed a lot of things. They needed more tools. They needed more hands to wield them. And Zeb had no idea when Hector would be back. Or if.

Three turtles, a big one and two little ones, had lumbered onto the island during the storm. Zeb killed one of them and stuck sticks in the meat to roast over the fire. The other two he meant to corral. It was Faith's job to keep them on their backs so they couldn't wander, their stubby legs waving in the effort to turn over. Livy and he made a flimsy fence out of palmetto stalks and fallen branches. It wouldn't have held anything more active than turtles, but they'd probably keep penned for a day or two. And they'd have three vessels, little pots or cups. He was sure Livy would have a dozen ideas of what to do with the shells.

Using the axe, he whittled a sapling into a spear and tried for an otter – when Faith wasn't there to see -- but they were wily and fast. Maybe next time.

Zeb thought about what else he could kill for something besides food. People made belts out of snake skins, but he'd heard the skin was too thin to do much else with. He had his axe. Occasionally a gator glided past, ignoring them. When he had the boat ready, maybe he'd get a gator. A small one, he said to himself.

After the sixth day, and no Hector, Zeb had to force the smiles Faith and Livy needed to see and hid the brooding going on behind the happy face.

If Hector abandoned them, they might be stuck on this little island, reduced to living like savages, their clothes rotted away, never seeing another soul. He could feed them, he wasn't worried about that, but what kind of life would Faith have growing up with nobody in her life but him and Livy. Nobody to play with. Nobody to have babies with. She had been safe at the white house, Mama had been right about that. Safe was looking a lot better than it had when he worried Faith was unhappy.

He was working hard as he could to get themselves a dugout made. He'd never done it before, but it wasn't hard to figure out. Trouble was, he needed more than an axe. The big trouble, however, was what to do once he had it ready to float.

He wouldn't dare paddle out of sight of this island. He might not find his way back and Faith and Livy would be here all alone. And if he took them with him, he still didn't know which way was what. All this dugout could do was give them someplace to stay if the water rose too high.

But he kept at it, chipping away at the log, making lists in his head of the things they needed. They had plenty of food – fish, crawfish, turtles, snakes if it came to that. But he needed a chisel, a saw, a hammer. And he needed to hunt. If he killed a deer, they could use the bones to make awls, needles, scrapers and more. With leather he could make string, even rope, and soft shoes like the Indians wore. He wondered if he could make a bow and some arrows. He didn't see how with just an axe and a knife, but he hadn't tried it yet.

Livy had her own list. Gourds, more seeds, baskets, shirts, pants, dresses. Come winter, they'd freeze to death in these threadbare summer clothes, she said. Nothing colder than a windy day on the water in December, even if the sun shone. But Livy was not complaining. Merely thinking out loud.

Zeb did not share his thoughts, but sometimes maybe Livy could see what he was thinking. She would squeeze his shoulder as she passed by, or bring him a cool drink in their one cup.

She never faltered, his Livy. The big rain had washed up the seeds she had planted. She sifted carefully and methodically through the sand and brush and gathered enough to replant. Faith, too, seemed happy enough. She hummed as she gathered moss, sat still as turtles when she fished, and made the day's fire with great concentration.

Zeb kept on smiling. In the evening, after they'd put the fire out, Livy told them stories, and he laughed when he should. He hugged Faith every night and sat with her, talking about Mama and Grandma and Hope till she grew quiet and her breathing was slow and even.

Faith sound asleep, Zeb lay down on his back next to Livy, his forearm over his eyes. Yesterday and today he'd felt like his guts were on fire. It wasn't anything he'd eaten. His belly was just eating on itself he was so worried.

"He'll come," Livy said softly. "We'll be fine, the three of us. We are fine."

She traced his lips with her finger tip. She lifted herself on top of him and kissed the underside of his jaw. When he just lay there, she licked his neck. Zeb felt the smile building in him, but he lay still.

She scooted down and licked the hollow in the center of his chest, stroked her fingers across his nipples, down his ribs. He flinched where it tickled, and she slid her hand down to his hip bone, circling it with her palm, licking and purring.

When she slipped her hand into his pants, he flipped her over onto her back and carried out his own seduction. Taking his time, he kissed behind her ear, at the corner of her mouth, behind her other ear. When his tongue touched her lip, she opened her mouth and drew him in.

He rubbed his palm against her nipple, catching it between his fingers, loving how she broke the kiss to breathe in rapid gulps. His mouth moved to her breast, his tongue swirling circles around the hardened bud. He drew it into his mouth and suckled her until she writhed under him.

"Get those pants off. Now," she hissed at him.

Chuckling, he obliged and pushed into her, his breath stopping at the soft, hot, tight feel of her taking him in.

He held himself still over her and in her, his body trembling with the effort not to pound himself against her. When he regained control, he moved over her, slowly, deliberately.

Her hands caressed and stroked, from his neck down to his buttocks. When she reached between them and cupped his balls, he gasped a breath. "Wait," he told her, and held still again.

She didn't wait. She stroked him, she ran her thumbnail around the base of his penis, she gripped him in her inner passage. He lost the last bit of his control and plunged into her hot and furious. She met every stroke with her hips, their bodies slapping against each other.

When Livy's breath turned to a pant, her moans into gasps, he reached between her legs and touched the little nub that sent her up and over, her hips desperately pumping against his. He let himself go, the rhythm taking him over as he plunged and battered himself against the willing cradle of her body. Everything went black and he fell into the darkness, a primitive creature mindless with need and pleasure. With a final shuddering pulse, he dropped his weight onto her for one delicious moment before he remembered he was crushing her.

He rolled off and pulled her to him. "My God, Livy. That was worth being born for."

In a little while, she touched his cheek. "It's God's promise, Zeb. You see that? Why else God give us each other, give us our freedom – we gone live, and we gone love each other, Zeb."

With Livy settled against him and asleep, peace crept in, and hope, and then he slept.

Chapter Seventeen

"Zeb!" Faith ran for him. "Somebody's coming."

Zeb felt the tension pouring right out of him. He left his axe stuck in the log, ready to help Hector beach his boat. But it wasn't Hector.

Flavian and a woman. A girl sat on the floor between Flavian's knees. Another child lay draped in the woman's arms, his long legs hanging off her lap. Zeb blinked and passed his hand over his mouth. That child didn't look right.

Flavian had a rag tied around his biceps. Dried blood streaked his face.

Zeb grabbed hold of the boat and hauled it up onto dry ground. He straightened then and looked again at the child so limp and still in his mother's lap. There was a round hole in his skull just behind the ear.

"They found us," Flavian said.

Zeb lifted the little girl out and set her down next to Faith. Flavian climbed out and reached for his boy. Cradling his child, he walked to the lean-to and sat down, the boy's head pressed against his bare chest. His wife sat next to him. She reached for her son's foot and just held it.

Livy came to the clearing from her little garden patch. She looked at Zeb then at the little family.

Faith had the girl by the hand and brought her under the shelter, too. The girl climbed into her mother's lap. They all sat there, no one saying a word.

Zeb thought about where they would bury the boy. What they'd use to dig without a shovel. There wasn't a scrap of extra cloth on the island. What would they use for a shroud?

The ground was soft. They could dig with their hands. They could weave a mat out of palmetto leaves and wrap it around the child before they put him to rest.

"He was running to get my tools. 'Luke,' I shouted. 'Get in the boat.' He was nearly there when the bullet got him. He had a hand saw with him. He died for a hand saw."

Zeb's gaze was on Faith. He opened his arm to her and she crawled to him and sat in the lap he made for her.

He had known there were risks to running away and trying to live out here. But there lay Flavian's boy in his daddy's arms, proving how dangerous this was. He was about Faith's age, and yesterday, he was just like her. Laughing, playing, working. Breathing.

He could take her back. They wouldn't punish a child for being taken away. Maybe he'd even go back himself. He could endure another whipping. Or whatever Benning and the master decided to do to him. Some places they branded runaway slaves when they caught them. Sometimes they maimed them. Nobody on this place had done anything like that though. Whatever they did, they wouldn't kill him. He was too valuable for that.

He looked at Livy. She gazed at the boy, her face blank. She'd lost a child, too, he reminded himself. But she wouldn't go back. Not Livy.

Then he'd take Faith back and come back to the island himself. He wasn't going to leave Livy, not ever.

"Faith, come help me," Zeb said.

Faith rose and held her hand out for the little girl. "You can come, too," she said.

Zeb got his axe and led them to a stand of palmetto near the middle of the island. He showed them how to peel the blades off the central stalks and how to weave them in a thatch. They wouldn't make a perfect mat, but it would do.

He dug a grave using his hands and one of the smaller turtle shells while the girls worked with the palmettos. When they were ready, they went back to the lean-to.

He sat down in front of Flavian. None of them had moved while he was gone.

"When you're ready," he said softly.

A single sob erupted from the mother, and then she was quiet.

They wrapped the boy in the matting and lay him in the grave. Zeb said a prayer asking God to take Luke to his bosom.

Livy took the mother and the girls back to the clearing while Flavian helped him fill the grave.

Walking behind Flavian on the way back to the beach, Zeb thought the man seemed to have shrunk since Zeb saw him on his own island. His shoulders slumped, and his head was bent. It was grief, that's all.

They emerged into the clearing and found two more dugouts pulled ashore.

Hector and three men were unloading the boats. "We've got a little food," Hector said. "Samuel over there managed to save a few tools." Samuel was the boy, about 12, that Zeb had seen when he went to Flavian's camp.

The other men were Derek, a short stocky man with two missing front teeth. Adam, slim, skinny even. And Cal, a man whose muscled shoulders showed he'd done hard labor all his life.

"Derek grabbed a cook pot," Hector went on. "Adam, he run just after you did. Brought an axe out with him."

"More than what we had," Zeb said.

Cal made a fire and they ate what they'd brought. They were going to have to hunt or catch their next meal, but they were fed, they were on dry land.

Finally Zeb turned to Hector. "What happened?"

"Slave trackers. They attacked at dusk, about a dozen of them, four in a boat. Don't know why they didn't wait until dark. Or until morning. It would have been worse for us."

"Birdie saw them coming when they were still a few minutes away. That gave us a chance," Samuel said.

"They came in with rifles and shotguns, shouting and hollering. Shooting. Mostly they didn't aim. A live slave is worth more than a dead one. But the bullets were flying. One of them got Flavian's boy, Luke. Randolph, he got shot right in the heart. I expect he was dead before he hit the ground. Dickie got hit in the neck. He lasted till all the blood ran out of him. "

Zeb could picture it, the confusion and noise, the blood.

"Three dead. Everybody else got away?"

"Yeah. We're all here."

"How? How did you get away?"

"Fools attacked, it was near dark. We had two rifles, a handful of bullets. Cal and me, we shot back. I think we killed one."

"Yeah. We got one of them," Cal said.

"Derek knifed another one. Everybody grabbed what we could and shoved the boats off. By then, it was early dark. The slavers were all on shore, and we got ourselves hid in the swamp before they come after us."

"They didn't want to be out there in the dark," Derek said. "That's why they attacked when they did, so they could spend the night on dry land."

"Likely right," Adam said.

"How safe is it here?" Livy asked.

"We're safe. We a long way from that camp, and Hector and Flavian the only ones knew where this one was. I imagine the slavers feel pretty good. They got two dead men to take back. There'll be some reward, even if they dead."

"It's cause you three run off from Dietrich's place, and Adam here run off from the next place up a few days later," Cal said. "That was more running off at one time than they could blink at." He looked at Hector. "Ought to have planned it better than that."

Hector's mouth tightened, but he just looked away.

"They likely burned our camp," Derek said.

"I imagine," Adam answered.

Flavian wiped his hands over his face. "Don't matter if they burned it. We built it once, we can build it again."

"This is a good island," Hector said. "Ain't it, Zeb."

He nodded. "The water ain't made us sick. Plenty of fish, turtles. Livy found a couple of patches of sunlight over that way and planted some seeds."

What Zeb most wanted to know was what kind of tools they'd gotten away with. They all knew they needed tools to survive out here.

Hector talked about it first. "You've got your axe, Zeb. And a couple of knives?"

"Zeb and me both got a knife," Livy said.

Zeb fished in his pocket and held up his two nails. "We got nails, for what they's worth."

"We'll use them," Hector said. "We've got Luke's handsaw." Hector looked at Flavian and his wife, Birdie, was quiet a minute, and then he went on. "Got a plane, a chisel. Got flint and steel. Got two rifles. No more bullets though. And we got another axe."

Zeb nodded. They could get by with those. "Anybody made a bow to hunt with?"

"I was trying to," Derek said. "Left it behind, but it wadn't any good no way."

"We can make some traps. There's otters out here," Zeb said.

"Steel trap be the best," Adam said.

"Well, we ain't got no steel traps," Cal snapped.

"Cal," Flavian said softly, and Cal shook his head and looked away. "Cal," he said again. "We fight amongst ourselves, we ain't gone make it."

~~~

That first night, Livy startled awake at every sound, somebody turning over, an owl hooting. Those slavers had found Flavian's camp, they could find this one. They could still be out there, in the swamp, smelling the air for smoke, listening for a voice or a snore.

All day the next day, she felt eyes on her, eyes hiding behind the moss and the cypress, and heard the slap of oars in the water. But it was only a fearful imagination. There was no one out there.

She felt better when Flavian set up a watch schedule. With six men, they could have a sentinel day and night, listening, watching. They'd gotten careless, Flavian said. That's why the slavers had found them. They wouldn't be careless any more.

Gradually, Livy quit looking over her shoulder and waking up in the night. She noticed some of the strain ease from around Zeb's eyes, too. She'd wondered if he would resent Flavian for assuming command of Zeb's island, but it didn't look like Zeb saw it that way. Neither did Hector even though this was to have been "his" island.

As for herself, she had been happy, just the three of them, but she liked Birdie, and it was good Faith had another little girl to play with.

It's a good life out here, Livy thought. All she'd ever wanted was her freedom, and she had so much more than that. She had a husband. She had a child.

And she had these new friends. Flavian was everybody's uncle, Birdie the aunt. Sam was the little brother, Faith and Millie the baby sisters. Zeb and the other men were like cousins. They were becoming a family.

In the evenings, they didn't dare have a fire that might be seen glimmering through the trees. They sat in the dark and told stories. Cal had a head full of stories, funny ones and scary ones where ghosts disguised themselves in the mist and floated through the swamp. Zeb sang, his voice so deep and smooth and rich, Livy
~~~

felt his tone wrap around her like warm arms. And then they would sing together, the church songs they all new, the songs they'd learned from their mothers.

It took a lot of food to fill eleven bellies. Everyone fished. Derek made traps and took a dugout around the hummocks and islets to scout for animal trails.

Then Adam declared they needed to kill a gator.

"What, are you bored?" Cal asked.

Adam looked irritated. Livy had noticed Cal irritated a lot of people. He was a good looking man, Cal was, but he had a way of curling his top lip that made the others narrow their eyes when they looked at him.

"Gator tails is good eating," Flavian intervened, ever the peacekeeper. "The hide's tougher than any leather you ever saw. We can use the bones, too."

So they were going gator hunting, just like that.

Livy pulled at Zeb's arm and said so only he could hear, "You ain't going, are you? You got your boat to work on. They don't need you."

Zeb bent his head to her. "You worried, Livy?" He licked her ear and grinned at her. "We gone use boats, woman. We ain't wading out there."

This was the Zeb she first knew. Smiling all the time, full of sunshine, but not simple. Not Zeb. These last weeks, he had wormed his way into her heart, and he knew it. That didn't mean she had to act the fool over him.

Livy shoved at him. "Go on then, but don't come complaining to me if some gator eat you up."

"That's a promise," he said.

He poked her in the ribs so there wasn't anything to do but let him go with a smile on her face.

They left in two dugouts, three men and an axe in each of them. Sam had to stay back so as not to overload a boat. "You go next time," Flavian promised him.

Livy couldn't keep her mind off Zeb out there hunting creatures with maws full of teeth and great slashing tails. She had seen gators no longer than her arm, but she'd also seen monsters nearly as long as the boats.

"They be all right," Birdie told her. "They got each other and two axes."

When they finally came back, Zeb's boat towed a gator behind it, belly-up, rope wrapped around its chest below the front legs.

Faith and Millie clung to each other, not nearly as frightened as they pretended, Livy was sure, but they craved Samuel's attention, so they shivered and whimpered. Disappointing for them, however, and amusing for Livy, Samuel was more interested in the gator than he was in little girls.

"How long is it?" Samuel called, crowding the men as they pulled the dugouts onto shore. He rushed to grab hold of the rope to help haul the carcass out of the water.

"What do you think?" Flavian said.

"He's longer than Zeb is tall, ain't he?" Sam guessed.

Livy had hold of Zeb's arm and gave him a look-over. "You ain't eat up then."

He dipped his head for a quick kiss. "Not this time."

"Oh my Lord!" Birdie yelled.

Livy jumped. "What?"

"Look there at the side of that boat."

The dugout Zeb had been in had great gouges along the top of one side.

"It bit the boat?" Livy said. "That's it. You ain't going on no more gator hunts."

"Livy, I hunted a dozen gators before now. Ever one of them killed just like that," Flavian assured her.

She breathed in noisily. Birdie didn't seem worried. Nobody seemed worried but her, and Faith and Millie with their pretend carrying-on. She was going to embarrass Zeb if she fretted any more.

"Well. What you gone do with that thing?"

"Gator tail steaks is good eating," Birdie said. "You girls come on. We need to get a fire going."

Zeb left her to help with the butchering. Cal stood close by coiling up the rope.

"You bleeding, Cal?" she said.

He looked at his forearm and then at her. "You ever stitch anybody up?"

"Sure. Let me see."

Three gashes still oozed blood, each of them only about three inches long, but they were deep.

"I get my needle. And some of that bark Birdie said goes good on wounds."

He sat on the end of a dugout while she cleaned the gouges and stitched them closed. "This claw marks? Not teeth?"

"Claw marks. I was stupid or it wouldn't have happened."

"Who axed it?"

"Adam did that. He brought that axe with him when he run, and he don't let nobody forget it."

"Long as somebody axe that thing dead."

She tied off the last stitch and bent over his arm to cut the thread with her teeth. "We got to watch that it don't fester."

She straightened up and found Cal looking at her with hot eyes. "Zeb man enough for you, Livy?" he asked softly. And Zeb not thirty feet away bent over the gator, helping to cut through the hide.

Livy stepped back, her mouth taut. "Zeb man enough for any woman on this earth," she said.

His gaze dropped to her mouth and then roamed over her breasts. "And you woman enough for two men. Ain't you?"

She ought to hit him. And scratch him. But people would see, and Zeb would know. Like Flavian said, they didn't want no fighting amongst themselves.

"I don't like you, Cal."

He chuckled. "I know how to make you like me. I know how to make you like me a lot." His voice was pitched low and brought up the hair on her arms.

Livy took another step back. "You leave me alone. Zeb ain't near as sweet as he seem. He beat you to death, I tell him to."

Cal laughed. "Thank you for stitching me up, Miss Livy." He sauntered over to the others and lent a hand pulling the hide off the gator.

Chapter Eighteen

Livy finger-combed Faith's hair and gathered it all up in a topknot tied off with the blue ribbon. That ribbon was Faith's prized possession and it was getting ragged. There wasn't any help for it though.

"What you and Millie doing today?"

"We gone make ourselves little baskets. Then we gone gather up all the wood shavings from where they smoothing out Zeb's boat."

"And what will you do with all them wood shavings?"

"Birdie finished making us a palmetto doll, one for me and one for Millie. And you seen how them wood shavings look like the curls on those white girls' heads? We gone stick them in the dolls' heads and they have pretty yellowy-red curls."

Livy kissed her cheek. "You got black curls and they just as pretty. Go on with you, I got to get doing."

There was so much more to eat out here than Livy had realized. Birdie had been in the swamp for years and showed her how to pick water cress growing in the shallows. There were cattails on the sunny side of all the islands out here, and turns out you can eat just about all of a cattail.

Today, Birdie was going to show her how to cut swamp cabbage.

They found Adam scouring the last bits out of a turtle shell using wet sand. "Adam," Birdie said. "We gone borrow your axe this morning."

He stopped what he was doing and looked at Birdie a minute. "What you want with my axe?" He said it with a teasing sort of smile, but Cal was right. Adam did keep his axe to himself. But he'd share. He always did, long as he kept up with who had it.

"We gone get you something else to eat besides fish and turtle, that's what."

Now he was interested. "Like what?"

"You like swamp cabbage?"

"Yeah, I like it fine."

"Well, we got to chop down one of them palms to get at the cabbage."

"You want me to come chop it down?"

"It ain't hard to cut a palm down. We bring your axe back after while."

They left the cleared beach, passing Derek and Cal constructing a trap they hoped would get them an otter. Derek threw a pre-occupied smile their way, but Cal's smile was one of those that only drew up one side of his mouth. His eyes drifted down Livy's body and lit on her hips as she walked. She felt how they swayed with every step and tried to walk straight, but she wasn't built to walk straight.

Those dark eyes roamed over her. She felt like he'd peeled the dress off her.

She gave him a hard look and followed Birdie into the woods.

"You got you knife on you all the time?" Birdie said.

"Yeah." She gestured at the sheath she'd woven out of palmetto leaves. "I begin to think them palmettos more use to us than fish hooks."

"You keep it on you. Cal might need reminding you belong to somebody else."

Livy felt the heat rise in her face. "You think he do anything? I done told him no."

"Don't know if he do something," Birdie said. "But he need a woman worse I ever seen a man. Some men, it takes them like that, and ain't no cure for it but gray hair or a woman. And it ain't just you."

"You had other women at your camp?"

"Me and another woman. Sam's mama. She dead now. Caught a fever and died. But Cal looked at her like he do you, and then he looked at me like that. But when he got too close, I cut him a little bit right here," she said, gesturing to her neck.

Livy didn't want to cut anybody. She just wanted him to quit looking at her like that.

"Flavian know?"

Birdie shook her head. "I didn't tell him. Didn't want him killing a man. And Cal left me alone after that."

Livy didn't want Zeb killing nobody either.

"That palm there, see it?" Birdie said. "It ain't a swamp cabbage palm. You want this kind right here."

It was one of those that had the prongs all over the trunk where the old fronds had come off. They were all over out here.

"So we gone cut this palm down, and then we gone trim off all these prongs."

"I'll do it," Livy said. She took the axe and started swinging. It wasn't hard wood like an oak or even a pine, but it still took her enough swings to make her shoulders burn.

It was awkward trying to cut the remnants of old fronds off the core using an axe, but Birdie was handy. What they ended up with was a white column maybe six inches across. Birdie carried the axe and Livy hoisted the three-foot core over her shoulder to take back to the camp where they could lay it on a palmetto mat out of the dirt.

"Here's your axe," Birdie said.

"I get the first piece?" Adam said.

Livy produced her knife and shaved a disc off the column.

Adam bit into it. "It's a good one. Got a nice crunch to it."

"We borrow your axe again sometime."

"That's fine."

~~~

The dugout was finished, and everyone gathered on shore to watch its first float. Zeb stepped in, paddle at the ready. "All right," he called soon as he was settled.

Adam and Derek shoved the boat off the sand and into the water. Faith and Millie and Livy yahooed and cried out hallelujah, the others clapping and carrying on.

It was a fine moment. Zeb was proud as he'd ever been in his life. He was glad he'd had help, glad he'd had the tools the others brought with them, but he had done most of the work – all the earliest, hardest work. And he hadn't done it for the Boss. He'd done it for himself and his own family. That was the most new thing of this whole new life.

The thing handled like an over-loaded cane cart, but he'd get the hang of it.

He paddled in close to shore and said, "Come on, Livy. You and Faith, come take a ride."
~~~

They made a circle around the island. At the pool, Faith pointed to an otter floating on its back.

"Can I have this one for a pet, Zeb? Please?" Faith begged.

"An otter don't want to be nobody's pet, honey."

Faith made a big pouty lip, but she didn't mean it. She knew otters weren't like dogs or cats.

Zeb looked at his family, both of them facing him where he sat in the back of the dugout. They were hot and skeeter-bit, but they were used to that. The wonder of it was they were both smiling in spite of how hard everything was out here.

Every single sunrise he woke up wondering what the day gone bring. That had never been true before. They always been told do this or do that, never decided none of it for themselves. And it always the same things. Hoe or pick or dig or saw. Cut the cane. Boil the cane. Whatever the Boss said do, that's what they done.

And Zeb, he'd smiled every day, whatever he'd been told to do. Didn't think about possibles cause he hadn't seen any possibles. Maybe Livy was right to think he was simple.

Out here, he and Livy and Faith only had leaf mats to keep them out of the dirt when they slept, they ate more fish than he had a taste for, but he more than wanted to smile. He wanted to shout. He wanted to sing.

That's how good it was to be free. When he opened his eyes of a morning, he'd ask himself, what I gone do first? Need to work on the boat. Need to catch some fish. Need to try making a fish net out of grass or blade leaves. However much he needed to do, he was the one decided if and when he'd do it.

This is what Livy wanted all along. How come she knew deeper in her bones than he ever did what it meant to be free? She was like Grandma. She was smart. And brave. If Zeb hadn't needed to save Faith from a life lived in that house without no love or friendship or laughter, he likely never would have run from there. He was glad he was woke up now. Glad he felt this constant thrum of excitement – what I gone choose to do next? What I gone *choose*.

He caught Livy's eye and she looked back at him with so much heart in her eyes he had to blink.

Last night she'd loved him like he was a sweet plum and she wanted to taste every bit of him. He'd built them another lean-to away from where the men slept. Flavian and Birdie slept in a new lean-to the other side of the big one. Faith slept like she turned into a log soon as it got dark, and he and Livy could have each other every night.

He wasn't ever gone get tired of making love to Livy. Seemed like it was different every time though they didn't do nothing new. She wasn't the same woman she'd been when he first saw her. Pretty as she was, she'd had a sour, sad, mean look to her.

Last night, he had teased her as they lay in each other's arms. Didn't matter how hot it was, they started the night cuddling. "You gone simple, Livy?" he whispered. "That why you smile all the time now?"

"I told you," she said, defending herself, "when I seen that wicked gleam in your eye, I knew you wadn't simple."

He'd gently traced her bottom lip with his thumb. "I liked you back when you didn't do nothing but scowl at me. But I like it even better when you smile."

She'd bit his thumb, gently. "How much you like it?"

"You need me to show you again?"

"I need convincing."

"You gone be quiet this time?"

"I show you if you come on over me and do what you supposed to."

"I'm supposed to, huh?"

She had kissed him and made him hush.

Paddling his new boat, he left the otter and finished circling the island. "And here we are back," he said. Hector was waiting for them and helped Faith and Livy climb out and wade back to shore.

"Let's go out again," Hector said. "I start showing you how to find your way around."

Zeb had been waiting for that. They paddled back into the stream again.

"You know where the sun come up."

"Sure." Zeb nodded his head toward the east.

"You know what that direction called?"

Zeb shrugged and said, "Sunrise."

"And over there?" Hector pointed north.

"Hector, I ain't been nowhere I needed to know what to call that way. I always just heard 'that way' with a pointed finger to go along with it."

"Well, I found out the names. That's north." He pointed to the other quadrants. "West, south, and east. You keep that in your head all the time, it help you not get lost."

They turned into a channel. "Which way the current going?" Hector asked him.

Zeb knew that much.

"And which way north from here?"

Zeb didn't take but a minute to figure it out. "That be north."

"Now we got to start noticing things. Like right there, see that cypress leaning into those other two? They's close together, and that leaning one looks like it wants to kiss the other two. See that?"

Zeb grinned at him. "Kissing trees?"

Hector wasn't mad, but acted like he was. "You want my help or not?"

"Yeah, I do. Okay. Them trees on my left leaving the island. They gone be on my right when I looking for the island and getting close."

"Keep going. I show you where this channel meets up with another one."

Zeb realized he hadn't ought to have been worried about getting lost. There were markers all around if you just learned to look for them. He could find his way back from wherever he took himself to fish or hunt.

"I still don't know how to get back to the plantation."

"You want to go back?" Hector asked, his brows raised.

"No. But Hector, someday, maybe it be best if Faith go back."

"Why?"

Not a day went by Zeb didn't remember seeing Flavian's boy Luke draped over his mother's lap when they came to the island. The slavers could come back, start searching again, start shooting bullets again.

"Things good now," Zeb said. "Faith happy. She safe. But maybe it not always gone be so."

"There's no way to know what gone be, Zeb. You know that."

"I just want to know I could take her back if I had to."

"One day I show you the way back, then," Hector said. "But it gone take from sunup to sunrise to go and come. Best we do it while the days are still long."

"You don't want to stay the night, see Tish and the boy?"

Hector stared off in that direction. "Yeah," he said. "I want to. But it's more dangerous now, especially for you. They be watching your Grandma to see if she taking food out to leave for you. And somebody like Weasel see you or me, he gone tell the Boss and get himself a extra something."

Zeb shook his head. "Not Weasel. He wouldn't turn nobody in." He told him what Weasel had done for him when he stole the axe.

"Weasel did that?"

"Yeah, he did. Surprised me, too."

"I think about Tish and Beesum coming out all the time, how I could make it safe for them. But she won't never come now. They'll all know about the raid, that some of us got killed. She won't come."

Zeb could see the hurt in him, but only for a moment. Hector wasn't one for sad faces. "I just need to find me one of them woman trees. Pick me a ripe one and take her to camp."

Zeb laughed.

Zeb began to go out alone, learning his way.

One night, with Livy in his arms, he told her, "You gone learn, too. I take you out and you can start noticing where we are, how to get around."

"Why I need to know that? I'm not going nowhere without you."

He didn't like to say it out loud, but she needed to think on it if she hadn't already. "Nobody not gone die, Livy. I want you able to take care of you and Faith something happen to me and the others."

"Nothing gone happen, Zeb. I never felt so safe in my life as I do now."

He wondered if that was true, if she had quit thinking about slavers raiding the camp. He'd squeezed her tight and said no more. But he took her out in the dugout and showed her how to get around anyway.

~~~

Livy had never been one to hum or sing, but she did both, off and on through the day. She'd even learned to ignore Cal. If she didn't look at him, she couldn't see the way he looked at her.
~~~

She took Faith with her to the bathing pool where the otters liked it best. They watched them play for a while and then Faith said, "I want to swim, too."

They left their dresses on – too many men around to go around naked, and the dresses needed a wash anyway.

They splashed and Livy showed Faith how to lie on her back, her arms and legs spread out, and just float.

Her little body was stiff as sticks at first. "You gone be just like that otter once you get this. I won't let go till you ready."

"Float like an otter," Faith whispered over and over, and then she loosened up and she had it. Livy lay back and floated with her.

When Faith shrieked, every nerve in Livy's body turned hot. She got her feet under her just as Faith leaped on her.

"What?"

"There's a bear over there."

"In the water?"

"No. On that other piece of land."

Livy saw it then, maybe a hundred feet away. A good sized black bear. It was looking at them, but it didn't seem all that interested.

"We better go tell Zeb," Faith whispered.

"All right. We'll do that." There was a lot of fat on a bear, even this time of year. They could cook with bear grease, rub it on their skin where the skeeters bit. No telling what all they could do with a bear.

Livy carried Faith out of the water and set her on her feet. And there was Cal.

"I heard somebody scream."

What was he doing this side of the island, by himself? Had he followed her, had he been watching them?

Livy tilted her head to the other shore. "There's a bear."

He squinted his eyes and watched it for a minute. It still wasn't interested in them. He turned his gaze back to Livy.

He didn't pretend not to look at her in her wet dress, his eyes turning that hot black like she'd seen before. She felt every inch of her skin, covered or not, where his eyes moved over her.

"We're going on back."

"We got to tell Zeb," Faith told him.

He didn't move. When Livy had to brush past him, his fingers grazed her breast and her arm as she passed. She ignored him even if his touch had felt like fire. She took Faith's hand and went on, knowing he watched her backside moving under the wet dress, making her whole body feel hot.

Chapter Nineteen

"A bear?" Zeb said.

"A big ole bear," Faith said. "He's big, Zeb. Big and black. And mean."

"Where'd you see it?"

Faith pointed to the trees across the channel.

"Over there."

"Adam!" Zeb called him over, then hollered, "Hector."

"Something happen?" Hector asked.

"Ever been on a bear hunt?" Zeb said, grinning.

Suddenly alert, Adam said, "You seen a bear?"

"Damn. We need dogs for a bear hunt."

"Well, we ain't got dogs," Zeb said. "And we ain't got guns. But it seem like six men ought to be able to kill one bear."

Sam had heard and came over, eager to go. "I got four spears made."

"They throwing spears, or just for jabbing?"

"Well, I ain't tried killing nothing but fish and turtles with them, but why couldn't you throw one?"

"And we got the axes."

"Hold on," Livy said. "You get close enough to use an axe, that bear close enough to use its claws and teeth." She glared at Zeb. "You come back half eaten by a bear, don't spect me to sew you up."

Zeb just smiled at her. "You would too sew me up, wouldn't she, Faith?"

"Maybe we just make a lot of noise and it go off somewhere else," Faith said.

Zeb put his arm around her slight shoulders. "You don't need to worry. We take all us men and bring you back a bear skin."

"And meat. I am sick to death of fish," Adam said.

"Well, let's get everybody rounded up."

Flavian had hunted bear, once. He insisted they come up with a few plans, depending on where they found this bear. "Sam, you coming, too. But you got to promise to stay back. You there to make noise if we decide to herd it toward the spears. You promise?"

"I promise."

He likely would have promised to wear bells on his head to get to go with the rest of them, Zeb thought. But he would have too at his age.

Hector and Adam took the boat to see if the bear was still where Livy and Faith had seen it. While they were gone, Zeb cut three more saplings and sharpened the ends with the axe. These were not fire-hardened like Sam's spears, but at least they'd all have a weapon. If they could corner it and get six or seven spears stuck in it, that bear would be theirs.

"Birdie and me and the girls, we go back to the pool so we can watch you," Livy said.

"Don't forget bears can swim. You see it get in the water, you don't wait to see if it coming to you. You run back here and I'll come with the boat and pick you up. Hear?" Zeb said.

Everybody took a few practice throws with their spears, and they were off. Livy was as excited as the men were, and only a little scared. There were seven of them, after all, and only one bear.

Birdie said, "Get you the biggest knife we got and come on. We got to cut ourselves some brush."

"What for?" Livy said.

"Zeb a fool he think we can run from a bear. If a bear decides to chase after you, it gone get you. So we gone make sure it don't want to come over here and chase after us."

"We could climb a tree, Mama," Millie said.

"Sugar, if we had any good climbing trees, that bear could climb it, too. But we got our own plan. You girls know how to make a torch?"

Livy had Birdie's plan figured out by the time they made it to the other side of the island. If the bear was still there, they'd see the whole hunt.

Zeb and Sam were in the boat, steady in the shallow stream, watching from the water. The other two dugouts were pulled ashore, the men creeping through the forest, their spears ready.

Zeb started thwacking the side of the boat with his paddle, and Sam did the same, encouraging the bear to head into the woods, toward the men.

On Livy's side of the water, she held the torch, Birdie and the girls held leafy branches on long limbs. If that bear tried to swim over here, they would light the leaves on fire and wave them like torches. It wouldn't be coming ashore over here.

The boat thwacking worked. Livy heard excited shouts, but no screams. Nobody hurt. It gone be fine.

She heard the bear roar, then the men yelling all at once. Next thing she knew, that bear came crashing through the woods and splashed right into the water, ignoring Zeb and Sam in the boat.

Faith squealed. Millie screamed. The bear was swimming right for them.

"Light them branches," Birdie said, calm as you please.

Livy held the torch low while they caught their leaves afire and waved them at the bear. It was swimming strong through the shallow water even with a spear in its back.

It smelled the smoke, its black nose quivering. It hesitated, then turned around to find another place to land. But Zeb and Sam were right behind it.

Sam had his and Zeb's spears, one in each hand, while Zeb paddled them closer.

"Here, give me those," Birdie said to Millie and Faith. "You gone catch your dress tails afire you ain't paying attention."

Livy hadn't planned to see Zeb chasing a bear, just him and Sam, and that bear wounded and mad. She held her breath.

Zeb pulled the dugout alongside the bear, it struggling now from panic and pain. They were not six feet away when Sam hurled the first spear. It went home in the bear's shoulder, inches from the other spear. He hurled his second spear and caught it in the ribs.

With a roar Livy felt in her bones, the bear stood on its hind legs, raised its front paws, and lunged for them.

Faith shrieked and covered her eyes.

Zeb was on his feet, legs spread wide. He swung the axe backward, the boat rocking under him, then put all his weight behind his swing and buried the blade in the bear's chest.

Cut through the heart, the bear's body kept coming, its momentum crashing it into the dugout.

Zeb and Sam both tipped out the other side. The bear's weight shoved the dugout on top of both of them.

Livy jumped over the dying flames of the brush and plowed into the stream. "Zeb!" She shoved through the water, paddling with her arms, pushing off the bottom with her feet. "Zeb!"

The bear slid off the boat and sank under the water. Sam surfaced, spluttering and gasping for air on the other side of the dugout.

Livy's mind darted from a Thank you Lord that Sam was safe to a shriek of fear. "Zeb!"

And then, right in front of her, Zeb popped up from the water, gulping air. She reached for him and hugged him to her. "Zeb," she cried, her fingers crawling all over him, looking for wounds. "Zeb."

"Shhh," he said. "I've got you. It's all over."

She shoved him away from her. "You idiot! There were supposed to be seven of you – seven – not two idiots in a boat."

Zeb grinned. "You love me anyway."

She punched him in the chest hard as she could. Then she grabbed him and held him tight.

Sam passed by them, wading to shore. Livy reached out and grabbed him, too, hugging the both of them.

"You an idiot, too, Sam."

They hauled the bear to the far shore to butcher it on the other island, butchering being a messy business. The leavings would attract all kinds of critters they would just as soon not encourage to visit their camp.

On their own island, they built a fire under a screen of palmetto fronds to dissipate the smoke, then draped strips of meat over a rack. For dinner, they had fresh bear steaks.

Zeb licked his fingers. "Anybody know how to tan a hide?"

"I done it a few times," Flavian said. "Me and Sam, we'll do it."

"Makes you think, don't it?" Zeb said. "How much we had and didn't notice. How much we don't know how to do. I don't know how to tan no hide. I can't make a horseshoe."

"Not that we got much call for a horse shoe," Cal said with a smirk.

"We could use a barrel of salt," Adam said. "Where's salt come from anyway?"

"From barrels, that's all I know. We can't even make candles. Less we use this bear fat."

"No," Birdie said. "We got better uses for that fat than candles."

"Can't make a fry pan, but I sure wish we had one," Livy said.

"I wish we had somebody knew how to make shoes. And had the nails and everything else to make them with."

"Another month or two, we gone wish we had blankets."

"I want to sit in a chair again. And eat at a table."

"I miss molasses."

"And walls."

"I miss my dog."

Out of nowhere, it seemed like, Faith geared up and bawled. "I miss my baby sister," she cried.

Zeb pulled her into his lap and cradled her. Here they were, one of the best days they'd had, their bellies full of meat, everybody healthy, and they were all feeling sorry for themselves. He guessed he'd started it himself, but he hadn't meant it to be complaining. He'd just been thinking how, poor as they were in the quarters, they had so much they never thought of. Like floors under their feet.

"I been wondering," Flavian said. "How much you think is left back at our camp? May be some stuff didn't burn up. May be we could find something – a pot, a tool."

"I left a length of rope back in the trees. Bet they didn't find that," Hector said. "Zeb, let's you and me paddle down there tomorrow and see what's there."

Zeb gave him a look. They could head on down toward the plantation. They didn't have to go all the way, just close enough Zeb knew where it was.

~~~

That night, Faith was clingy. Livy and Zeb both petted her and let her cry over little Hope. And then over Mama and Grandma. And the kittens Auntie Jean's cat had. When she finally went to sleep, Livy felt like clinging, too.

She'd been terrified in those moments when Zeb had stood up in the boat, swung back with that axe, the bear rearing up and roaring close enough Zeb must have felt its breath.

But he was safe. Not a scratch on him.
~~~

"Guess you proud of yourself, killing that bear," she said to him, real low so nobody else spread out asleep in the clearing could hear her.

"Yeah," he said. She could feel his grin against her cheek. "You proud of me, Livy?" He feathered kisses along her jaw, down her neck. "Hm?"

"Am I proud of you for nearly getting your fool self killed? That what you mean?"

He tickled her ear with his tongue and she shivered. "I can't stand it when you do that. And you know it."

"Where you want me to kiss, then?"

She brought his fingers to her mouth. "Right here," she whispered. While he nibbled at her lip, she dragged his fingers down to her breast. "And here."

By the time he moved over her and slid inside her, she was near mindless with wanting him. When the moment came, Zeb opened his mouth over hers, helping her keep her cries in her body. She marveled at how his whole body could convulse over her, spasm upon spasm, and hardly make a sound. Whenever her time came, exploding, erupting, seizing, she wanted to scream and thrash.

Lying half asleep in his arms, she murmured, "Someday when we got walls and a roof around us, I'm gone make you scream, Zebediah."

He chuckled in her ear. "That be a relief, then, letting out all those shouts I been saving up."

She shifted her head on his arm, ready to sink into sleep with Zeb's warmth behind her.

But over where the men slept in the big lean-to, somebody was sitting up. Facing their way. Watching them.

It'd be Cal. He'd been watching her all through dinner. Not so anybody noticed, but Livy noticed. Probably Birdie did, too.

Cal likely heard them making love, quiet as they were. She didn't much like him, but she knew what it was to be lonely, to need somebody to touch. And a little piece of Livy wanted to lay him down and ease him.

She turned over and pressed her face into Zeb's side. It was a long time before the rise and fall of his big chest lulled her to sleep.

Chapter Twenty

"Don't worry if we don't make it back tonight. We may decide to wait till morning."

"Why would you stay out another day?"

"Depends on what we see at the old camp. Could be there are lots of things left we can gather up."

He gave Faith a hug and Livy a quick kiss, shoved off his dugout with Hector already in it, and he was gone.

They paddled without a word, Zeb all the time remembering sights he could use as markers. They were heading north and east it seemed like. So south and west would take him home.

Well, he thought. When had their primitive little camp become a home? Maybe after that first big rainstorm. They were soaked. The ground was sodden. They were cold. And Livy had looked at him and smiled. "Can't get any wetter than this," she'd said, "and we still here. This is a good place, Zeb. See how the water run right back into the bayou?"

So he had a home. If they didn't find anything to collect at the old camp, they'd turn around and he'd be home with Livy and Faith before dark.

Late in the morning, Hector stilled his oar. "See that magnolia tree?"

"Yeah, I see it."

"It not the only magnolia out here. What else you see?"

"That one got a dogwood off to the left."

"What else?"

"That ground a little higher than most of the islands out here. And the tip of the island, it got a funny shape, like the magnolia the heel of a boot, and the tip of land be the toe."

"All right. This is it. This where you turn right, like you going south, to go to Flavian's camp. But if you keep going straight, you be at the plantation in a few hours."

Hector's paddle was still, his head turned toward the plantation.

Zeb could understand the pull Hector felt, his woman and boy back there, but the plantation was not so peaceable a place as it had been, not with three slaves having run off. He pictured him and Hector creeping through the dark toward the cabins and setting off a passel of dogs. Running blind through the night, the dogs baying and gaining on them. Just imagining it caused his belly to tighten.

"I got to try one more time, Zeb. See if Tish come with me."

Zeb wished he could see Mama, Grandma, and Hope, but it wasn't worth getting caught for, not with Livy and Faith waiting for him back on the island. Orchid Island, that's what Faith called it. It looked prettier to him all the time.

Maybe what he should do is just let Hector go ashore after dark and then paddle the dugout a ways off, wait on the water where he'd be safe until Hector gave him the signal to pick him up. That would be smart, cause if there was anything in this world Zeb needed to do, it was to get home to Livy and Faith.

He gave Hector a single, decisive nod, and they continued straight on.

~~~

It didn't take much notice to clean fish, and Livy's mind wandered. She wished she could take Zeb to visit her mama and her sisters. They'd like him. They'd be glad she had herself a good man. But that wasn't gone happen.

How many fish had she cleaned these last weeks? They was good, but boring. Lord, what she wouldn't give to bite into a big juicy red tomato.

"Mama, come see," Faith called. Livy smiled to herself. Faith had started calling her that when the bear scared her half to death, and she'd kept right on with it.

At the edge of the water, the girls were making turtles in the mud. The turtle back was a real turtle shell; the legs, tail, and head they'd shaped out of mud.

"What you gone feed these turtles?"

Cal walked into the clearing, an axe over his shoulder. He glanced around and came over.
~~~

"What you think we ought to feed these turtles, Cal?" Millie had known Cal a long time. She liked him better than Faith did.

"They need something pretty to eat. Something blue. Like them flowers around the side of the island."

"The iris flowers," Millie said. She hopped to her feet, Faith too, and they were off to collect irises.

Livy didn't trust him one bit. "That was smart, getting the girls to run off."

He grinned at her. "These turtles gone love irises."

Livy went back to her fish scaling. Cal made himself comfortable on the ground not three feet away.

He didn't say anything, and finally Livy snapped at him. "What you want, Cal?"

"Just wanted to be with you a little while." He spoke softly to her. Did he think she was an ornery mule needed to be gentled?

"I'm not interested in you, Cal."

"I think you are."

She put her fish down and looked straight at him. "No. I am not." She picked the fish up again and said, "Go on with you."

He stayed right where he was. She decided to ignore him. Watching her clean fish wasn't gone hold his interest for long.

"When I make love to a woman, she cry out like she calling the sky down to her. She don't be able to stifle herself like you do with Zeb."

Heat flushed from Livy's breasts right up into her hair. She picked up another fish to scale.

"I'd kiss you everywhere, Livy. Everywhere," he said, looking at her lap, then into her eyes.

She knew what he meant, of course she did, but doing a thing wasn't the same as talking about it. Her face got even hotter. Nobody had ever talked to her like that in her life.

"You bother me again," she said, "I gone know what to do with this knife."

He got up slowly, ignoring the knife in her hand. "You and me, Livy, we be good together. I gone make you sing when I touch you."

He picked up his axe and sauntered back toward the fourth dugout they were working on.

Livy's fingers trembled when she picked up the next fish. She hated him for making her breasts ache, making her wet down there. But it didn't mean anything. He was a man and she was a woman, so what? There was more to loving than that.

~~~

Middle of the afternoon, Zeb and Hector tied up to a tupelo and ate their bear jerky in the shade. That was the only stop they made, and they were seeing their way by starlight by the time they got to the back of the plantation.

They listened for a long time. Nothing to hear but bats and owls and frogs.

"All right," Hector whispered. "I'm going in. Two owl hoots, a quiet, then two more hoots. That mean I'm back for you to come get me."

"I'll be here."

Hector stepped out of the boat and disappeared into the woods. Zeb paddled off, a hundred yards, maybe more, where he found shadows even starshine didn't reach.

What if they had new dogs on the place that didn't know Hector's scent? What if the master had hired guards patrolling at night?

Zeb listened hard. No dogs barking. No rifle shots. Hector was in the cabin by now. He'd made it.

Zeb stretched out in the bottom of the dugout and tried to get comfortable. He was going to be here for hours, just him and the skeeters and the bullfrogs.

Everybody in Mama's cabin probably asleep by now. Except maybe Grandma. Sometimes she'd get up and sit on the porch a while, just to think. He wondered if she'd had trouble after he'd run off with Faith. Benning already knew she helped runaways. He likely kept on her all the time trying to get her to tell him where Zeb had run to. She didn't know, but even if she did, the Boss would never get it out of her.

What if Benning decided to try making her tell it? What if he locked her in the old stocks for a day and a night? What if he whipped her?

Zeb sat up and rubbed his hands on his face. He had to go in. He had to see if anything happened to her, or to any of them, because of him.
~~~

He paddled back across the black water, his oar as quiet as nothing. He pulled the dugout up under the willow tree and groped his way to the path where he let his feet and hands find the way because he couldn't see a thing.

When he emerged from the tree cover, he was almost to the end of the lane. He stopped and listened. The only sound from the quarters was a baby crying like maybe it had the colic. It seemed foreign to him now, this place. All the familiar shapes and smells like long-ago memories. He realized he didn't miss it – he missed his family, but not this place where he'd grown up.

With starlight to guide him, he glided through the grass and into the lane between the cabins.

Aunt Jean's dog stretched and sauntered out to sniff his hand, then went back to his bed under the porch.

He stepped quietly onto the steps and eased himself in the cabin. "Mama?" he whispered.

He heard the corn shuck mattress rustle. "Son? That you?"

"Yeah, Mama, it's me."

He heard her stifle a cry like she had her hand over her mouth, then she rushed across the floor and grabbed him to her. He wrapped his arms around her and held her while she cried.

"Minnie? What you doing?" Grandma said.

"Get up, Eva. It's Zeb," Mama whispered.

"Oh my Lord," Grandma said. "Let me get the candle lit so I can see you."

"No, Grandma. Don't light the candle."

"Course not. What am I thinking?" She groped her way to them, gave him a big hug, and felt of his arms. "You all right? Where's Faith?"

"I left her at home, Grandma. She's good."

"'Home,' is it? That sound like it's all right out there."

"It is, Grandma. You and Mama and Hope? Everything good here?"

"Come sit down, Zeb. Minnie, be careful you don't knock into anything in the dark."

"Benning give you trouble cause of me running?"

"Things was a little tight for a while, that's all," Grandma said.

"They was more than tight, and you know it," Minnie said. "Master hisself come down here and made a fuss. Sissy say it cause his missus fit to be tied Faith run off with you. Benning, he so mad I thought he gone whip your grandma."

Zeb searched for Grandma's hand in the dark. "He hurt you, Grandma?"

"Nah. Just a lot of hollering. Tore up the cabin some like he thought you hiding in the stew pot or something."

"He put her in the stocks all one day. That's what he did to her."

"And that was one day I didn't have to work. I just fine, Zeb."

"You know why he didn't whip her?" Mama said.

"Now Minnie, you don't go telling that."

"It was Weasel, that's why. He told Benning he been courting Eva and that she'd come and spent the night with him in that old empty cabin other end of the lane. That morning when everybody wake up and you and Livy and Faith gone off, he said Eva just as surprised as anybody on the place. He said she liked to cried her eyes out."

"Don't know why Benning believe a thing like that. But he didn't whip me. Now I got to let that Weasel kiss me all the time."

"She likes it, I think," Mama teased.

"I thought he was with Fancy."

"She tired of him and that's the truth. She too young for him anyway," Grandma said.

"Mama. I worry about you."

"I'm all right, son, long as you and Faith all right. Tell us what she doing out there."

Zeb described their life on the island, told them about Livy being a mother to Faith, about Flavian and the others coming to them.

"We heard they raided out there. Didn't know how many got away."

"Eight of them, Grandma." He didn't tell them about Luke dying and them burying him on the island.

"You safe, where you are?"

"We're safe. We got plenty to eat. Livy and me, we good together, Mama."

"Then you did right, running off," Grandma said.

"Can I wake Hope up?"

"Just pick her up and hold her. Let her wake up if she wants to."

Zeb lifted her into his arms and carried her back to the chair.

"She been cutting a new tooth in the back. Don't make her sweet natured, I tell you."

She was warm and soft and limp against his chest. He held her gently, carefully, and ran his fingers down her leg to cradle her foot in his big hand.

"I miss this child, Mama. Mostly I think about her in the morning when she'd get up, all smiles, toddling around the place. You know how sometimes she come pat my face till I wake up?"

They ought to know what he planned. He looked at his Grandma first. He knew she'd back him up. Mama, though, needed to get used to the idea. "Someday, Mama, I aim to come back and get Hope. When she's old enough."

Mama put her face in her hands. Grandma Eva touched her shoulder. "That years away, Minnie. We got years yet to raise her up."

Mama breathed out. "Let's talk about something else."

"I'm glad Livy got another woman with her," Grandma said. "That many men, you gone need more women."

"That's why we come in. To see if Tish would come out with Hector. He don't reckon she will, but he had to try one more time."

"Nah, I don't reckon she will, either. After she heard about that raid out in the swamp, I think Tish decided she wadn't Hector's woman no more." Grandma hesitated. "Jubal been going over there of a night."

"Well," Zeb said. "That sound like Jubal."

"I don't blame her none, I don't," Mama said. "Not everybody made to live out there in the swamp, and she got a little boy to think of."

"You hungry, Zeb?"

"I could eat, you got something left from supper. Don't light no fire though."

"I got cornbread and a sweet potato. You can eat that cold."

They talked the rest of the night, Hope still asleep, still cuddled in his lap. When Zeb judged it might be another hour before daylight, he set Hope on her cot.

"Here, Zeb." Grandma fumbled in the dark to get him a candle. "You take this. What else you need?"

"We need everything, and we don't need nothing, Grandma. We getting along."

"Your mama and me, we been collecting ever since you left. Case you ever come back. We spread everything around the cabin so if Benning come in here again – you know how he do -- he won't see nothing gathered together."

"We got an extra pot out of the big cookhouse. That's first."

"How'd you get a pot out of there?"

"Never you mind about that. I got a scrap of canvas, too. Don't know what you gone do with it, but it for you. Minnie, where's that piece of rope?"

"It sewn into my mattress. I get it out."

"I found a nail and a horseshoe over by the blacksmith shop."

When he took those, Mama said, "Give me your hand, Zeb. This here for Faith."

He rolled a little sphere in his fingers. "What is it?"

"It's a glass button. Kind of yellow. Something pretty for her."

He put it in his pocket with the nail.

"Ya'll done good, Mama. We use every bit of this."

"We'll keep on collecting, just in case you come back. But, Zeb, we don't want to see you caught," Grandma said. "You don't be coming back again."

"But Lord, Zeb," his mama said. "It done us so much good to see you made it, that you and Faith doing good. I won't be so heart sore knowing you happy."

He wrapped the horseshoe in the canvas, put it in the pot, and coiled the rope on top with the candle. "This pot, Mama, that's a fine thing to take back. Livy gone thank you every time she cook with it."

He kissed them and hugged them. Eva told Mama to hush up, don't cry, just like she always done. It hurt him to leave, but he had to go.

He got back to the dugout before Hector did and pushed off into the water to wait. It was still dark when Hector hooted for him. He paddled in to shore and picked him up. Just Hector, alone.

"Hold on," somebody said.

Zeb felt all the hair on his head stand up. "Who's there?"

"It's just me," Weasel stepped out from the trees so they could see him.

"What you doing out here?" Hector demanded. "How you know we here?"

"Just settle down. I don't sleep much, that's all."

Weasel carried something in his arms. "Brought you something, Zeb, for you to take to Faith."

He hesitated only a moment and paddled the ten feet back to shore.

Weasel waded into the water to his knees and handed Zeb a half-grown puppy. "His name's Jimbo, but I reckon you can call him what you want."

Zeb took the sleepy pup in his arms. Been a long time since he'd had his own dog. He stroked Jimbo's silky ears, and Jimbo licked his hand.

"Why you giving us a dog, Weasel?" Hector said.

"I ain't giving it to you. That dog for Faith."

"Why?" Hector said again.

"Cause I gone tell Eva I give her grandbaby a puppy, and that gone make Eva happy. And when I make Eva happy, she make sure I'm happy."

"You old goat," Zeb said without heat. "You sleeping with my Grandma?"

"That not something we grownups talk about with the youngsters." He waded back to shore and disappeared in the darker woods.

~~~

Livy was lonesome when the sun went down and it was time to go to bed. She wished she had a bed, anyway. She lay down on her mat, missing Zeb. It was the first time she'd had to sleep without him since they'd married each other.

She hadn't kept count how long they'd been on this island. Before, she always knew what day it was. It had seemed important to know that, but she didn't know why, now. And she was just as happy not knowing. A body didn't need to know whether it was Sunday or not to pray, so what difference did it make?

If she had to guess, she'd say it had been two months. The days were a little shorter, the night air a little cooler.

If she were inclined to worry about something, she supposed she could worry about that. Hot as the summers were, the winters
~~~

could be cold enough to freeze water. And none of them had nothing to wear in the cold. Faith's pretty leather shoes were all torn up from the wet and the mud, and anyway, they was probably too small for her now.

Maybe Derek and Adam would figure out how to get those traps to work. Then they could all dress in otter fur. Or if they killed another bear – well, while she was thinking about *ifs,* then why not another four or five bears -- then there would be enough for everybody to have leather shoes with soft fur on the inside.

She listened to the camp settling in for the night. Faith was sound asleep, and from the quiet, most everybody else was, too. Livy turned onto her side, her eyes heavy and ready to sleep. She was just dozed off when she felt a light hand on her hip.

She startled, but Cal's hand was on her mouth. "Shh," he whispered.

The hand on her hip smoothed up over her ribs and cupped her breast. Livy shoved at his hand, but he moved his weight onto her and clamped his hand over her mouth again.

"Shh, Livy. Listen to me," he whispered in her ear. "I got us a place cleared out in the woods. We'll go there, and when I make you come, you can scream to high heaven if you want."

He kissed her neck. "I'm gone take my hand off your mouth now. Nod your head you gone be quiet."

Livy nodded. She didn't mean to make any noise at all, cause then the others would know, they'd tell Zeb, and Zeb would kill him. She didn't want Zeb killing anybody, not Zeb.

Cal moved his hand off her mouth, his lips taking their place. His tongue probed, trying to get in her mouth, and then he stiffened.

"What you doing, Livy?"

"You feel that, Cal?" she said quietly. "That's my knife. You don't get off me and go on, I'm gone it slide it between your ribs and cut your liver out."

He let out a great sigh. He tried to kiss her again, and Livy slid the knife into his flesh a quarter of an inch. His body trembled, but she kept the knife steady.

"Livy," he said.

"No."

He rolled off her, got to his feet, and walked off into the dark.

~~~

By the time the sun rose, Hector and Zeb were deep into the swamp, Jimbo curled up asleep between Zeb's bare feet. At the tip of the island shaped like a boot, Zeb noticed the dogwood was not visible from this direction. He'd remember that. They turned south and in another hour they were at Flavian's old camp.

They pulled the boat ashore and stood with their arms crossed, looking at the devastation. The cabins were burned to the ground except for the mud chimneys. The nearest trees were still scorched.

Jimbo danced around, excited at all the new smells, but he kept close to Zeb as he explored.

"I expect they burned the garden, too. We ought to go look."

The raiders had not burned the garden. They'd gone through with machetes, looked like, and chopped down the growing corn, the bean poles, the squash and cucumber vines. But the squash had come back, the beans had sent their tender green vines to climb back up the poles. They found pumpkins ready to pick.

They decided to have a look around before they gathered whatever there was out here.

Hector found his rope, then walked into the cold ashes of the first cabin, sifting through the mess with his foot. "Well, look at this." He bent over and picked up a hunk of blackened metal. He hefted it in his hand and showed Zeb.

"An axe head? How'd they miss that?"

"Don't think they went in the cabins. Just torched them."

If there was that kind of salvage to be found in the ashes, it was worth getting down on their knees and searching every part of the remains. They turned up a paring knife, probably usable once it was scraped clean and whetted. A chisel. An iron fry pan. The saw blade they found was warped and half melted, but they took it anyway.

"You know what?" Hector said. "Derek was tanning a deer hide back away from the cabins cause of the stink. Maybe it's still there."

While Hector hunted for the hide, Zeb filled the pot and the square of canvas Mama had given him with every bit that could be gleaned from the garden. They were going to feast tonight.

Zeb whistled for Jimbo and headed back to the shoreline.
~~~

They loaded the dugout with the hide and everything else they could find, even the stones that had been laid out to make the firepit.

And so they headed home with a full dugout, leaving only ashes behind.

Chapter Twenty-One

When Faith saw them coming, she leapt to her feet and splashed into the water, calling "Zeb! Zeb's home!"

Zeb stepped out of the dugout and grabbed her for a big hug. "I brought you something."

"What?"

He set her down in the water and reached into the dugout. "This is Jimbo."

Faith's eyes rounded and she took in a huge breath. "A puppy," she breathed. "Can I hold him?"

When she had him in her arms, Jimbo licked her chin and she squealed. Was there ever a happier sight than a child with a puppy, Zeb thought. Faith carried him to shore like he was precious. She set him on the ground next to Millie and the two of them crouched down for him to get to know them.

Everybody who'd heard Faith hollering came to greet them. Zeb stood at the boat's stern ready to shove it onto the sand, but he looked for Livy, too, and here she came, striding toward him, with the biggest grin on her face. She didn't stop till she was knee deep and she could throw herself at him.

He caught and whirled her in a big splashy spin.

"I missed you," he said into her ear.

"I didn't miss you a bit," she said, his ear lobe caught in her teeth.

"Not even a little bit?" His hand cupped her bottom and gave it a squeeze.

"Zeb," she said. "There's people right here."

"But I got to remind you what you missed."

"You let me go, you awful thing."

He squeezed her butt again before he let go.

She saw the girls playing with Jimbo. "A puppy? Where'd you get a puppy?"

"Back at the plantation. Now don't get mad. Nobody seen nor heard us. We got in and out fine."

Livy scowled at him, and it was not a teasing kind of scowl. "What if you'd got caught? What if they'd had dogs waiting for somebody to come sneaking into the quarters in the night? What happen to you then?"

She was getting hotter and more worked up. "Livy. Look at me. Look at Hector. Nothing bad happened. Nothing." He pulled her back into his arms. "You don't scowl at me no more. I'm home, ain't I?"

"I missed you," she said against his chest.

"I'll make it up to you, tonight," he whispered.

She gave him a little slap against his chest and helped him unload the dugout.

"A fry pan!" she said, holding it aloft. "Birdie! Come look. They found your fry pan."

They laid everything out on the beach for everybody to see.

"Rope," Adam said. "A hundred times I wished we had some rope."

Flavian picked up a red potato, rubbed it clean with his calloused palms, and bit into it raw. He closed his eyes and smiled.

Birdie and Livy sorted through the foodstuffs to separate what wouldn't keep from what would. "Feels like Christmas, don't it?" Birdie said.

"You even got my deer hide," Derek said. "That come in handy for sure."

Zeb draped an arm over Livy's shoulders as they watched Faith and Millie play with the puppy. "We gone be fine out here, Livy." He gave her a squeeze. "We got us a good life."

Not as good as it ought to be, Livy thought. She felt Cal's eyes on her, watching her like he always did. Something was gone have to happen.

They didn't wait to be called to supper this evening. Everybody gathered round and talked while Birdie fried up sliced potatoes and onions in bear grease. Livy boiled a mess of squash with the dozen okra pods they brought back.

"We need to get some goods to take to town," Flavian said. "It's time."

"We got plenty of turtles. Alive, for meat. Or we could trade turtle shells."

"What anybody want with a turtle shell?" Cal scoffed.

Adam looked at him. "We using them, ain't we?"

"I been thinking," Flavian said. "We get that bear hide cured right, it worth a lot more to us for trade than it is here on the island. We can't all lie under a bear rug when it get cold."

They listed more things they could gather or make. Then Flavian asked, "What we gone bring back with us? We need to decide what we need first."

"Bullets and powder. No doubting that," Cal said.

"Yeah," Derek said. "He's right. Bullets and powder number one thing we need."

"A hammer be good."

"We gone need clothes and shoes for the winter. If you bring back cloth, Livy and me, we can sew up coats. But you got to bring thread, too."

"A pair of scissors be a help," Livy said.

"Maybe some cornmeal and flour."

"We need another saw we gone finish these cabins before it get cold."

"We not likely gone get all that. Let's give ourselves three weeks," Flavian said. "Then we take what we got and get what we can."

The next weeks, enthusiasm ran high. They finished the fourth dugout. They kept the axes and the one saw busy sun up to sun down building the first cabin. They cut a big cypress on the next island since they weren't positive they would get it to fall where they wanted it to. Over there they hewed out bins and small vats the mill used in quantity.

Zeb's particular project was collecting turtles to take to the market, Flavian telling him he could maybe get a machete for nine or ten turtles. He built a kraal to hold as many turtles as he could get in there and fed them fish guts and wild parsnips, water cress, whatever he could get them to eat, and that was most everything.

He enlisted Faith and Millie to dig earthworms, and it was their favorite pastime, holding up a long wiggly earthworm for a turtle to snatch out of their hands.

"What you doing?" Livy yelled.

She rushed over from the cook fire and dragged both girls away. "You don't know that's a snapping turtle? You practically feeding him your fingers."

"He likes worms," Faith said.

Livy shook her head. "Don't you feed that one no more worms, not like that."

"Turtles don't bite. Sam said so."

Livy looked around. Sam wasn't far off, braiding palmetto leaves to make a hat. "Sam, bring me a good strong stick."

He brought the stick.

"Now you watch, all of you," Livy said. She held the stick in front of the snapping turtle. Fast as a snake, it latched on and snapped the stick in two.

"See that? That turtle be just as happy if that stick was your finger."

"But Sam said . . . "

Sam gulped. "I didn't know turtles would do that, Livy, honest I didn't."

"That kind over there won't," she said, pointing to the rounder turtle half submerged in the water. "But this here kind, with the long neck. You treat it just like a snake cause it's just as mean."

So they tossed the worms into the kraal from then on, careful to keep their hands out of reach of those snapping jaws.

~~~

Zeb had been out in the boat through the morning. He came back to the island hungry and hot, but he had three more turtles.

He was pulling the boat up on the sand when Livy came striding into the clearing from the garden path, her face furious. As soon as she saw him, she stopped. She cleared her face and plastered on a too-big smile. "Did you catch any?" she called.

And here come Cal from the same path, striding just as hard, long legs catching up to her. He had four bright scratches on his cheek, all of them oozing blood. Looked like one whole side of his face starting to swell up and there were claw marks on his neck, too.

"Livy, wait," Cal said. Then he saw Zeb. He froze and his eyes widened.

Zeb looked from Cal's bloodied face back to Livy. Now he saw her sleeve was near torn off, the top button of her dress gone, and her lips were red and swollen.

She was watching him, scared.
~~~

His mind seemed to shut down, like a red curtain had fallen over his senses. He charged Cal, head lowered like a bull on the run.

Livy screamed. "No, Zeb. No!"

Cal hardly had time to put up his hands before Zeb plowed into him, knocking him to the ground. Zeb threw himself on him, got his hands around Cal's throat and squeezed.

Cal's fist beat at him, his hips bucked to get him off, but Zeb held on.

Livy pounded his back, screaming at him, but he couldn't stop. "Don't Zeb. Oh don't!"

Strong hands tried to pull Zeb off, but he wouldn't let go.

Cal's eyes rolled back in his head and his body went slack, and still Zeb squeezed.

Somebody finally punched Zeb in the jaw and somebody else in his ribs while another two pulled him off. They took Zeb down to the ground and two of them piled on top of him.

"I'll punch you again you don't stop thrashing," Derek shouted at him.

"Is he dead?" he heard Livy say.

Flavian stood up from feeling the pulse in Cal's throat. "No, he ain't dead."

"Oh thank God," she said.

Zeb's chest was working like a bellows, his teeth clamped. He tried to roll Derek off, but there were two of them with their feet dug into the earth, pushing themselves onto his torso.

Livy knelt on the ground next to him and grabbed for his fisted hand. He jerked away from her, but she grabbed it again and held on.

"Zeb. Listen to me. You got to stop this. Stop it."

He tried again to throw Derek off, but Livy let go of his fist and grabbed his head with both hands. "Look at me," she said. "Look at me, Zeb. I ain't hurt. I ain't hurt at all. You hear me?"

She kissed him on the lips. "It's all over. You come back to me now." She kissed him again, and the red haze in his mind began to clear.

"Get off me," he muttered to Derek.

The breath shuddered out of his chest when Derek and Adam rolled off. He wrapped an arm around Livy and held her tight.

"He hurt you?" he said into her hair.

"No, Zeb. I told you. I ain't hurt."

He heard Cal coughing and gasping. So he hadn't killed him. He supposed he'd be glad of that, later on.

He put his hand over his eyes. "Did Faith see this?"

Livy looked around. Faith was on the other side of the clearing, her face buried against Birdie's bosom.

"Yeah. I think she seen some of it."

"I better talk to her."

"We'll both talk to her. Just lay here a minute first. We all got to calm down."

"He didn't hurt you, Livy?"

"No. I told you."

He got himself up off the ground and walked over to where Cal still lay in the dirt. He wanted to kick him in the head, but he just stood there looking at him.

"You pretty near killed him, Zeb," Flavian said.

"I would have." His knees began to tremble, then his hands and arms.

"Now's when we need some moonshine," Birdie said. "Get him on away from here and give him some water. Water always good."

"Come on, Zeb," Livy said. Derek took his other arm, and they walked him out of the clearing all the way to the otter pool. "You can go on back," Livy told Derek.

When he was gone, she took his arm. "Come in with me." They walked into the water without taking their clothes off. The coolness shocked him. When did the water get so cold? He shivered and Livy took him in her arms and lay back.

"Float with me," she said. "Just close your eyes, let the sun warm your front and the water cool your back. See? It feel good, don't it?"

Zeb's trembling stopped. The shivering stopped. He let the sun warm his eyelids and his lungs began to breathe regular, in and out, slowly.

"Why didn't you want me to kill him, Livy?" he asked, his eyes still closed.

He was so afraid. Afraid she wanted Cal. Had they been meeting in the garden while he was stupidly off hunting turtles or working on the cabin? And he'd come up on them after they'd had a quarrel, like lovers do.

"Do you want him, Livy?" He didn't know if she heard him, there was so little breath in him.

She heard. She reared up out of the water. "I could slap you, yes I could. Did you see the scratches on his face? Did it look to you like I wanted him?"

She stormed off, pushing her way through the water and back to shore.

The water ran off his arms, down his neck as he stood up. "Livy," he said. He felt like his heart was stuck in his throat. "Why didn't you want me to kill him?"

She whirled around to face him. "Why didn't I want you to kill a man? What you think it do to you to kill a man? How you gone sleep at night, how you gone be the Zeb I love, once you kill a man? You think it wouldn't change you? You think you still be the sweetest, smilingest man ever was if you kill a man?"

She caught her breath. "I don't need Cal dead. I just need you, Zeb. The way you are."

Zeb scooped water up in his two hands and splashed his face. He put his hands on his hips and looked up.

There were white egrets perched in a tree nearby. A single white fluffy cloud broke the expanse of blue sky, the only sound the plop of a fish jumping. Zeb breathed deeply. There was ugly in the world, but most of it was in men. Out here, there was beauty and if men would let each other alone, there was peace.

What would it feel like to stand here under God's heaven having killed a man? Would the sky turn gray, the water and the bright birds, too? For ever after, a gray world?

Zeb walked through the water to stand with her. "I'm glad I didn't kill him, too."

"Come on. We'll go back and talk to Faith. She needs to know you the same Zeb you always been."

~~~

Just before dark, everyone gathered in the clearing. "Don't put the fire out," Flavian said. "We need to be able to see each other for this."

Livy sat cross-legged on the ground next to Zeb, close enough their elbows bumped. Faith sat in Zeb's lap. She had been a lot more upset by what she saw Zeb doing to Cal than she had been
~~~

when the bear had gone after him. Zeb cuddled her, and she had her cheek pressed into his chest.

On the other side of the circle, Cal sat between Flavian and Hector, waiting to hear what they were going to do about this.

Now she'd settled down, Livy felt sorry for Cal. She'd found out it was hard to resist somebody who wanted you that bad, who seemed to yearn for you every minute. But that's all it was when she felt the pull of him, feeling sorry for him, and she had resisted him every time he came to her. She had never given him any reason to think he could touch her, and she would do it again, kicking at him and scratching his face like she did in the garden. If she hadn't left her knife in the basket, she would have stabbed him. Not to kill him, maybe in the leg or something.

When she glanced at him, he was staring at her. He was gone get himself beat again he didn't stop it. She looked away.

Birdie didn't wait for Flavian to speak and she didn't wait for any kind of convening like they did in church when they had to talk something over. She went right to it.

"Cal has to leave."

Zeb turned his head to look at Livy. He still wondering if she wanted Cal? He'd know different when they went to bed tonight. She slipped her arm through his.

"He didn't do rape, Birdie," Derek said.

"If he'd done rape, I'd be saying kill him," she said, not a hint of feeling behind her words.

"Where is there for him to go? We cain't just send him back to the plantations."

"That gone be Cal's problem," Birdie said.

The entire group was silent, thinking about how it would be with no safe haven, the slavers after you, and all on your own.

"Livy? This what you want?" Flavian asked.

She looked at Cal and he was still staring her right in the eye. Still trying to tell her she belonged with him. He wasn't persuaded to leave her alone.

"I want him to go."

"Zeb?"

Livy could see the muscles work in his jaw. "He's leaving."

They were all quiet again. Flavian's group had been living with Cal for several years. He wasn't well-liked, but he was one of them, like a brother or a cousin who wasn't no one's favorite, but he still belonged to them.

"This what comes of not having enough women," Derek said. "It's a problem for all of us men."

"I don't know what we gone do about it," Hector said. "Like I told Zeb, I been looking, and I ain't found no tree with women ready for picking."

Flavian assumed the leadership, effortlessly. It's what they all wanted from him, Livy thought.

"All right," he said. "Here's what's gone happen. We don't wait any longer to go to the market. Day after tomorrow, we take what we have, and we take Cal with us. We leave him in town."

Cal stood up, the only one on his feet. "I want that dugout I been working on."

Flavian shook his head. "You ain't the only one worked on that dugout. You take your knife. That's yours. As much food as you can carry. And if I get any money trading in town, I'll give you some of it. That's all you gone take with you."

Flavian got to his feet. "You done wrong, Cal. You know you have." He reached a hand down to help Birdie rise and the two of them left the fire.

The man needed sense knocked into his head. There he was, purple black bruises all around his neck, and he still stood there and looked at her with hungry eyes. How much more no it take to get through his thick head? He'd grabbed her and kissed her, hard, back in the garden. She'd pushed at him, and he wouldn't let her go. She kicked at his shins, she scratched his face. She couldn't get him to let go until she kneed him in his privates. And he still looking at her like that. She wasn't gone waste another minute feeling sorry for him.

Zeb handed Faith over to Livy's lap, then he stood up. His fingers curled and he squared his shoulders at Cal.

"Zeb," Livy hissed. "Don't you start up now. It's settled. He's leaving."

Hector took hold of Cal's shoulder and turned him. "You done caused enough trouble. You come on with me and Derek. We gone stay with you every minute till you gone."

Hector gave Cal a shove and the three men walked out of the circle of light into deep dark.

Adam poured water onto the fire from one of the big turtle shells, and the whole clearing was dark, but Zeb still stood poised for battle.

"Zeb," Livy said firmly. "Take Faith. We three going to bed."

Zeb lifted Faith and helped Livy up. She held on to his hand and the three of them walked through the dark to their own lean-to.

Faith sandwiched between the two of them and sound asleep, Zeb asked her, "Why didn't you tell me he been looking at you like that?"

She couldn't see him. No moon, no stars tonight. It would probably rain before morning. "I felt sorry for him, Zeb. It ain't easy being lonely."

"I could have talked to him, scared some sense into him."

"Zeb, Cal just as big as you. And he don't act like he got room in his head for sense."

"You should have told me."

Livy sighed. "I spect you're right." She stretched her arm over Faith and stroked his shoulder. "It's good you didn't kill him, Zeb."

He breathed in and out like the air was heavy. "Yeah. It's better like this."

"Zeb?"

He turned his head toward her.

"Faith asleep good now."

He got up on his elbow and looked at her. She couldn't make out his eyes in the dark, but she could see the flash of his white teeth.

"You trying to tell me something, Livy?"

She rolled away from him like she was in a huff. "You cain't figure it out, Zebediah, then I'm just gone go to sleep."

He goosed Livy with a finger in her ribs before he lifted Faith carefully and laid her down on her own sleeping mat.

"Well, you figured it out," Livy said and held her arms up to him.

Chapter Twenty-Two

Early morning, they all gathered to see the dugouts off. It would take them most of the day to get to the market on the back side of town. The morning mist still hovered above the water and the air had a little nip in it. Summer was about over.

Birdie made Flavian give her a hug before he left. "We be gone three days," he said. "Maybe four if the weather turns on us."

"Come home, Flavian. That's all I want."

Flavian rocked her in his arms a minute before he let her go. It was a risk, going to the city market. Livy knew he'd done it before, just sidling into the market like he was one of the free blacks selling anything from shoe strings to tea cups to saddles. Nobody had ever bothered him, but that didn't mean they never would.

Birdie walked over to Cal and considered him a minute.

"You make a life for yourself out there. Don't get caught."

Livy thought he was a little too choked up to answer her, but he nodded.

Then Cal stared right at Livy. *You could come with me,* he said with his eyes. *Please, come with me.*

Livy turned away.

Flavian and Derek pushed the first boat out, Hector and Cal the second one. Everyone else waved them off.

"You wish you was going?" Livy asked Zeb.

He shrugged and smiled at her. "Never been to no town. Might be interesting. But life out here pretty interesting, too."

The smile slid off his face. "How about you, Livy? You wish you was going?"

He meant did she wish she were going with Cal. She stared at him like he was a worm. Half a worm. How could he still not know she loved him? Her teeth clamped tight, she gave him one more glare and was about to turn on her heel to walk away from him when she saw Faith looking from her to Zeb.

The worry line in that child's face twisted Livy's heart. She didn't want Faith scared the two of them were going to have at each other. She held her arm out for Faith. They ended up in a three-way hug, Faith's face pressed to Livy's breast.

"I ain't never going nowhere without the two of you. You hear me?"

Zeb leaned over Faith and kissed Livy under the ear. "You like the swamp, huh?"

She didn't feel like being soothed. She'd rather punch Zeb in that big hard shoulder. If Faith weren't right there, she would lay into him good.

"Hmm, Livy?" he murmured in her ear. Then he startled her – he licked his tongue all the way across her face.

She couldn't help herself. She laughed and shoved him away, but he wouldn't stay away. He grabbed her tight, a big old Zeb smile on his face.

"Don't you got nothing better to do?" she said.

"Yeah. Me and Faith gone go fishing. You come, too."

"We gone catch a big ole eel we saw last time," Faith said.

Livy made a face. Ugly things looked like snakes.

"We need you," Zeb wheedled.

Faith tugged on her arm. "Come on, Mama."

Well, anybody called her mama got what they wanted. She let Faith drag her to the dugout. "I'm not cleaning no eel," she said.

"I'll do it," Faith said.

Adam was off a ways working on their first cabin. The walls were finished, just logs, no windows, and Adam was laying saplings across the roof poles and lashing them together. He was still skinny, but he was strong, and moved around up there like it was easy.

"Got to take these women out," Zeb called to him. "I help you when I get back."

Adam looked briefly at Livy and shook his head like he was disgusted, but she knew he wasn't. Adam and Zeb seemed to be the best friends on the place, finding something in each other nobody else did.

There it was. Adam didn't have a woman. Derek neither. And now Hector didn't even have Tish to see once in a while. And not one of them looked at her like Cal had. This gone be a better place without him.

She waved at Adam and he gave her a little wave back.

They caught not one but two eels. Livy simmered them in a little water with a handful of crawdads for flavor, then added water cress at the last minute.

Using a turtle shell as a ladle and more turtle shells as bowls, Livy dished up supper. Sam had carved them each a spoon in the last weeks, so Birdie and Millie, Sam and Adam, Zeb, Faith, and Livy sat down to eat.

"You know what this needs?" Livy said.

"Same thing you always say everything needs. Onions, peppers, tomatoes," Birdie guessed.

"Yeah, it needs that. But what else it needs is rice. Wonder if wild rice grow out here anywhere. Birdie, you ever see any?"

"Nah, this ain't good rice country. You got to have the water just deep enough, just the right time. This here swamp water too changeable."

"I want me a hunk of corn bread, that's what I want," Zeb said, and they were off again on a favorite pastime, cataloging all the foods they missed.

Zeb looked at the clouds gathering above. "What you think, Adam? We get the cabin thatched before it rain?"

"Let's be trying."

"Come on, Sam. You hand them palm leaves up to us."

"I gone hand them to Sam, then," Millie said.

When Millie had happily traipsed after her hero, Faith shook her head and said, "That girl a fool for that boy."

Birdie laughed out loud and Livy didn't even try to cover her smile.

"Someday you be a fool for some boy, too," Livy told her.

"Maybe we'll find a boy tree like that woman tree Hector always looking for," Birdie said.

Faith put her hands on her hips. "You just funning. There ain't no boy tree, is there, Livy?"

"Well, I never saw one, but the world's a big place."

About an hour before dark, the rain commenced. Not one of those friendly rains that start with sprinkles for a few minutes. This one was a sky flood, the rain coming down like there was a river up there spilling onto them.

They worked in the rain tying big palm branches onto the sapling poles until it got too dark to work. Then the men joined the women and girls inside the cabin. The roof wasn't finished, and what they thought they'd finished leaked, but it was more shelter than they'd had for months.

The rain didn't let up. Livy always liked listening to it when she'd had a real roof over her head. It hadn't been such a pleasure in the lean-to, and wasn't any great pleasure in the unfinished cabin either. It brought the cold, this rain did. Livy and Faith were both snuggled up with Zeb to share their body heat. Sometime in the night, she heard Birdie say, "Adam, we coming over to lay with you, Millie and me. Sam, you come on over here, too."

"All right," Adam murmured, hardly awake.

The next morning, the rain was gone, but the air was not just cool, it was cold. And they were wearing every stitch they owned, one worn layer of cotton, nothing on their feet.

"We got plenty of firewood," Zeb said. "You all get in the cabin and build you a fire."

So Livy and Faith, Birdie and Millie passed a restful day, tearing palmetto blades into strips for lashing the fronds on the roof. At the same time, Birdie told stories. Livy told stories. The girls made stories up. They had a fine time sitting around the fire, the smoke sifting lazily through the leafy roof.

Zeb, Adam, and Sam cut more palmetto fronds and finished thatching the roof. When it rained again that night, not a single drop of rain trickled down on them.

The next day was warmer. Livy waved Zeb and Adam off in the boats. They were looking for trees just the right size to make the next log cabin with. They hoped to have three of them finished in a few weeks, one for Zeb and Livy and Faith, one for Flavian, Birdie and Millie, and a bachelor cabin for Sam, Derek, Adam, and Hector.

Now all they needed was for Flavian to bring them some warm clothes, Livy thought. That and a hundred other things, but they could make do if they didn't freeze to death.

The fourth day, late in the afternoon, Jimbo barked in ecstasy, alerting everyone that all his friends were returning.

Birdie ran straight into the water to get at Flavian. Livy hadn't realized how worried she was, but she could see why. They didn't none of them have any friends in town.

They pulled the two dugouts up onto the shore and everyone helped unpack the goods, excited and exclaiming over everything they'd brought back.

"That bear skin brought us more than all the rest put together," Hector said. "Reckon we gone have to go hunting for another one."

"You even got scissors!" Livy said.

"And blankets. Some calico. Some canvas. Didn't get no shoes, but we can make some out of otter hide if we catch some more."

Livy looked up from happily snicking the scissors in the air to see Zeb looking at her with a strange little smile.

"What?" she said.

Zeb walked over to her and leaned down. She felt his breath on her neck, felt his lips brushing against her ear. "Don't know what I done for God to send me you, Livy."

"So I'm God's gift, huh?" she murmured.

"Yes, you are."

She turned into his arms and wrapped hers around his waist. "Then I thank God for sending me to you."

Zeb had changed, out here. He smiled, still, but not like he used to. He used to be a smiling fool, she thought, smiling over every little thing, even smiling in the hot sun with the sweat rolling into his eyes. Life on Orchid Island wasn't easier than being on the plantation, and it required more planning, more worrying. He didn't smile so much, but she trusted him more now because she felt he finally understood what she'd yearned for, what he'd been missing. Her Zeb had finished growing up, she supposed.

"Look here, Livy," Birdie called, holding up a sack. "We got corn meal."

Hector held a hand up, looking at Birdie and then at Livy to claim their attention. With great fanfare, he reached into his pocket and produced – an onion!

There was a time Livy didn't want no onions, but that time was long past. Her mouth watered, and then Hector, still silent, held up his other hand to say "wait," and fished out a single tomato from his other pocket.

"Zeb," Livy said. "I'm through with you." She walked over to Hector and kissed him right on the mouth, relieving him of onion and tomato while she was at it.

When she backed away, grinning at him, Hector turned wide eyes on Zeb and held his hands up in defense. Zeb just laughed, as Livy knew he would. Hector knew it, too, she figured.

Turned out there were a few more onions and tomatoes in a sack. Livy mixed chopped onion into the corn meal and made corn cakes. Every slice of fish had a juicy slice of tomato on top. It was a feast.

When they were finished, it was nearly dark. Birdie put the fire out as usual, but everyone lingered to hear about the trip into town.

"Nobody look at you funny?" Birdie asked.

"Nobody did. Don't know why the slavers don't hang around the markets, but they wadn't none there."

"What about Cal? He give you any trouble?"

Derek exchanged a look with Hector. "Some. He ought to have one of the boats, he said. Argued about it pretty hot. But Flavian wadn't having none of it. We gave him the two dimes we got trading and told him to go on."

"Might as well tell them the rest," Hector said.

Derek didn't want to, Livy could see that. "We had a scuffle at the bayou when we got ready to go. Cal knocked Flavian down with a punch in the gut. Shoved Hector into the water. Him and me beat each other up a while, then these other two," he said, gesturing at Hector and Flavian, "got hold of him and put a stop to it."

"I never saw nobody any madder than that. His face was a sight, what with his busted lip already swelling up, but the mad in his eyes, that made me step back, I'll tell you."

"Well, he's good gone by now."

"What you think he gone do?"

"He know which way is north. He maybe make it."

Livy looked at Zeb. When he returned her gaze, she didn't see any bad feeling in him. Cal was gone, and Zeb was through with it,.

They snuggled up in the blankets that night, more comfortable than they'd been in a long while. For one, the mosquitoes died off in a cold spell like this, for another, the morning dew didn't chill them come dawn.

The next several days, life on Orchid Island was good. The men worked on the cabins. Birdie and Livy made canvas pants. They had to think on how to cut the pieces out for shirts and dresses, drawing patterns in the dirt, neither of them claiming any talent for it. Faith got stung by a bee, and it hurt, but she didn't complain overmuch.

Livy had given up praying all those months of misery when she was dragged away from her sisters and her mother, when she had seethed with anger, yearning to run for it. But she had taken it up again these last weeks, sending up prayers of pure thankfulness. Loving Zeb, being a mother to Faith, living on Orchid Island -- as close to paradise as a body could get this side of heaven, she figured.

Chapter Twenty-Three

Millie was persuading the dog to come out of the rain and play with her under the lean-to when Jimbo suddenly whirled away from her, ran to the shoreline, and barked furiously. She peered through the rain -- four boats of white men came paddling around a bend.

Millie screamed.

Hector and Flavian ran for the two guns and got them loaded.

Livy's mind took time for an instant's thought: Adam and Eve didn't get to stay in their paradise either. And there was Cal in one of the slaver's boats, Orchid Island's own serpent.

Livy grabbed Faith, Birdie had hold of Millie, but there was no point in running to the middle of the island. It wasn't that big an island. The women had their knives at the ready, but if the men couldn't stop the raiders, they had no hope of fending them off.

Zeb ran into the clearing with his axe. A man who's killed a bear with an axe, Livy thought, don't think it's just for chopping wood.

There were two white men in each boat, Cal in the prow of the first boat. The white men opened fire as they landed.

Livy pushed Faith to the muddy ground and threw herself on top of her, the rain beating on her back. Flavian and Hector, aiming from the shelter of the first cabin, fired, reloaded, fired, reloaded, but they were slow at it and their powder got wet in the rain. They used their muskets like clubs and swung at the white men, but there were too many of them, and they already had Adam and Derek on their bellies.

A white man fell to the ground and writhed, screaming out in agony. The smell of his blood and bowels sickened her, but Livy was glad, glad he would suffer before he died.

She heard the clang of a shot hitting metal and from the corner of her eye saw the axe fly from Zeb's hand. Two men were on him, and one of them thunked the stock of his gun into Zeb's head and he lay still as death.

Another man grabbed at her. She slashed out with her knife, catching him on the forearm. "Damnation and Hell!" he yelled, his blood splattering her face.

He twisted the knife out of her hand and socked her in the jaw. While she was dazed, he grabbed her hair, yanking it and pulling her head back so the rain fell hard onto her face.

"I just as soon stick this little gal with your knife as stick you. You want her to live, you settle down." He yanked on her hair again. "You gone settle down?"

She managed to move her chin enough to nod yes. Then quick as you please he released her and clapped hand cuffs on her, snapped the short chain from the cuffs to one ankle bracelet, and she was hobbled. Faith huddled close to her, both of them trembling more from shock than from the cold rain.

Livy craned her neck to see that Zeb still hadn't moved. Hector and Sam were fighting with their fists. Likely the slavers didn't want to kill any of them. They were all worth more alive than dead.

Birdie was trussed up just like she was. Flavian lay on his back, a shotgun poking at his chest.

Seemed like forever, or maybe only seconds, and it was over.

"Don't want to shoot any of you," a slaver said over the sound of rain slapping into the water and onto the trees, "but we have plenty more ammo if we need it. You people are breaking the law, and you know it, so come on peaceful like, and nobody has to get hurt."

Livy crawled over to Zeb and put her mouth to his neck. There was a pulse, and she gulped for breath for a moment. He was alive. She hadn't lost him. Not yet.

All around her, she heard the snick of manacles clicking shut. They came to Zeb and chained him before he even woke up.

"We don't have enough irons, Boss."

"Use your head. Use one cuff on one man, the other on another man. Choose one of them to put the ankle bracelet on."

"Boss," a slaver said. "Lawrence here is dead." He meant the man whose belly was torn up with buckshot. Flavian and Hector's muskets hadn't done that.

The one they call Boss walked over and stared at the body, the rain falling into the dead man's wide-open eyes. Boss knew one of their own shotguns had caught this man in the belly. He could easily say one of them had done it, though. Livy watched his face, but she couldn't tell whether he had any fairness in him or not.

Faith cried out. Livy startled and whirled around to see Faith cradling Jimbo. They'd shot the dog, maybe on purpose, maybe not, but his body was bloody and limp. Adam, too, was bloody, a wound on his upper arm, but none of them could help him bind it with their hands and legs in chains. The slavers cuffed Zeb and Adam together.

Every single one of Orchid Island's people, lying or sitting on the ground, focused on Cal still in one of the slavers' boats. He had brought the whites to them. He had betrayed them all.

He had not helped the slavers once they got to the camp, but he had not helped his people either. Livy guessed Cal didn't have any people now.

His gaze ran over all of them bound and chained without focusing on any of them. She didn't see anything in his face, not shame or sorry or glad or mad. Then he looked her full in the face.

His gaze softened. He looked at her like she was his love, like he knew she'd love him too if she just would.

"Come with me, Livy." He didn't care who heard him. "I'll take you north, you be free. And you won't have to live in no swamp."

She stared at him, hardly believing he could ask her this after what he'd done.

"Come with me, Livy," he pleaded.

Livy spat on the ground and turned away.

The slavers came for Livy first. They hauled her to her feet and dragged her to the boat, mud thick on her dress, on her calves and arms. They headed for the skiff Cal was in. "Don't you put me in the boat with that snake," she snarled. "I kill him first chance I get."

The white man laughed at her and put her in another boat, Faith next to her. They loaded Birdie and Millie in a different one. At least they hadn't put irons on the girls. Adam and Zeb went into the boat with Birdie, the others distributed amongst the other skiffs.

"You want us to fire these cabins?" one of the white men said.

"Nah. Everything out here's too wet to burn. Let it go. They aren't coming back out here anyway."

Cal climbed out of the skiff, his hands still bound.

He held them out to the one they called Boss. Boss looked at his cuffs, then at him.

"You promised," Cal said.

Boss snorted a sort of chuckle. "Not yet." He turned his back on Cal and got into a boat.

"Tie that dugout to the skiff," Cal demanded, just like he wasn't a man with manacles on his wrists. "I'm gone need it."

Boss stared at him for a long moment. Then he nodded to one of his men to tether a dugout to one of the boats.

They all shoved off, the hiss of rain hitting the water loud now there was quiet enough to hear it. Livy stared at Orchid Island until the byway curved around another island and she couldn't see it anymore.

Faith leaned into her, but she straightened and said, "Zeb's awake!"

He shook his head. He blinked. He was confused, she could tell. He looked around him, took in the chains, the white men. Suddenly he jerked his head around, scanning the boats until he found her and Faith.

He stared at them, all the grief in the world on his face. She gave him what she could, a smile that said *I love you.*

Another man might have slumped then, his shoulders and head bowed. Not her Zeb. His jaw hardened as he looked more closely at the white men. She figured he was counting heads, counting guns and knives, judging how they were bound. She didn't know whether to be cheered by the calculation in his eye or frightened. He could get himself killed yet.

Cal sat in the bow of one of the skiffs. Livy wouldn't give a handful of beans for his chances of coming out of this a free man. The fool.

Chapter Twenty-Four

Zeb had never felt such pain, not even when Benning had lashed him with the whip. His head felt like somebody took an axe to it, all his wits spilling out into his lap. He closed his eyes against the rain, shivering, yearning to yield to the darkness threatening him, as if he could sleep away the pain and all the despair.

He forced his eyes open again and focused on Livy in the next boat. She had been watching him every time he opened his eyes. She had to be scared, but she didn't show it. He nodded to her, hoping that was reassurance. That was all he could offer her now, a tight-necked nod of the head.

Adam sat across from him, their cuffs requiring them to stretch their arms along the gunwale toward each other. Adam's skin was gray and his arm was still bleeding, dripping onto both his and Zeb's feet.

Adam was trying to tell him something without saying anything. Zeb narrowed his eyes and tried to pay attention. Adam kept cutting his eyes toward the water, then back to Zeb. He tried to understand, but inside his head there were a thousand bells ringing.

Adam widened his eyes and cut them to the water again. Then he looked at his bloody arm and back to Zeb with his brows raised.

Zeb gave his head the littlest shake to show Adam he didn't understand. Adam's mouth thinned, then he mouthed a word at him.

Dead? Was he saying dead?

Adam did the other thing, cutting his eyes to the water, to his arm. Then again he shaped his lips to say dead.

All right. Even through the fog in Zeb's brain, he got it. He gave one tiny nod and looked away. Out of the corner of his eye, he saw Adam give a little kick to Birdie's leg, a purposeful, very much alive kick.

Suddenly, Adam slumped over, letting his body fall across Birdie. She screamed. "Oh my God," she wailed. "He's dead. He's dead. My God, Flavian, Adam's dead."

The white man poling the skiff behind Adam gave him a shove with his foot. "Bled to death, I reckon," he said. "Shut up, woman."

Birdie's scream turned into keening. Zeb caught Livy's eye and shouted out his grief, hoping she'd start into wailing, too. She understood him well enough and keened as loudly as Birdie.

With all the noise and confusion, the white man said, "God Almighty, stop your carrying on."

They kept on wailing.

Finally Zeb shouted out, "Get him away from here. Get him out!"

"What are you talking about?" the slaver said.

"Get him off of here! He died bad, he gone come back and haunt every one of us. Get him out of the boat."

The slaver looked at him like he was a crazy man, so Zeb acted even crazier. He let out the kind of scream that rose the hair on the backs of every human that heard it and liked to have cleaved through his own swollen brain.

"He's rising! I see him! Oh Lord, don't let him get me." He screamed again since the slaver still hadn't done anything.

"What you want me to do, Boss?" the slaver called to the next boat. His white skin had paled like he'd seen Adam's spirit rising himself.

"Get these people quiet! Toss him over!" Boss commanded.

The slavers hauled on Adam's carcass, taking his arms and his legs. Suddenly Zeb realized he was going to have go into the water with him, chained together like they were.

"Hold on there!" Boss cried. "Those manacles cost me $10. And I don't want that big fella going over the side, too. He's worth too much. Unchain him and toss the dead one over."

They dropped the manacles on the floor at Zeb's feet and threw Adam overboard.

Adam sank straight to the bottom. The water was dark here with the rain coming down, no sun penetrating the surface.

Zeb tapered the wails down to whimpering, all the while scanning the water through slitted eyes. He didn't see Adam surface, but he believed in his bones he'd drawn enough breath to get him out of sight.

They hadn't gone far from Orchid Island. If Adam could make his way back, he could save himself. Gather up tools, take one of the dugouts, and move off into the swamp, maybe down south where they say the Houma Indians lived. Lots of the time, the Indians took in escaped slaves, didn't matter to them that their skin was black. Zeb prayed to God that Adam would make it.

The rain didn't let up. They made a soggy camp, everyone cold and wet and hungry. All of the islanders huddled together for warmth – except Cal. He sat with his back against a tree, very much alone.

The white slavers managed to build a fire by sheltering it under a tarp. Wet wood, lots of smoke, but at last they had enough fire to make coffee. They gave one cup to share amongst their prisoners, happy to refill it, but only the one cup. They handed out beef jerky and cold grits cake.

There was no way to get dry, no way to get warm. Zeb tore giant heart-shaped leaves off their stalks to lay over them for a little cover, then lay down. He cuddled Faith against his chest and then Livy lay down with her back pushed up to both of them, making a sandwich of Faith. Eventually Faith stopped shivering, but Livy never did.

One of the white slavers kept guard, the rifle cradled in his arms. He didn't look that attentive to Zeb and he wondered how any kind of weapon could fire in this wet.

He stretched his unchained arm across Faith, his hand on Livy's waist. "Livy. You want to turn over?" he whispered. "Get your front warmed up?"

She shifted so she faced him. "It won't get me no warmer, but at least I can see you a little bit." She reached her arm over Faith too and stroked his face.

His heart swelled, grief and love all mixed together so he could hardly speak. "I'm sorry, Livy."

"No, Zeb. Don't be sorry. These been the best months of my life."

"We should have killed Cal."

"I didn't want you killing nobody. And none of us guessed he was bad as this." She spoke so softly, he could barely hear her.

"I get the chance, I'm gone kill him. You understand that, Livy."

"Zeb! Somebody coming up from the water. Don't look."

"It ain't one of the slavers?"

Livy gripped his arm, hard. Looked like she closed her eyes. What didn't she want to see?

"What?"

"Adam cut that guard's throat. Wait. Be still."

Zeb waited, all his senses keen to hear, to see, but the rain covered the sound and obscured his vision.

"He got another one," Livy said, the sound barely coming out of her mouth.

Two slavers dead. That left five. Plus Cal.

Adam crouched next to him, followed Zeb's wet arm, and pressed a knife into his hand. But Zeb still had a chain from one arm to one leg. He rolled up carefully, holding the chain taut to keep it from rattling.

Adam bent down and gave the other dead man's knife to somebody, Zeb couldn't see who.

"Winston, you moving around like it time for somebody to spell you," the one they called Boss said. Zeb froze. "Wake Manson up."

When nobody moved to wake the other man, Boss called out, "Winston?" He sat up and looked around. It was dark, and it was raining, but Zeb could make out the man's shape, and no doubt he'd see them too.

The man jumped to his feet, tossing the tarp off him. "Winston! Everybody, get up!"

Zeb leapt at the nearest slaver lying under his tarp. The man was half roused, pushing the oiled canvas off, when Zeb got to him and knifed him in the throat. Even over the sound of the rain pattering against the leaves, he heard the man's breath gurgle through the blood flooding his throat. Zeb slashed the man's neck to put an end to it.

They were all on their feet now, and it was hard to know who was slaver and who was friend.

He went for the man fumbling with a shotgun. Zeb knocked him down and plunged the knife into his chest. That wasn't enough. Zeb stuck him again and the man's body went limp.

It was all confusion, grunts, cries, shouts. Zeb didn't find another slaver on his feet and turned to where Cal had been. He wouldn't have to choke the life out of him. He had a knife this time.

But where was Cal? He could make out men straightening up, looking around. Were there no more slavers to kill, then?

"Call out your name!" Zeb shouted.

"Sam," the boy said, his voice high and terrified.

The rest called out – Adam, Derek, Hector – Zeb himself.

"Flavian?" Zeb called.

No answer. Birdie shrieked, "Flavian, where are you?"

"Where's Cal?" Zeb shouted.

Birdie screamed. Zeb ran toward her voice and could make out two men lying in the mud. Both of them motionless.

The others crowded around. Birdie had thrown herself over the man on top, Flavian by the size of him. She was sobbing, calling his name over and over.

"See can you get another fire started," Zeb told Derek. "We got to have a little light."

Zeb knelt and rubbed his hand over Birdie's cold wet back. He let her cry, her grief shaking her small body. Livy came and gathered Birdie into her arms.

They never did get a fire started, but Zeb made out what happened with his hands. Flavian lay on top, his hands clamped around Cal's neck. Cal had to have got a knife off one of the dead slavers – the handle of it protruded from Flavian's ribs.

"Let's gather up these tarps," Zeb said. "Everything else gone have to wait till morning."

They put the first tarp over Livy, Birdie, and the girls, the second over Flavian, even if that meant they had to cover Cal, too. Flavian, even dead, was too vital to them to leave in the rain. Then the men paired up, huddled under two more tarps. It was a relief not to have the rain rolling down their backs, but they were still all sitting in mud.

The sound of the rain pelting on the tarp felt like hammer blows to Zeb's head. Nausea and pain and cold wracked him. It was a long time before the rain stopped.

The sun rose on a grisly scene. The seven white slavers lay contorted on the ground, every one of them killed by a knife. "Livy, ya'll stay under the tarp. Faith and Millie don't need to see this."

Flavian and Cal lay locked together a ways off. As Zeb's hands had found, Flavian had lived long enough after Cal stabbed him to choke the life out of the traitor.

They looked through the white men's pockets and found the keys to the manacles. With cold wet fingers, they freed one another from their chains.

"What we gone do with all these bodies?" Derek asked.

"Don't much feel like digging with my hands to bury a bunch of slavers," Hector said.

"I ain't digging for none of them," Adam said. "Leave them for the gators."

Zeb thought about it. It wasn't Christian, leaving them out in the open. But he decided that's what they would do, and he didn't much care what the preacher would say about it.

"Let's get away from here," he said.

They were now four men and a twelve year old boy, the two women and the two little girls. "Can you pole one of these skiffs, Sam?"

"I can do it, Zeb."

"Good." Zeb didn't want to leave any boats out here for the next wave of slavers to find. They'd come, but by then, the gators would have done their work.

Zeb was afraid he'd have to break Flavian's fingers to get them off Cal's neck, but he managed by mashing the neck. It couldn't do any more harm to a dead man.

They loaded Flavian into the first boat with Birdie and divided themselves among the other three skiffs and the dugout Adam had used to follow them.

Not a one of them looked back at that blood-soaked island. With the tarps and knives, guns, ammunition, and shoes of the dead men, they paddled and poled their way home.

In the soft earth of Orchid Island, they buried Flavian next to where his son Luke had been buried not so many months before. Sam climbed a tree to bring down a cluster of orchids to decorate the grave. Zeb spoke over the body, asking God to take his soul, then Derek and Hector told how Flavian had taught them how to live out here, about how he made them into men. Birdie stood at the foot of the grave, calm, silent, her eyes on her husband's shrouded body.

Livy led Birdie and the girls away before Zeb and the others filled in the grave.

Back at the clearing, Zeb said, "We can't stay here."

"No, we can't stay," Hector said.

"We can stay the night, nobody knows all those men ain't coming back yet, but tomorrow, good light, we leave. That gives us the rest of the day to gather what we can take with us."

"We got to eat first, Zeb. Let's have a fire, get warm, and eat," Livy said. "Then we start collecting."

"Yeah. We'll eat."

It didn't take long to get all their belongings together and packed in the boats. Their tools. The cloth Birdie and Livy dried and folded. A few pumpkins.

Livy carefully wiped the wet mud off her scissors. "You reckon they'll rust?"

"You drying them soon enough. They'll be fine."

"I hope so. I prize this pair of scissors more than any other thing I ever had."

Before dusk, Birdie took the girls into the cabin to bed down. Faith had not left Millie's side all day, had let Millie cling to her when Birdie had to work in the garden.

Zeb took Livy across the island to the swimming pool. An otter was frolicking with his friends, but the three of them swam away when they saw them.

They waded into the water. It was cold now, after all the rain, and winter coming on.

Body to body, their tenderness warming them, Livy said, "I been so happy here, Zeb."

"We'll find another place. We be happy again." His fingers held her jaw, his thumb caressed her lips. "You hear me, Livy? We be happy again."

Zeb kissed her, promising her.

They wrapped themselves in one of the sun-dried blankets and watched the sun set. Then Zeb lay her down one last time on their island home and loved her.

Chapter Twenty-Five

They headed south, deeper into the Atchafalaya, further from the plantations. The sky was bright and clear, the sun welcome on their backs whenever they emerged from the tree canopy.

They were a strange sight, Livy thought. Nine raggedy people in four skiffs towing four dugouts. They had more than when she and Zeb had started out though. More strong backs. Tools. Blankets. And hard-won knowledge of how to live out here.

They were a quiet bunch. Birdie and Millie acted like they couldn't see nothing they were so grieved. Faith, bless her, sat with them, silent, there for Millie to hold on to.

Adam's arm was bandaged. It didn't seem to pain him. He poled his boat through the shallows as readily as the other men.

Livy had tried to spell Zeb earlier. She knew his head bothered him. Sometimes he was dizzy and had to catch himself. But when she tried poling, she'd nearly lost the pole and she couldn't keep up with the others. So she watched him and made sure he kept drinking water. There didn't seem to be nothing else to do for him.

And so her Zeb had killed after all. Not Cal, but two of the slavers. He had to do it. He was right to do it. But she worried. Would those two slavers' souls cling to him, sucking the joy out of him?

Sam trolled off the back of one of the boats and caught enough fish to feed them. They stopped just long enough to roast the fish on sticks, then went on until an hour before dark. In the thick growth of a piece of land, they built hasty lean-tos for the night.

Livy lay awake until past moon-rise, listening to the bats and the owls, the raccoons rustling in the brush. She'd kept Millie and Faith from looking at all that death back at the slavers' camp. The rest of them though had seen the sprawled bodies, the puddles under them pink with watery blood. Likely none of them would forget it.

She guessed everybody was capable of killing. If Livy had had a knife, she'd have been willing to use it. Even Sam. She'd seen him with a knife in his hand. Maybe he had killed, too.

She kept her hand on Zeb's chest, feeling for his heart beat. His chest moved easy with his breathing, but nobody never knew what a blow to the head gone do to a person. Back on her first place, a fella named Beau got knocked down when somebody dropped a hammer from the roof they were putting up. He'd been a big strapping boy, strong as anybody, and looked like he was fine after the first hour or so. And that night he died in his sleep.

"Zeb, you don't die," she whispered.

In the morning, Livy changed the bandage on Adam's arm. The gash was red and a little puffy.

She touched it gently. "It hurt, Adam?"

"Nah. It's nothing."

She put the rest of Birdie's salve on the wound and tied a strip of calico around it.

Through the day, they moved the boats into shade, out into sunlight, back into the shade. The birds were on the move, feeling winter coming. Overhead, geese flew in an arrow pointed south. At one open stretch of water, a whole flock of brown and green ducks glided down and lit on the surface.

"Hold up here," Zeb said quietly. They had dried powder, they had shot, and they had guns.

Derek, Hector, and Zeb loaded up and waited for Zeb's signal cause once the first shot fired, the ducks would spiral into the sky and they wouldn't get a second chance.

Zeb sighted along the barrel. Blinked his eyes and shook his head and sighted again.

"What's wrong?" Livy asked quietly.

He wiped his hand over his eyes. "Everything's still blurry."

"Pass it over to me," Adam said.

Zeb gave Adam time to sight the gun, then said, "Ready? When I say three. One, two . . . "

The sound echoed across the water and bounced off the trees. The ducks leapt into the air and a hundred wings flurried and whirred, lifting the flock up into the blue sky.

Livy hoped nobody said anything about needing Jimbo to swim out there and bring the dead birds back to them. At least not so Millie and Faith could hear him. They'd both tune up and start crying again.

They moved the boats toward the kill and collected eight ducks. They'd eat good tonight.

The next morning before they got off, Zeb called Faith to him. "Sit down here and let me fix that rat's nest on your head."

Livy watched him settle her between his legs and patiently unsnarl her hair. She still had her blue ribbon, raggedy and faded, and he used it to tie her hair in a bushy knot on top of her head.

"Don't you look pretty," Livy told her.

Zeb gave his girl a big hug and patted her bottom. "Go see if Sam wants some help."

"You look like you feeling better," Livy told him.

"Feel like I'm gone live after all," he smiled.

That was the first smile she'd seen since the raid. She drew a deep breath and let it out. Then she walked around behind him and hugged him. She couldn't tell him what she wanted to, her heart filling up her throat. She nuzzled his neck and let him go.

These days of moving through the swamp eased everybody from the shocks and fears left over from the slavers' raid. The weather stayed fine, their only company the birds and an occasional gator swimming through the water. They ate fish and turtles, plenty for everyone.

Of an evening, they talked about Flavian, remembering something he'd said that made them laugh, or something he'd taught them. Nobody ever said a word about Cal.

The nights were cool, but they had the blankets Flavian had traded for in town. A blanket wasn't enough for Adam though when he started having chills and fever. His arm was festering and hot.

When the chill came on him, Birdie moved over to his blanket, she and Millie. They curled their bodies around his, keeping him warm.

That morning, they took the time to work on his wound. They boiled water and pressed hot cloths against it, drawing the poison out. Birdie found the herb she wanted growing along the edge of the shore and ground it into a paste to plaster on it.

That night Adam's fever flared up again. Livy and Birdie wiped his face and chest with cool water. Then the chills came and

Birdie called Millie to lay to his front while she wrapped her arms around him from the back.

"Where we going, Zeb?" Livy asked him. "We got to find a place, get some cabins built before winter."

He shook his head. "I just following my nose, Livy. Waiting till I see the place we supposed to be at."

"I'm scared we gone lose Adam."

He held her close. "I'm scared of it, too. He saved every one of us, Adam did. And look like that gone kill him."

"What if we took that arm off?" Livy could hardly say it. She couldn't do it, she knew she couldn't. But Birdie probably could. She was a woman made out of steel.

"I been thinking about it," Birdie said. "That might save him. Or it might kill him."

"We best wait a while," Zeb said.

"One more day. I think that's all the time we can wait or the poison finish him off."

They made a camp and stayed put the next day. They fished, made a raised mat for Adam to get him up off the ground. Improved the previous night's lean-tos. Kept the fire going to have hot water for bathing his wound.

Nobody talked much that whole day. They hovered where Birdie tended to Adam, everybody just waiting. Late that afternoon, the clearing was filled with the *ssshhp* of Hector sharpening his big knife. When he was satisfied with that, he honed the edge of his axe.

During the night, Adam muttered and hollered nonsense. He called out "Birdie!" and Livy heard her murmuring to him, calming him.

Everybody was up soon as the sky lightened enough for them to see where they put their feet.

Adam lay tangled in the blankets, his head thrashing back and forth.

"It's gone have to be done, or he gone die today," Birdie told them.

Nobody wanted to say what they were all thinking: if they took his arm, he could still die.

"Sam," Livy said, "you take the girls off in the skiff a ways. Do some fishing."

Sam nodded to Faith and Millie to come on. "Don't get lost, Sam," Birdie called after him. "Pay attention where you are."

"Who gone do it?" Zeb asked. "Who got the steadiest hands? The best nerves?" Livy read the message behind Zeb's words. He hoped it wasn't him, and she didn't blame him.

"Birdie and me, we done talked about it," Hector said. "We do it, but we gone need every one of you to hold him down."

Every one of them. That only meant Zeb and Derek and her. She was gone have to see it through, just like Zeb was. She closed her eyes and tried to keep her gorge from rising.

Livy built up the fire. She boiled Hector's sharpened knife and the axe head. For good measure, she threw her threaded needle in there, too.

"What good that gone do?" Derek said. "He likely bleed to death. What good boiling the knife gone do?"

"I don't know, Derek," she snapped at him. "I seen it done before, that's all. It can't hurt."

Adam didn't know what was going on. Sometimes he was awake and groaning, sometimes he looked like he was dead already. They talked over how they were gone do it.

Birdie had seen an amputation once before, a woman's leg had to come off. She told them what they had to do, how to stop the bleeding with a hot blade, how to make a skin flap, how to sew it closed. Livy kept swallowing hard and trying to keep her hands from trembling.

"Zeb, you the biggest," Birdie said. "I want you holding down both legs. Livy you use your weight and all the strength you got on his body. Derek, you hold down his other arm cause he gone use every bit of muscle he got to get away, and that arm gone be dangerous. Everybody ready?"

Hector gathered the second axe and fished the knife and the other axe head out of the cooling water. They washed the wound, and they began.

Livy didn't watch. She wished she could close her ears and her nose, too. With the first cut, Adam screamed and a flock of egrets swarmed out of a nearby tree in a swift cloud. The smell of blood and piss rose all around her.

Adam bucked and fought, but they held him, Zeb helping her keep his hips down with one of his big hands.

By the time they were ready to cut through the bone, Adam had passed out.

"Like this," Livy heard Hector say.

She turned her head and saw him placing the axe blade against the white bone and using the back of the other one to bang it straight through.

Livy threw up, heaving nothing but bile, but she didn't leave off pressing her weight on Adam's body. Derek was shivering all over, his breath shuddering in and out. She couldn't see Zeb, and didn't want to. She squeezed her eyes shut tight and wished it was over.

Adam came to while Birdie was sewing the wound closed. He knew what had been done to him. He didn't scream so much as groan from deep in his chest, the panic making a scream more than he had breath for. The whites of his eyes showed as he rolled his head back and forth. Livy held on, just like Zeb and Derek did, but after only a few minutes, Adam's eyes rolled up and he lost consciousness again.

"Cut through this thread, right there," Birdie said to Hector.

Then it was finished.

"Ya'll get off him now. I sit with him."

"We call you if we need you," Hector said, and he walked toward the woods.

Livy went cold all over, catching sight of Hector carrying Adam's arm away. She was trembling like Derek had a while ago.

Derek stumbled off into the bushes and vomited.

Livy rolled off Adam, careful not to look at his stump. Zeb still straddled Adam's legs, his head bowed to his chest.

"Zeb?" she said.

He didn't look up, and his voice came out harsh. "You all right, Livy?"

She nodded and then realized he couldn't see her. "I'm all right."

Abruptly, Zeb stood up and strode to the boats. He heaved a dugout into the water and climbed in. Without looking back he paddled hard till he was around the corner of the island where nobody could see him.

Livy was sorry he didn't take her with him. She could have held him while he went to pieces, cause that's what she thought he was doing. She wouldn't think any the less of him if he cried and carried on just like she and Derek been doing.

They kept camp the same place, waiting till Adam was well enough to move. Two days later, he still had fever. They could still lose him. The fifth day, he woke up clear-eyed and cool to the touch.

He was going to live. He still had terrible pain, and it was still a horror to him to see where his arm had been. It was a horror to Livy, too, but she had to get over it. She meant to help Adam get through this, not let him see how her stomach heaved every time she looked at him.

They made a pallet out of all the blankets in the bottom of the dugout where he could stretch his full length. Birdie rode along with him, towed by one of the skiffs.

He began to eat a little. Still wouldn't talk. But he was alive. In the evenings, Zeb stayed close to him, doing the talking for both of them. He told him about the first time he killed a squirrel with his sling shot. About when to cut the cane at its sweetest, which of course Adam already knew. The important thing was Zeb was with him and just kept talking.

Everyone else had lay down to sleep and Zeb stayed with Adam, still talking. Livy couldn't hear what they said, just the soft drone of Zeb's voice. All of a sudden, Adam let out a yelp of laughter. Zeb laughed, too, the both of them laughing fools.

When Zeb finally came and lay down next to her, she whispered, "What'd you say that was so funny?"

"I told him about the first time I ever did it with a girl," Zeb whispered back.

She tried to see him. "And that was funny?"

Zeb chuckled. "It was."

"Tell me about it," she murmured in his ear.

"Never in your lifetime or mine," he murmured back.

Chapter Twenty-Six

The world began to look different the further south they traveled. Fewer cypresses, more willows, more oaks. More open marsh and more dry land, too. Sometimes Livy could smell salt in the air.

"There's supposed to be a big ocean down this way," Zeb said.

"How do you know that?"

"Don't know it. Just heard it."

"You reckon they got slavers waiting all along the coast?" Hector said.

"I think this supposed to be Indian country."

"Who told you all that?"

"Noah did. Back when I was a boy. He had it from a slave ran off and was a sailor till they caught him and brought him back."

They found a pecan tree at one of their stops. Sam and the girls collected two big turtle shells full and everyone gorged on this welcome alternative to fish.

Sitting in a patch of sunshine with pecan shells in her lap, Livy looked around. "I like this place," she told Zeb. She'd said that about the last place they camped, too. But Zeb just shook his head.

"We gone have to stop some time." She was tired of moving camp every night, of sitting in the boat the live-long day.

Zeb just smiled. She'd worried he'd be a changed man if he killed Cal. Maybe he would have been. But he didn't seem like having killed those two white men bothered his conscience at all. He'd been quiet, and solemn, the first days after the raid. And Adam's ordeal had shaken him. But seem like the more they got out from under the cypress canopy, the sunnier Zeb was.

"We gone stop," he told her.

She gave him a mock scowl. "When?"

"Don't know. Haven't found it yet."

"We haven't, huh?"

"Nope. Know it when we see it."

They saw it that same afternoon. They rounded a bend in the narrow bayou and there it was. A whole village of huts, smoke coming out of chimneys, children playing.

The Indians left off what they were doing and came to the banks to watch them.

"I don't see no bows and arrows. No guns neither," Derek said. "Maybe they not gone kill us."

The huts were wattle and daub, arranged in a circle. Beyond the village there were fields, past harvest now, but these people had gardens. They ate something besides crawfish, fish, and turtles.

Livy's heart sped up. Not out of fear, but out of hope. The women wore their straight black hair parted in the middle and braided down their backs. Some of them wore short capes over their shoulders, some of them only skirts. They didn't smile, but they didn't look mean either.

"Now that looks mighty welcoming to me," Hector said, eyeing the bare-breasted women on the bank.

"Hector, you hush," Birdie told him.

"You think we be welcome here?"

"I don't see why not," Zeb said. "We got all these boats. We got tools. And we all be good people."

They pulled into shore and some of the Indians helped slide the boats up on to the banks.

All of the Orchid Islanders stood together, Zeb standing out in front. "Hello," he said, and raised his hand in greeting.

An older man stepped forward. He wore his hair in a long braid with a band around his forehead. He had on a calico shirt, a breechcloth down to his knees, and soft leather shoes.

He spoke rapidly, incomprehensibly. Zeb looked over his shoulder at his friends. "Don't suppose any of you speak Indian."

Livy rolled her eyes and he turned back.

Zeb talked, pointing back north toward the swamps, toward Orchid Island. He held up his fingers to show how many days they'd traveled, making rowing motions.

Zeb used his arms and hands some more, talking all the while. What he was telling the Indians was that they had four skiffs, four dugouts, two axes, and guns. And they would like to stay awhile.

Livy thought he was doing a pretty good job until all the men walked away. The women and children stayed on the banks, staring at them.

The men congregated about fifty yards off. Talking about what to do with them, Livy thought.

Seeing that group of nice huts, four walls, roofs, windows, chimneys. All these people. Livy surprised herself at how much she wanted this, to be part of a community, to know they didn't have to invent how to live every day in a place as hard as the swamp.

When a toddler wandered close, his fingers in his mouth, Livy acted on what felt natural. She fell to her knees and held her arms open, and the little boy walked right into her hug.

She could have cried, feeling this child happy to put his arms around her neck. She stood up with him, smiling, and carried him to the women. One of them laughed and took the boy from her. The women chattered at her. All she could do was smile and nod.

One of the women pushed three little girls forward, talking and gesturing toward the boats where Millie and Faith stood.

Livy held her hand out. "Come here, Faith. You too, Millie. Come say hello."

There was an awkward moment while the girls looked each other over. Then the Indian girls took Millie and Faith's hands and scampered off with them.

Livy pointed to herself and said, "Livy." She pointed to Birdie and said, "Birdie."

She didn't introduce Zeb or the other men standing behind her. This was women's time. When the Indian men came back, that would be men's time again.

But one of the women had other ideas. A young bare-breasted woman with clear skin and bright eyes broke away from the others and walked slowly over to where Zeb stood with his arms crossed. She gave him a sly smile and squeezed his biceps.

The Indian women were laughing, but Livy didn't think it was funny. She was gone make Zeb pay for smiling at that naked woman. Taking her time, she walked over to Zeb herself and put her arm through his. Very carefully, keeping a smile on her face, she pointed to Zeb, pointed to herself, and said, "This one is mine."

The young woman put her hands on her hips and all the women giggled and pointed at her. Livy hoped she hadn't made an enemy the first two minutes on dry land, but she wasn't handing Zeb over to nobody else.

Hector stepped forward and presented himself to the Indian woman with his arms spread out. He turned all the way around for her to see what a fine man he was and waited for her response, smiling into her eyes.

She grinned, looked back at her friends, and then laughed with her hands over her mouth. Instead of taking hold of Hector, like Livy supposed he was hoping she would, the girl scurried back to her friends.

By the time the men returned, the atmosphere was not only friendly but even jolly.

The older man eyed all the laughing and smiling women and scowled. They quieted, but they didn't stop nudging each other and whispering behind their hands.

The Indian began a lengthy speech, none of which they understood, but Zeb looked attentive and nodded now and then. Best any of them could do.

Finally, the Indian held out a smoking pipe with both hands, then opened his arm to direct Zeb toward the huts. All the men filed off, leaving Livy and Birdie with the women.

What now?

Birdie reached back into one of their skiffs and lifted out the shell full of pecans. She walked over to the women, sat on her heels, and gestured for them to take what they wanted.

In a few minutes, a dozen women sat cross-legged around the turtle shell, cracking nuts and chattering. Nobody seemed to mind that Birdie and Livy didn't understand a word they said, so Livy decided she didn't mind either. She said whatever she wanted to say when she wanted to, and that seemed to work just fine.

Eventually, Zeb, Adam, Derek, Hector, and Sam came back to them.

"We're invited to stay!" Zeb said. "These here are Houma Indians. They got other black slaves come to live with them, and they can talk to us! Some of them even got little children look like they both black and Indian."

He grabbed Livy up and whirled her around. "This is it, Livy," he said in her ear. "I feel it. This gone be home."

She kissed him on the mouth, right in front of all those people. The Indian women all giggled and pointed, but she didn't care. She kissed him again, his face cradled in her hands.

Everyone gathered in the common area in the center of the huts. Seated on a raised platform, Zeb smoked the calumet with Tonti, then it was passed to Tonti's lieutenants and to Adam, Hector, and Derek.

Next the Houma women gifted them with feathers, an iron pot, a tin spoon, and baskets full of food.

Zeb was a gracious guest. Livy looked at him, wondering when her humble, unassuming man had learned to act the proud, masterful leader. He conferred with Hector a moment, said a few words to Adam and Derek, and gave Livy a wink.

He stood and announced that he wanted the Houma to accept their best dugout, a skiff, and an axe.

Livy wasn't surprised he would offer them boats. They had eight after all. But an axe! They could not produce an axe head themselves; this was a very valuable gift.

After Zeb presented the boat down at the landing, Tonti led Zeb and their other men to a long hut with a fire burning in the center. The women stayed outside, listening to the ritual prayers the men performed around the fire.

What followed was a celebration with drums and whistles and singing and dancing. She got separated from Zeb in all the commotion, and was with a group of Houma women dancing in a circle.

When she looked for him, that girl who had given Zeb's arm a squeeze was dancing circles around him, her bare breasts on display. Zeb didn't seem to mind either.

Livy pushed through the crowd, glowered at the girl, took Zeb's arm, and dragged him off. When she looked over her shoulder at him, the fool was grinning. She dug her fingernails into his arm.

"Ow," he complained, but she didn't let up and hauled him away from the festivities.

"Livy," he said. "You gone draw blood you don't let loose."

She turned on him. "You were watching that girl's breasts jiggle."

Zeb swallowed. Good. She meant for him to be sorry scared.

"I was, Livy."

So he didn't even deny it. She crossed her arms and glared at him.

"It gone take some getting used to, all these women not wearing a stitch above the waist," he said. That didn't sound like an apology.

"You never looked at me like that."

"If you walked around without nothing covering you up, right out in the sunshine, I would."

She raised an eyebrow at him.

"Besides, you don't know how I look at you when you turned away, bending over with your backside in the air."

He was just this close to smiling at her. If he did, he was a dead man.

"I don't like that girl. She too forward."

"Not as pretty as you, either," he said. "Just naked, that's all."

He touched her under the chin. "You the woman I want, Livy. You're my wife, and I'm your husband. Nothing on this earth mean more to me than that."

She cocked her head and narrowed her eyes. "You promise not to look at those naked women anymore?"

Zeb drew in a big breath and blew it out. "How about I promise not to touch none of them? I can promise that."

"You better keep that promise."

He stepped in close and ran his hands up her arms. With his forehead touching hers, he said, "I will."

She raised her face to him and let him kiss her till she believed him. Then she kissed him until she was sure he remembered he belonged to her, body and soul.

They walked back to the celebration hand in hand, Zeb's smile lighting the way in the gloaming.

~~~

In the next days, Birdie found the old woman who knew all the herbs. Livy went along as Birdie took Adam to her and made him show her his stump, still raw and painful. The old woman made a foul-smelling concoction Livy thought she would smear on the wound, but instead she brewed a tea and made Adam drink it.

He grimaced, but he drank it. Then the woman showed Birdie how she made a medicinal paste and that they put that on the raw places. Adam winced with the pain of being touched, but he allowed both of them to fuss over him. It looked to Livy like Adam
~~~

was ready to do whatever Birdie told him to. They'd started out sharing a blanket when Adam was chilled and fevered, but now he was better, they were still sleeping under the same blanket.

Soon enough, working together, the men put up a small hut for Zeb and Faith and Livy, one for Adam, Birdie and Millie, one for Hector and Blossom, the young woman he'd tried to impress the first day. Derek and Sam bunked with other young men who hadn't yet claimed, or been claimed by, a woman.

The first night in their hut, Livy wept.

"What?" Zeb said.

Faith was also staring at her like she was a crazy woman.

"Look at all this," she said and waved her hand to indicate everything in the hut.

The floor was dirt, but it was dry. The roof was thick-thatched with reeds. They had a door and a window with a leather cover to open and close. They had sleeping mats. Blankets. A cook pot. Three spoons. Their turtle shell bowls. A bag of corn meal, a bowl of nuts. And outside, they had old friends and new friends.

Zeb smiled at her. Her Zeb, smiling.

"We're rich. That what you mean?"

She threw herself into his lap and hugged him. "Faith, come hug your mama and daddy. We're home."

Chapter Twenty-Seven

The Orchid Islanders prospered with the Houmas. In their sixth year living with the Indians, Faith took a husband, one of Tonti's sons with a black woman who'd escaped from a plantation to the east. Not long after, Faith and Hotti's first child was named Hope. The second one was Tonti, the third was named after Hotti's mother Ohoyo.

Millie took a husband the same year as Faith, a young Houma man whose mother was a shrew, but Millie just shrugged off her complaints and demands and did as she pleased. Her husband found that more beguiling than her pretty smile or voluptuous figure.

Adam and Birdie had a hut full of children. Hector and Blossom had two of their own. Derek took up with a widow woman who already had six children. He and his woman never had any children between them, but Derek seemed content to be daddy to her six.

Sam was a grown man, already had a wife and lost her in childbirth. He was still grieving, but that didn't mean he couldn't enjoy the attentions of half a dozen young girls who'd love to share his hut.

Livy birthed a set of twins, both boys, a few months after they'd joined the Houma. Zeb named them Noah and Abraham. Their next child Livy named Rosemarie after her mama. The fourth, a boy called Tonti, was still at the breast.

That's when Zeb sat her down once the children were all asleep. "I been thinking," he said.

"You always thinking."

"I been thinking about Hope."

"Faith's baby sister?"

"She about thirteen years old now, near grown."

Livy looked at him, feeling trouble coming.

"I'm gone go after her."

Livy got to her feet in one swift move. "No you are not. They catch you, they chain you up, they whip you half to death, your children won't never see you again. I won't have it. You are not going."

"Hector say he go with me. He got a boy back there, remember? He about the same age as Hope."

"She might not even be there anymore. She could be sold off, Hector's boy, too."

Zeb pulled her back down and held her hands. "What if it was Rosemarie, Livy? What if your baby girl was still a slave, gone always be a slave, the rest of her life? What would you say then?"

She bowed her head. He knew he'd said the one thing that could persuade her, the one thing as close to her heart as him and their children. She remembered how she'd burned to be free those years before she finally ran off with Zeb and Faith. How she'd thought she would burst into flames if she couldn't get loose.

"It's dangerous, Zeb. What if she don't know you no more? What if she don't want to come? And you likely to be dead trying when you got a wife and four children needing you home."

He pulled her into his arms and held her like she was a child. "Don't cry, honey. I know it's dangerous. I know you need me here. That's why I'm gone be careful. If I can't get to her, well then, I can't. But I have to try."

Livy sobbed and clung to him. She begged him not to go, but he was resolute.

He and Hector took a day to prepare. Sam came to them as they loaded their dugout, one of the ones they'd made back on Orchid Island.

"I'm going along, that be all right," Sam said.

Zeb and Hector talked it over in that way they had, using their eyes and maybe a tilt of the head instead of words. They knew well enough Sam had been lost since his wife and the baby died.

"You're just bored," Hector said. "You could take another wife, let her keep you occupied."

Sam just shook his head. He didn't need words, either.

"All right," Zeb said. "In the morning, first light."

That night, Livy took him, fierce and hot and desperate. Zeb absorbed all her heat, all her fear, and helped her find her way up and over the crest of her intolerable need. Coming down from such tumultuous intensity, she wept against him soundlessly. He soothed her, his hand tracing circles over her back.

Then Zeb loved her his way, slowly, tenderly. Every kiss was his promise to come home to her. When they'd both reached their fulfillment, Livy sighed, turned into his arms and slept.

The next morning, Livy stood on shore, Tonti in her arms, Rosemarie, Noah and Abe gathered around her. She didn't cry, for Zeb's sake. She smiled, for the children's sake. Her heart pushed off, waved to her and the children, and paddled north, back into the swamps.

Maybe he wouldn't even find the way. It wasn't like there were road signs out there in the swamp. And in all these years, the trees would be different, maybe the channels would run by different islands. Then they'd have to give up and come home, safe.

Livy went home to their hut and fed the baby. Once Tonti was sleeping, she made a single clay bead and placed it on the hearth to dry. Every day, she would make another clay bead until Zeb came home to her. It was all she could do.

~~~

Zeb felt hollow, paddling away from Livy and the children. But he had thought about this for months, years, really. He'd always meant to go back for her, even when he and Livy and Faith were new in the swamps, new in their freedom. He had to do it. Hope belonged to him, just like Faith and his own babies.

By the fifth day, the cypress canopy closed over them and they were back in the swampland.

"I don't remember none of this. Just one tree after another," Sam said.

"I'm counting on the sun to show us the way," Hector said.

"It ain't changed, at least."

In the third week, they found Orchid Island, by chance more than by reckoning. The log cabins were still there, no roofs anymore. That was all there was to indicate anyone had ever been here. They camped two nights, then moved northeast, Hector fairly sure of his directions now.

The magnolia tree with the dogwood behind it was still there. They were close to the old plantation then, only a few hours away.
~~~

They waited till good dark to pull close to the willow where Hector used to pull his dugout ashore.

"Sam, you got no reason to risk going in," Zeb said. "You stay back, pull the dugout behind that patch of trees. You hear shouting, shots, dogs – you get out. Go home."

"You think I'd run off and leave you? I go off when I know you're dead."

"Sam, you get caught – " Hector's voice faltered. "I kill you if you get caught, you understand?"

"I'm sitting out here in the dark. How'm I gone get caught? Go on."

Zeb's heart beat so hard he could hardly hear over the rush of blood in his ears. He crept alongside Hector, stopping to listen, to smell, to strain to see through the night. This was the field where he'd watched Livy hoeing, the hat he'd made for her on her head. The same field where she'd given him the onion from her dinner pail. The same field where Noah had got himself rattler bit.

When they reached the lane running through the quarters, they didn't speak. Hector scurried from shadow to shadow toward Tish's old cabin.

Zeb moved quietly toward his mama's. To was no surprise when a dog came out to inquire who he was. Zeb held his hand out to be sniffed and spoke softly. The dog was satisfied. Useless thing, let a stranger come sneaking in, but Zeb was grateful.

He let himself into the cabin quiet as any thief.

"Who's that?"

Zeb froze. A man's voice? Who lived in this cabin now? "It's me," he said. That was a fool thing to say, but he couldn't think of nothing else.

Nobody said anything for the longest time.

"Zeb?" A woman's voice this time.

Zeb let out the breath he'd been holding. "Yeah. It's me."

There was rustling as they climbed out of their bed. He heard flint strike steel, and a candle flared into the dark.

"Oh my Lord," his grandma said. "It is you." She threw herself into his arms and held on tight, her chest heaving with sobs.

And there stood Weasel, still skinny, but stooped now. And a girl with big eyes, staring at him.

"Hope," he said. She didn't nod, didn't speak.

And then he asked, "Mama?"

"She's gone, Zeb. Caught a chill two winters back."

They sat down to talk, to tell each other their news, Eva never letting go of Zeb's hand.

"Grandma, we better put the candle out."

Weasel shook his head. "Benning don't come down here no more. His rheumatiz got too bad. Can't hardly get up of a morning."

"You got four youngsters of you own? What you name them, Zeb?"

He told them all about his children, about Livy, about living with the Houma. He told especially about Faith, how she grew up so fine, how she had her own family.

He watched Hope watching him as he talked. If she guessed why he was here, she didn't say. Hope didn't say anything, in fact.

Zeb hadn't gone to her, hadn't insisted she give him a hug. She needed to know him a little bit before he expected that of her. "Hope, what kind of work they got you doing?"

"Mr. Benning put me in the laundry."

"That's hard work, but it better than the fields, I think."

She nodded.

"You know why I'm here?"

She stared at him. "Grandma Eva always said you come back for me someday. Mama Minnie always said that was nonsense."

"I used to rock you to sleep in my arms. I used to feed you pap with a spoon and tickle your feet. I love you like my own child, Hope."

Hope looked at Grandma, then at Weasel, who'd probably been a father to her these last years.

"I come back to get you. To take you with me so you can be a free woman. So you can have babies born free."

"Mama Minnie said it ugly living in the swamp."

Zeb could just hear his mama saying that, and he smiled.

"Look there, Weasel. Ain't that our Zeb? Ain't nobody smile like Zeb."

Zeb laughed. "We don't live in the swamp no more, Hope. But I tell you, living in the swamp, we was happy, Livy and me and Faith. Do you remember your sister?"

She shook her head.

"Hope don't remember you either, Zeb," Weasel said. "You got to give her time to get used to the idea."

"We ain't got much time, Hope. We got to be back at the boat soon as we can."

Hope's eyes opened wide. Weasel said, "Honey, we ain't gone make you go. You got to make up your own mind."

"Our Hope a little bit like Minnie," Grandma Eva said. "Kind of timid. But maybe she a little bit like me, too."

Hope sat down on her cot and looked at her hands. It was a lot for a girl to think on. Zeb gave her time, all the time he could.

When she looked up, she gazed at him. What did she see, he wondered? A stranger, but could she see that he loved her?

"Come with me, Hope. You got a family waiting for you. A whole life, as a free woman."

Hope looked at Grandma Eva a long time. Her eyes filled with tears, but she didn't shed them.

She nodded.

Eva clapped her hands over her face and let out one great sob. Then she wiped her face. "Good," she said, her voice quavering. "That's settled then."

Eva began bustling around the cabin, gathering things for Hope to take with her.

"No, Grandma," Zeb said when Eva wrapped up all their candles. "It ain't like before. I'm taking Hope to a home. All she need is her clothes."

"Well, she got her own needle. She ought to take that."

Hope's bundle was meager, even after she stuffed her old rag doll in with her other dress. "I'm ready," she said, her voice very small.

"What you gone say when Hope gone in the morning? Hector's boy Beesum, too."

"I think of something. Those scalawag children run off, thinking they gone have a possum hunt in the dark, and got lost. Something like that. I'll work on it, talk to Jubal when it get daylight."

"Jubal raising Hector's boy?"

"Tish and Jubal had themselves two babies before she died. Jubal and Ruby raising all them children now, hers and Tish's."

"Jubal always wanted to get free, too," Zeb said.

"Well, he got so many children on this place, how many, Weasel?"

"I don't know. Nine, ten. Couple of grandchildren. I don't think he want to leave a one of them."

While Eva hugged Hope and murmured her last loving words to her, Weasel opened his arms and Zeb stepped in to hug the old man. "Thank you," he told him. He owed Weasel – for all those years ago, helping him get free, for keeping his grandma from being lonely, for helping raise Hope.

"I thank you, Zeb. It's a fine thing, you coming back for Hope."

Weasel hugged Hope, rocking her in his arms, and Zeb went to his Grandma. She cupped his face in her hands, studying him.

"I never been so proud," she said.

He kissed her and held on to her for a long time. When he let her go, he said, "You ready, Hope?"

She nodded and walked with him to the door.

"Wait, Zeb," Eva said. She brought him her little box off the shelf. "Your granddaddy's pipe. Remember it? It belongs to you, always has."

Zeb bowed his head, nearly overcome.

"You put that in your pocket, show it to your sons when you get home."

He kissed Eva one more time, touched her cheek, and then he put his hand on Hope's shoulder. "Let's go."

He closed the door softly and heard his grandma sob. He was glad Weasel was there for her, that she wasn't alone.

Chapter Twenty-Eight

Livy drilled a hole in each new bead before it hardened. She had forty now, which she wore around her neck. She never took the necklace off except to add a new bead.

The first week Zeb was gone, she hadn't been able to sleep or eat. She nearly made herself sick, but Birdie sat her down and they talked away a long afternoon.

Birdie left her with the special tea that helped a body sleep, and stopped by every day until Livy seemed like herself again. She wasn't herself, though. The terrible fear burned like a firebrand she carried inside her gut for days. Birdie's medicine eased that pain, but then she felt like her chest was filled with hard gray stones, and Birdie had no medicine for that.

Some days she was so angry with Zeb it was all she could do not to tear the house down, not to take an axe and chop it to bits. Faith brought her babies over and sat with her in the evenings. She loved Zeb, too, but Faith didn't need him. Livy needed him like she needed air.

Came an evening, Livy rolling a lump of clay in her fingers to make yet one more bead, Birdie came running to get her.

"They're here. Livy! They're back!"

Livy grabbed up the baby and ran for the landing, the older children overtaking her and running ahead.

The dugout was crowded with five people. They'd done it. They'd brought back those children.

Three of the girls in love with Sam stood shyly on the shore, waiting for him to notice them.

Hector held out his arm to his son Beesum and presented him to Blossom and their children.

Zeb scooped up each of his children in turn. He hugged them, rubbed the top of their heads too hard, kissed them. He glanced at Livy, but she didn't put any welcome in her face.

He came to her, his hand on the girl's shoulder. Hope. But Faith came running now and grabbed Hope up, turning round and round with her, crying and laughing.

That left Zeb standing there. He might have been the only one on that shore, for Livy's eyes alone.

He came to her slowly, watching her. When he was close, he reached out a hand to stroke Tonti's cheek. Tonti hid his face against Livy's shoulder, not so sure he knew this man.

"Livy," he said.

"There's stew left in the pot. Come on home, you can eat." She turned away and walked back to the huts.

He walked beside her. When he reached for her hand, she moved away.

Dark fell. Zeb kept Noah and Abe up, entertaining them with tales about gators chasing them, about bears big as trees coming after them, till the boys were so wound up Livy couldn't get them to sleep. Zeb lay down with them, then, and told them that was all nonsense, the bears weren't hardly as big as a house, which earned him some giggles. They snuggled up close to him and finally slept.

Tonti and Rosemarie were long asleep, Livy lying with Rosemarie on her pallet. When Zeb untangled himself from his boys, he walked over to his and Livy's bed.

"Livy," he said.

She pretended she didn't hear him.

She did the same thing the next night, and the next.

During the day, she acted like everything was fine, except that every time Zeb tried to touch her, she moved away from him.

Hope spent most of her time at Faith's house, but Livy sincerely welcomed Hope into their home, too. She was a quiet girl, sweet with the younger children. Livy liked her and was glad to be her aunt, her mama too if she wanted.

She'd grown close to her Uncle Zeb during the weeks they paddled and poled through the swamp to get here, but Hope most of all wanted to be with Hector's son Beesum. If anyone went looking for Hope during the day, they found Beesum, too.

The fourth day, in the middle of the afternoon, Zeb came in from working on his boat, Hope in tow.

"Livy," he said.

She was stirring a pot, a task much more interesting than looking at her husband. "What," she said.

"Hope is here to look after the children."

Livy stilled. "They too much for Hope to handle."

"I'll take them over to Faith's, Aunt Livy."

"Leave off stirring that pot, Livy. We gone take a walk."

That was a new note in Zeb's voice. A command, not a request. Well.

She stood up, straightened her skirt, and walked out the door. Zeb caught up with her and directed her toward the grove on the other side of the gardens. When he tried to take her hand, she didn't jerk it back, but she let it lie in his hand like some dead thing till he let go.

Among the trees, where they had some privacy, Zeb put his hand on her shoulder and pressed gently. "Sit down, Livy."

She sat and arranged her skirt around her ankles.

"You never gone look me in the face again, Livy?"

She jerked her chin up and looked him in the eye, her face as blank as she could make it.

"Well, that's something, then. Look, Livy. I know you mad at me for going. I know you was scared."

"You don't know nothing about how scared I was."

"Then tell me."

She clamped her jaw shut and looked away.

"I missed you, Livy, you and the kids. I counted the days till I could get home to you. Forty-one, just like the number of them beads around your neck."

"Faith told you how many beads there were."

"I guessed. Cause I was counting the days too."

Zeb plucked a tall blade of grass and fingered it. "It was like leaving one of my own back on that place, Livy. Hope was my child, just as much as if I'd been her real daddy. I had to go get her."

Livy gave him a nod. She could do that much.

"I'm sorry it hurt you so much. It hurts me, to see how much it hurt you."

"She's a fine child," Livy said, her gaze on the row of trees to her right.

"I love you, Livy."

She raised her chin and closed her eyes, but she couldn't stop the tears from rolling down her face. She turned away from him instead.

He moved next to her. "Will you let me put my arm around you?"

She didn't answer him. She didn't think she could.

He eased his arm around her shoulders and she heard his breath hitch. Good. As much pain and worry he caused, he ought to be too sorry to breathe.

She cried, her back stiff, her head turned from him. Zeb waited a while, then he pulled her into him and pressed her face against his chest. He kissed the top of her head and held her while her body shook in his arms.

"I'm safe, Livy. I'm with you. And I'm gone make you feel safe again. Cause I'm not going anywhere, not ever again."

She shivered, getting herself under control.

"You got to promise, Zeb. You won't leave me again, ever."

"I promise." He held her hand against his heart. "I promise."

He kissed her swollen eyes. "I gone be right here, keeping you safe. Livy, my wife, my love."

"If you'll just stay home," she said with a shaky laugh, "I keep you safe, too."

She let him kiss her then, the sweetest kiss she could remember. She wrapped him in her arms, hunger rising in her.

"Livy," he laughed, breathless as she was. "This ain't that private out here."

"I don't care." She pushed him back and covered his face with kisses, ran her hands over his chest, over his ribs. She reached further down and stroked him.

"Livy," he said, holding her arms, "you got to stop now, or we ain't gone stop."

"Then we ain't gone stop."

~~~

The requisite number of months later, Livy delivered another set of twins, girls this time.

Drowsy and happy after her labors, she asked Zeb, "What we gone call them?"
~~~

"My turn to name them? All right. I think what we got here," he said, looking at the bundles in his lap, "is Minnie and Eva. What you think?"

"I think that's fine."

He placed the babies between him and Livy, lay down, and stretched his arm across to rub her tummy.

"You all right, Livy?"

She rolled on to her side so she could see him. Her simple Zeb, her beloved Zeb. She brought his hand to her mouth and kissed it.

"Zebediah, I love you so much I cain't hardly stand it."

He moved over across the babies, across Livy, and curled himself around her back. "What would happen if you loved me too much to stand it?"

"I'd have to run away into the swamps. Find me another Orchid Island and live on fish and turtles."

He nuzzled her neck. "I'd come looking for you." He kissed her neck and ran his hands over her big breasts and her big tummy.

"Zeb, I ain't making no more babies tonight."

He chuckled in her ear. "I got all I want right here."

Livy fell asleep in his arms, her babies snuggled close. Zeb stared up at the thatched roof for a long time, holding his beloved Livy as she slept against their baby girls.

There wasn't any finer life than this. Lying there in the dark, he smiled.

The End

Bonus Section:

An excerpt from Gretchen Craig's novel of old Louisiana.

Tansy

Chapter One

For weeks, before she slept, Tansy Bouvier imagined herself dancing with an elegant, handsome man whose gaze promised love and forbidden pleasures – only to waken later in a tangle of sweaty sheets, shaken by dreams of laughing men and women whirling around her, herself in an over-lit circle, alone, isolated, and unwanted.

But this was not a dream. The dreaded moment was upon her, the moment she had prepared for all her life, and she must smile. Maman gave her elbow a pinch, a final warning to sparkle. Tansy raised her chin and followed her into the famous Blue Ribbon Ballroom.

Droplets of fear trickled down her spine as she fought both the dread and the foolish romanticizing of what was essentially an evening of business. A beginning, not an end, she whispered to herself. Time to forget girlhood dreams, time to forget Christophe Desmarais. This night, she entered the world of plaçage in which a woman's *raison d'être* was to please a man, a very wealthy man. In return, she gained everything – riches, security, status.

In spite of the fluttering in her stomach, she found herself captivated by the glamour of the ballroom. Gas lamps glowed like yellow moons between the French doors, and crystal teardrops in the chandeliers sparkled like ice in sunshine. And the music.

Tansy's chest lifted at the power and fire of a full orchestra, strings and reeds and percussion propelling the dancers around the floor.

Maman chose a prominent, imminently visible position near the upper curve of the ball room to display Tansy and her charms. Tansy's task tonight was to make a splash, to outshine every other girl who'd entered the game earlier in the season. No, she thought. Not a game. Tonight, Tansy would meet her fate: luxury or destitution, security or whoredom.

What if none of the gentlemen wanted her? What if none of them even noticed her? What then?

"Smile," Maman hissed from the corner of her mouth.

"I am smiling," Tansy replied through wooden lips.

"That is not a smile. Look like you're glad to be here. Watch the dancers."

White men in stiff collars wove intricate steps and turns through the line of women, every one of whom wore a festive tignon over her hair. Tansy squinted her eyes so as to make the dancers and the chandeliers a blur of lights and swirling colors. Such a grand, beautiful sight, as if the most renowned ballroom in New Orleans were not the scene of business and barter.

She had imagined the men as leering and brash. Instead they seemed aloof and slightly bored. The young women, though, were as she expected. They wore masks with bright smiles and welcoming, deceiving eyes that promised gaiety and delight. She was meant to do the same.

"Loosen your grip on that fan," Maman whispered. "It is not a sword to be brandished at the enemy."

Tansy swallowed and opened the fan with cold, stiff fingers. She spied her friend Martine on the dance floor, vibrant in a red velvet gown. How splendid she looked in the red tignon wrapped in intricate folds around her head. She laughed, her eyes sparkling as her partner leaned in to speak into her ear. Martine had already been to several balls and had regaled Tansy with tales of handsome gentlemen who whispered love and promises as they twirled her around the ballroom. She was having a grand time waiting for the right protector to offer for her, but Martine had a boldness, a carelessness, Tansy could not match. And Martine had never been kissed by Christophe Desmarais.

Tansy glanced again at her own yellow silk, the neckline cut so deep she felt indecent. If Martine was a vibrant scarlet tanager, she felt herself to be a mere mockingbird masquerading as a canary. She touched her matching tignon, terrified it might slip on her head. "I'm too conspicuous in this dress," she whispered to her mother.

"Nonsense. No other girl here can wear yellow like you can."

A Creole gentleman, dark haired, dark eyed, no doubt very charming, bowed to Maman. "Madame Bouvier."

Tansy breathed out in relief. She might feel conspicuous, but at least she was not invisible. The gentleman was tall and handsome, his nose straight and long, his brow rather noble. For a moment, she let herself believe this handsome man would fall in love with her, and she with him, and they would dance and laugh and feel drunk with love, together, forever. She wanted to believe it.

Tansy's foolish moment passed. Maman knew every gentleman in New Orleans and the status of his bank account. If the suitor were wealthy enough, he would be encouraged.

After the merest glance at Tansy, the gentleman murmured something polite to Maman, who nodded her approval.

He bowed to Tansy. "May I have the honor of this dance, Mademoiselle?"

With a curious feeling of detachment, she accepted his arm and followed him onto the dance floor. It was only a dance. She liked to dance. She'd let the music carry her.

The gentleman wore an expertly tailored coat of deep maroon paired with gray satin knee breeches. He did look very fine, but more to the point, very prosperous. He smiled at her. "Lovely evening."

I mean you no harm she interpreted. See how nicely I smile? See how I have not once gazed at your plunging neckline, eyeing the wares?

"Yes," she managed to say. "Lovely weather."

The dance led them near the orchestra's platform. Tansy darted a glance at Christophe, sitting among the violinists. Oh God, he was watching her. Her stomach dropped and heat rushed to her face. For the rest of the dance, she focused a frozen gaze on her partner's ear, and if he said anything else, she did not note it.

At the end of the set, the gentleman returned her to Maman, tossed a bow at her and went in search of more pleasing company. Maman scowled. "If you don't stop acting like a dry stick, I will take you home this instant."

Like the puppet she felt herself to be, she loosened her shoulders, unclenched her teeth, and obeyed. No dry sticks allowed. She would be a willow branch, graceful, pliable. Yes, that was her. Pliant Tansy Marie Bouvier, a willow to be bent to fit her destiny.

Tansy had a moment to collect herself as another Creole gentleman bent over Maman's hand and made the customary flattering remarks. He seemed pleasant, not inclined to devour young women at their first balls. He smiled. No, no fangs, no sharpened canines.

"Monsieur Valcourt, my daughter, Tansy Marie."

He was of medium height, medium build, medium dark hair and medium brown eyes. Not handsome, not ugly. Maman raised an eyebrow. Such a wealth of information in that eyebrow: this man is rich, this man is a catch, and if you know what's good for you, you'll make him fall in love with you.

"Mademoiselle, will you dance?"

Squaring her shoulders, she followed him onto the dance floor.

Tansy's resolve to ignore Christophe faltered and her eyes found him again. His focus was on the music, his brow creased in concentration. She knew men didn't set so much store in a kiss as women, but she would never forget it. She gave herself a mental shake. It was because of that kiss that her mother had dragged her here, two weeks before her seventeenth birthday, to ensure they both understood that Christophe, a mere fiddler, could not afford a beautiful canary like Tansy Marie Bouvier.

Monsieur Valcourt's attention seemed to be on the music, his gaze primarily directed over her shoulder as he moved her through the steps. He danced well. She liked the fact that he didn't try to charm her, nor did he seem to expect her to dazzle him.

They joined hands as they moved into a turn. Her cold fingers warmed in his palm, and his assumption of connection, of ease in their touch loosened her reserve. A comfortable man, this Monsieur Valcourt.

An older gentleman circled through the line to partner Tansy with a turn through the dance. He leered at her décolletage, yellow teeth on display, and he held his mouth slightly open with the tip of his tongue visible. The thought of his tobacco stained fingers in intimate contact with her skin sent a shiver of revulsion through her.

Or else, she remembered her mother's threat. Find a protector, or else face a life of penury, a few years in a brothel until your looks fade, and then what, eh?

The dance moved on and Monsieur Valcourt reappeared at her side. When he took her hand with no leer, no meaningful squeeze of her fingers, she breathed in freely for the first time all evening. The music ended. He bestowed on her an open, guileless smile that warmed his brown eyes.

Yes, she could live with this man. She didn't need to survey, and be surveyed by, a dozen or two other gentlemen. And if Maman was right, that her looks would assure her any man she chose, then she would as soon choose this one and have it done with. He seemed nice. They would likely have a family together. They would be happy enough.

She allowed herself one last glimpse of Christophe among the violinists. He met her gaze over his bow, and for a moment her vision tunneled so that all around him was hazy darkness, Christophe himself bathed in light. She closed her eyes and turned away.

Perhaps no woman could choose her own fate, but she would take control of what she could. She would be the placée of Monsieur Valere Valcourt.

Tansy opened her eyes and bestowed on Monsieur Valcourt her most dazzling smile.

ABOUT THE AUTHOR

Gretchen Craig's lush, sweeping tales deliver edgy, compelling characters who test the boundaries of integrity, strength, and love. Told with sensitivity, the novels realistically portray the raw suffering of people in times of great upheaval. Having lived in diverse climates and terrains, Gretchen infuses her novels with a strong sense of place. The best-selling *PLANTATION SERIES* brings to the reader the smell of Louisiana's bayous and of New Orleans' gumbo, but most of all, these novels show the full scope of human suffering and triumph. Visit Gretchen's Amazon Author Page at

www.amazon.com/author/gretchencraig